Anton Chekhov The Black Monk & Other Short Stories

The short story is often viewed as an inferior relation to the Novel. But it is an art in itself. To take a story and distil its essence into fewer pages while keeping character and plot rounded and driven is not an easy task. Many try and many fail.

In this series we look at short stories from many of our most accomplished writers. Miniature masterpieces with a lot to say. In this volume we examine some of the short stories of Anton Chekhov.

Russian Literature is probably more known for the sheer length, scope and breadth of its novels. Chekhov was no exception to this with such masterpieces as War And Peace. But he also wrote such plays such as Uncle Vanya, The Cherry Orchard and The Seagull. But he also sits atop most literary critics as one of the greatest short story writers ever.

Anton Chekhov was born on 29 January 1860, the third of six surviving children, in Taganrog, a port in the south of Russia.

Chekhov attended a school for Greek boys, followed by the Taganrog gymnasium, where he was kept down for a year at fifteen for failing a Greek exam. Despite having a religious background and education, he later on became an atheist.

In 1876, Chekhov's father was declared bankrupt after over-extending his finances building a new house. To avoid the debtor's prison he fled to Moscow, where his two eldest sons, Alexander and Nikolay, were attending university. The family lived in poverty in Moscow, Chekhov's mother physically and emotionally broken. Chekhov was left behind to sell the family possessions and finish his education.

In 1879, Chekhov completed his schooling and joined his family in Moscow, having gained admission to the medical school at Moscow University

Chekhov now assumed responsibility for the whole family. To support them and to pay his tuition fees, he wrote daily short, humorous sketches and vignettes of contemporary Russian life, many under pseudonyms. His prodigious output earned him a reputation as a satirical chronicler of Russian street life, and by 1882 he was writing for Oskolki (Fragments), owned by Nikolay Leykin, one of the leading publishers of the time.

In 1884, Chekhov qualified as a physician, which he considered his principal profession though he made little money from it and treated the poor free of charge. In 1884 and 1885, Chekhov found himself coughing blood, and in 1886 the attacks worsened; but he would not admit tuberculosis to his family and friends.

In the next twenty years his writing was to elevate him to that of a literary giant though he continued to practice medicine "Medicine is my lawful wife", he once said, "and literature is my mistress. When I get tired of one, I spend the night with the other"

One of the first to use the stream-of-consciousness technique, later adopted by the modernists, combined with a disavowal of the moral finality of traditional story structure. He made no apologies for the difficulties this posed to readers, insisting that the role of an artist was to ask questions, not to answer them.

But his health continued to deteriorate; he moved on doctors advice to a warmer climate at Yalta but yearned for Moscow and travel. Though the tuberculosis was to gradually worsen he kept working, his output prodigious but exemplary. But by May 1904, the outlook was terminal. Mikhail Chekhov recalled that "everyone who saw him secretly thought the end was not far off, but the nearer he was to the end, the less he seemed to realise it."

In 1908, Olga wrote this account of her husband's last moments: Anton sat up unusually straight and said loudly and clearly in German): Ich sterbe ("I'm dying"). The doctor calmed him, took a syringe, gave him an injection of camphor, and ordered champagne. Anton took a full glass, examined it, smiled at me and said: "It's a long time since I drank champagne." He drank it, lay quietly on his left side and died.

Chekhov's body was transported to Moscow in a refrigerated railway car for fresh oysters. Some of the thousands of mourners followed the funeral procession of a General Keller by mistake, to the accompaniment of a military band.

Chekhov was buried next to his father at the Novodevichy Cemetery.

Some of these stories are also available as an audiobook from our sister company Word Of Mouth. Many samples are at our youtube channel http://www.youtube.com/user/PortablePoetry?feature=mhee The full volume can be purchased from iTunes, Amazon and other digital stores.

Index Of Stories

THE LADY WITH THE DOG

I

It was said that a new person had appeared on the sea-front: a lady with a little dog. Dmitri Dmitritch Gurov, who had by then been a fortnight at Yalta, and so was fairly at home there, had begun to take an interest in new arrivals. Sitting in Verney's pavilion, he saw, walking on the sea-front, a fair-haired young lady of medium height, wearing a *beret*; a white Pomeranian dog was running behind her.

And afterwards he met her in the public gardens and in the square several times a day. She was walking alone, always wearing the same *beret*, and always with the same white dog; no one knew who she was, and every one called her simply "the lady with the dog."

"If she is here alone without a husband or friends, it wouldn't be amiss to make her acquaintance," Gurov reflected.

He was under forty, but he had a daughter already twelve years old, and two sons at school. He had been married young, when he was a student in his second year, and by now his wife seemed half as old again as he. She was a tall, erect woman with dark eyebrows, staid and dignified, and, as she said of herself, intellectual. She read a great deal, used phonetic spelling, called her husband, not Dmitri, but Dimitri, and he secretly considered her unintelligent, narrow, inelegant, was afraid of her, and did not like to be at home. He had begun being unfaithful to her long ago—had been unfaithful to her often, and, probably on that account, almost always spoke ill of women, and when they were talked about in his presence, used to call them "the lower race."

It seemed to him that he had been so schooled by bitter experience that he might call them what he liked, and yet he could not get on for two days together without "the lower race." In the society of men he was bored and not himself, with them he was cold and uncommunicative; but when he was in the company of women he felt free, and knew what to say to them and how to behave; and he was at ease with them even when he was silent. In his appearance, in his character, in his whole nature, there was something attractive and elusive which allured women and disposed them in his favour; he knew that, and some force seemed to draw him, too, to them.

Experience often repeated, truly bitter experience, had taught him long ago that with decent people, especially Moscow people—always slow to move and irresolute— every intimacy, which at first so agreeably diversifies life and appears a light and charming adventure, inevitably grows into a regular problem of extreme intricacy, and in the long run the situation becomes unbearable. But at every fresh meeting with an interesting woman this experience seemed to slip out of his memory, and he was eager for life, and everything seemed simple and amusing.

One evening he was dining in the gardens, and the lady in the *beret* came up slowly to take the next table. Her expression, her gait, her dress, and the way she did her hair told him that she was a lady, that she was married, that she was in Yalta for the first time and alone, and that she was dull there. . . . The stories told of the immorality in such places as Yalta are to a great extent untrue; he despised them, and knew that such stories were for the most part made up by persons who would themselves have been glad to sin if they had been able; but when the lady sat down at the next table three paces from him, he remembered these tales of easy conquests, of trips to the mountains, and the tempting thought of a swift, fleeting love affair, a romance with an unknown woman, whose name he did not know, suddenly took possession of him.

He beckoned coaxingly to the Pomeranian, and when the dog came up to him he shook his finger at it. The Pomeranian growled: Gurov shook his finger at it again.

The lady looked at him and at once dropped her eyes.

"He doesn't bite," she said, and blushed.

"May I give him a bone?" he asked; and when she nodded he asked courteously, "Have you been long in Yalta?"

"Five days."

"And I have already dragged out a fortnight here."

There was a brief silence.

"Time goes fast, and yet it is so dull here!" she said, not looking at him.

"That's only the fashion to say it is dull here. A provincial will live in Belyov or Zhidra and not be dull, and when he comes here it's 'Oh, the dulness! Oh, the dust!' One would think he came from Grenada."

She laughed. Then both continued eating in silence, like strangers, but after dinner they walked side by side; and there sprang up between them the light jesting conversation of people who are free and satisfied, to whom it does not matter where they go or what they talk about. They walked and talked of the strange light on the sea: the water was of a soft warm lilac hue, and there was a golden streak from the moon upon it. They talked of how sultry it was after a hot day. Gurov told her that he came from Moscow, that he had taken his degree in Arts, but had a post in a bank; that he had trained as an opera-singer, but had given it up, that he owned two houses in Moscow. . . . And from her he learnt that she had grown up in Petersburg, but had lived in S---- since her marriage two years before, that she was staying another month in Yalta, and that her husband, who needed a holiday too, might perhaps come and fetch her. She was not sure whether her husband had a post in a Crown Department or under the Provincial Council—and was amused by her own ignorance. And Gurov learnt, too, that she was called Anna Sergeyevna.

Afterwards he thought about her in his room at the hotel—thought she would certainly meet him next day; it would be sure to happen. As he got into bed he thought how lately she had been a girl at school, doing lessons like his own daughter; he recalled the diffidence, the angularity, that was still manifest in her laugh and her manner of talking with a stranger. This must have been the first time in her life she had been alone in surroundings in which she was followed, looked at, and spoken to merely from a secret motive which she could hardly fail to guess. He recalled her slender, delicate neck, her lovely grey eyes.

"There's something pathetic about her, anyway," he thought, and fell asleep.

II

A week had passed since they had made acquaintance. It was a holiday. It was sultry indoors, while in the street the wind whirled the dust round and round, and blew people's hats off. It was a thirsty day, and Gurov often went into the pavilion, and pressed Anna Sergeyevna to have syrup and water or an ice. One did not know what to do with oneself.

In the evening when the wind had dropped a little, they went out on the groyne to see the steamer come in. There were a great many people walking about the harbour; they had gathered to welcome some one, bringing bouquets. And two peculiarities of a well-dressed Yalta crowd were very conspicuous: the elderly ladies were dressed like young ones, and there were great numbers of generals.

Owing to the roughness of the sea, the steamer arrived late, after the sun had set, and it was a long time turning about before it reached the groyne. Anna Sergeyevna looked through her lorgnette at the steamer and the passengers as though looking for acquaintances, and when she turned to Gurov her eyes were shining. She talked a great deal and asked disconnected questions, forgetting next moment what she had asked; then she dropped her lorgnette in the crush.

The festive crowd began to disperse; it was too dark to see people's faces. The wind had completely dropped, but Gurov and Anna Sergeyevna still stood as though waiting to see some one else come from the steamer. Anna Sergeyevna was silent now, and sniffed the flowers without looking at Gurov.

"The weather is better this evening," he said. "Where shall we go now? Shall we drive somewhere?"

She made no answer.

Then he looked at her intently, and all at once put his arm round her and kissed her on the lips, and breathed in the moisture and the fragrance of the flowers; and he immediately looked round him, anxiously wondering whether any one had seen them.

"Let us go to your hotel," he said softly. And both walked quickly.

The room was close and smelt of the scent she had bought at the Japanese shop. Gurov looked at her and thought: "What different people one meets in the world!" From the past he preserved memories of careless, good-natured women, who loved cheerfully and were grateful to him for the happiness he gave them, however brief it might be; and of women like his wife who loved without any genuine feeling, with superfluous phrases, affectedly, hysterically, with an expression that suggested that it was not love nor passion, but something more significant; and of two or three others, very beautiful, cold women, on whose faces he had caught a glimpse of a rapacious expression—an obstinate desire to snatch from life more than it could give, and these were capricious, unreflecting, domineering, unintelligent women not in their first youth, and when Gurov grew cold to them their beauty excited his hatred, and the lace on their linen seemed to him like scales.

But in this case there was still the diffidence, the angularity of inexperienced youth, an awkward feeling; and there was a sense of consternation as though some one had suddenly knocked at the door. The attitude of Anna Sergeyevna—"the lady with the dog"—to what had happened was somehow peculiar, very grave, as though it were her fall—so it seemed, and it was strange and inappropriate. Her face dropped and faded, and on both sides of it her long hair hung down mournfully; she mused in a dejected attitude like "the woman who was a sinner" in an old-fashioned picture.

"It's wrong," she said. "You will be the first to despise me now."

There was a water-melon on the table. Gurov cut himself a slice and began eating it without haste. There followed at least half an hour of silence.

Anna Sergeyevna was touching; there was about her the purity of a good, simple woman who had seen little of life. The solitary candle burning on the table threw a faint light on her face, yet it was clear that she was very unhappy.

"How could I despise you?" asked Gurov. "You don't know what you are saying."

"God forgive me," she said, and her eyes filled with tears. "It's awful."

"You seem to feel you need to be forgiven."

"Forgiven? No. I am a bad, low woman; I despise myself and don't attempt to justify myself. It's not my husband but myself I have deceived. And not only just now; I have been deceiving myself for a long time. My husband may be a good, honest man, but he is a flunkey! I don't know what he does there, what his work is, but I know he is a flunkey! I was twenty when I was married to him. I have been tormented by curiosity; I wanted something better. 'There must be a different sort of life,' I said to myself. I wanted to live! To live, to live! . . . I was fired by curiosity . . . you don't understand it, but, I swear to God, I could not control myself; something happened to me: I could not be restrained. I told my husband I was ill, and came here. . . . And here I have been walking about as though I were dazed, like a mad creature; . . . and now I have become a vulgar, contemptible woman whom any one may despise."

Gurov felt bored already, listening to her. He was irritated by the naive tone, by this remorse, so unexpected and inopportune; but for the tears in her eyes, he might have thought she was jesting or playing a part.

"I don't understand," he said softly. "What is it you want?"

She hid her face on his breast and pressed close to him.

"Believe me, believe me, I beseech you . . ." she said. "I love a pure, honest life, and sin is loathsome to me. I don't know what I am doing. Simple people say: 'The Evil One has beguiled me.' And I may say of myself now that the Evil One has beguiled me."

"Hush, hush! . . ." he muttered.

He looked at her fixed, scared eyes, kissed her, talked softly and affectionately, and by degrees she was comforted, and her gaiety returned; they both began laughing.

Afterwards when they went out there was not a soul on the sea-front. The town with its cypresses had quite a deathlike air, but the sea still broke noisily on the shore; a single barge was rocking on the waves, and a lantern was blinking sleepily on it.

They found a cab and drove to Oreanda.

"I found out your surname in the hall just now: it was written on the board—Von Diderits," said Gurov. "Is your husband a German?"

"No; I believe his grandfather was a German, but he is an Orthodox Russian himself."

At Oreanda they sat on a seat not far from the church, looked down at the sea, and were silent. Yalta was hardly visible through the morning mist; white clouds stood motionless on the mountain-tops. The leaves did not stir on the trees, grasshoppers chirruped, and the monotonous hollow sound of the sea rising up from below, spoke of the peace, of the eternal sleep awaiting us. So it must have sounded when there was no Yalta, no Oreanda here; so it sounds now, and it will sound as indifferently and monotonously when we are all no more. And in this constancy, in this complete indifference to the life and death of each of us, there lies hid, perhaps, a pledge of our eternal salvation, of the unceasing movement of life upon earth, of unceasing progress towards perfection. Sitting beside a young woman who in the dawn seemed so lovely, soothed and spellbound in these magical surroundings—the sea, mountains, clouds, the open sky—Gurov thought how in reality everything is beautiful in this world when one reflects: everything except what we think or do ourselves when we forget our human dignity and the higher aims of our existence.

A man walked up to them—probably a keeper—looked at them and walked away. And this detail seemed mysterious and beautiful, too. They saw a steamer come from Theodosia, with its lights out in the glow of dawn.

"There is dew on the grass," said Anna Sergeyevna, after a silence.

"Yes. It's time to go home."

They went back to the town.

Then they met every day at twelve o'clock on the sea-front, lunched and dined together, went for walks, admired the sea. She complained that she slept badly, that her heart throbbed violently; asked the same questions, troubled now by jealousy and now by the fear that he did not respect her sufficiently. And often in the square or gardens, when there was no one near them, he suddenly drew her to him and kissed her passionately. Complete idleness, these kisses in broad daylight while he looked round in dread of some one's seeing them, the heat, the smell of the sea, and the continual passing to and fro before him of idle, well-dressed, well-fed people, made a new man of him; he told Anna Sergeyevna how beautiful she was, how fascinating. He was impatiently passionate, he would not move a step away from her, while she was often pensive and continually urged him to confess that he did not respect her, did not love her in the least, and thought of her as nothing but a common woman. Rather late almost every evening they drove somewhere out of town, to Oreanda or to the waterfall; and the expedition was always a success, the scenery invariably impressed them as grand and beautiful.

They were expecting her husband to come, but a letter came from him, saying that there was something wrong with his eyes, and he entreated his wife to come home as quickly as possible. Anna Sergeyevna made haste to go.

"It's a good thing I am going away," she said to Gurov. "It's the finger of destiny!"

She went by coach and he went with her. They were driving the whole day. When she had got into a compartment of the express, and when the second bell had rung, she said:

"Let me look at you once more . . . look at you once again. That's right."

She did not shed tears, but was so sad that she seemed ill, and her face was quivering.

"I shall remember you . . . think of you," she said. "God be with you; be happy. Don't remember evil against me. We are parting forever --it must be so, for we ought never to have met. Well, God be with you."

The train moved off rapidly, its lights soon vanished from sight, and a minute later there was no sound of it, as though everything had conspired together to end as quickly as possible that sweet delirium, that madness. Left alone on the platform, and gazing into the dark distance, Gurov listened to the chirrup of the grasshoppers and the hum of the telegraph wires, feeling as though he had only just waked up. And he thought, musing, that there had been another episode or adventure in his life, and it, too, was at an end, and nothing was left of it but a memory. . . . He was moved, sad, and conscious of a slight remorse. This young woman whom he would never meet again had not been happy with him; he was genuinely warm and affectionate with her, but yet in his manner, his tone, and his caresses there had been a shade of light irony, the coarse condescension of a happy man who was, besides, almost twice her age. All the time she had called him kind, exceptional, lofty; obviously he had seemed to her different from what he really was, so he had unintentionally deceived her. . . .

Here at the station was already a scent of autumn; it was a cold evening.

"It's time for me to go north," thought Gurov as he left the platform.

"High time!"

III

At home in Moscow everything was in its winter routine; the stoves were heated, and in the morning it was still dark when the children were having breakfast and getting ready for school, and the nurse would light the lamp for a short time. The frosts had begun already. When the first snow has fallen, on the first day of sledge-driving it is pleasant to see the white earth, the white roofs, to draw soft, delicious breath, and the season brings back the days of one's youth. The old limes and birches, white with hoar-frost, have a good-natured expression; they are nearer to one's heart than cypresses and palms, and near them one doesn't want to be thinking of the sea and the mountains.

Gurov was Moscow born; he arrived in Moscow on a fine frosty day, and when he put on his fur coat and warm gloves, and walked along Petrovka, and when on Saturday evening he heard the ringing of the bells, his recent trip and the places he had seen lost all charm for him. Little by little he became absorbed in Moscow life, greedily read three newspapers a day, and declared he did not read the Moscow papers on principle! He already felt a longing to go to restaurants, clubs, dinner-parties, anniversary celebrations, and he felt flattered at entertaining distinguished lawyers and artists, and at playing cards with a professor at the doctors' club. He could already eat a whole plateful of salt fish and cabbage.

In another month, he fancied, the image of Anna Sergeyevna would be shrouded in a mist in his memory, and only from time to time would visit him in his dreams with a touching smile as others did. But more than a month passed, real winter had come, and everything was still clear in his memory as though he had parted with Anna Sergeyevna only the day before. And his memories glowed more and more vividly. When in the evening stillness he heard from his study the voices of his children, preparing their lessons, or when he listened to a song or the organ at the restaurant, or the storm howled in the chimney, suddenly everything would rise up in his memory: what had happened on the groyne, and the early morning with the mist on the mountains, and the steamer coming from Theodosia, and the kisses. He would pace a long time about his room, remembering it all and smiling; then his memories passed into dreams, and in his fancy the past was mingled with what was to come. Anna Sergeyevna did not visit him in dreams, but followed him about everywhere like a shadow and haunted him. When he shut his eyes he saw her as though she were living before him, and she seemed to him lovelier, younger, tenderer than she was; and he imagined himself finer than he had been in Yalta. In the evenings she peeped out at him from the bookcase, from the fireplace, from the corner—he heard her breathing, the caressing rustle of her dress. In the street he watched the women, looking for some one like her.

He was tormented by an intense desire to confide his memories to some one. But in his home it was impossible to talk of his love, and he had no one outside; he could not talk to his tenants nor to any one at the bank. And what had he to talk of? Had he been in love, then? Had there been anything beautiful, poetical, or edifying or simply interesting in his relations with Anna Sergeyevna? And there was nothing for him but to talk vaguely of love, of woman, and no one guessed what it meant; only his wife twitched her black eyebrows, and said:

"The part of a lady-killer does not suit you at all, Dimitri."

One evening, coming out of the doctors' club with an official with whom he had been playing cards, he could not resist saying:

"If only you knew what a fascinating woman I made the acquaintance of in Yalta!"

The official got into his sledge and was driving away, but turned suddenly and shouted:

"Dmitri Dmitritch!"

"What?"

"You were right this evening: the sturgeon was a bit too strong!"

These words, so ordinary, for some reason moved Gurov to indignation, and struck him as degrading and unclean. What savage manners, what people! What senseless nights, what uninteresting, uneventful days! The rage for card-playing, the gluttony, the drunkenness, the continual talk always about the same thing. Useless pursuits and conversations always about the same things absorb the better part of one's time, the better part of one's strength, and in the end there is left a life grovelling and curtailed, worthless and trivial, and there is no escaping or getting away from it—just as though one were in a madhouse or a prison.

Gurov did not sleep all night, and was filled with indignation. And he had a headache all next day. And the next night he slept badly; he sat up in bed, thinking, or paced up and down his room. He was sick of his children, sick of the bank; he had no desire to go anywhere or to talk of anything.

In the holidays in December he prepared for a journey, and told his wife he was going to Petersburg to do something in the interests of a young friend—and he set off for S----. What for? He did not very well know himself. He wanted to see Anna Sergeyevna and to talk with her—to arrange a meeting, if possible.

He reached S---- in the morning, and took the best room at the hotel, in which the floor was covered with grey army cloth, and on the table was an inkstand, grey with dust and adorned with a figure on horseback, with its hat in its hand and its head broken off. The hotel porter gave him the necessary information; Von Diderits lived in a house of his own in Old Gontcharny Street—it was not far from the hotel: he was rich and lived in good style, and had his own horses; every one in the town knew him. The porter pronounced the name "Dridirits."

Gurov went without haste to Old Gontcharny Street and found the house. Just opposite the house stretched a long grey fence adorned with nails.

"One would run away from a fence like that," thought Gurov, looking from the fence to the windows of the house and back again.

He considered: to-day was a holiday, and the husband would probably be at home. And in any case it would be tactless to go into the house and upset her. If he were to send her a note it might fall into her husband's hands, and then it might ruin everything. The best thing was to trust to chance. And he kept walking up and down the street by the fence, waiting for the chance. He saw a beggar go in at the gate and dogs fly at him; then an hour later he heard a piano, and the sounds were faint and indistinct. Probably it was Anna Sergeyevna playing. The front door suddenly opened, and an old woman came out, followed by the familiar white Pomeranian. Gurov was on the point of calling to the dog, but his heart began beating violently, and in his excitement he could not remember the dog's name.

He walked up and down, and loathed the grey fence more and more, and by now he thought irritably that Anna Sergeyevna had forgotten him, and was perhaps already amusing herself with some one else, and that that was very natural in a young woman who had nothing to look at from morning till night but that confounded fence. He went back to his hotel room and sat for a long while on the sofa, not knowing what to do, then he had dinner and a long nap.

"How stupid and worrying it is!" he thought when he woke and looked at the dark windows: it was already evening. "Here I've had a good sleep for some reason. What shall I do in the night?"

He sat on the bed, which was covered by a cheap grey blanket, such as one sees in hospitals, and he taunted himself in his vexation:

"So much for the lady with the dog . . . so much for the adventure . . . . You're in a nice fix. . . ."

That morning at the station a poster in large letters had caught his eye. "The Geisha" was to be performed for the first time. He thought of this and went to the theatre.

"It's quite possible she may go to the first performance," he thought.

The theatre was full. As in all provincial theatres, there was a fog above the chandelier, the gallery was noisy and restless; in the front row the local dandies were standing up before the beginning of the performance, with their hands behind them; in the Governor's box the Governor's daughter, wearing a boa, was sitting in the front seat, while the Governor himself lurked modestly behind the curtain with only his hands visible; the orchestra was a long time tuning up; the stage curtain swayed. All the time the audience were coming in and taking their seats Gurov looked at them eagerly.

Anna Sergeyevna, too, came in. She sat down in the third row, and when Gurov looked at her his heart contracted, and he understood clearly that for him there was in the whole world no creature so near, so precious, and so important to him; she, this little woman, in no way remarkable, lost in a provincial crowd, with a vulgar lorgnette in her hand, filled his whole life now, was his sorrow and his joy, the one happiness that he now desired for himself, and to the sounds of the inferior orchestra, of the wretched provincial violins, he thought how lovely she was. He thought and dreamed.

A young man with small side-whiskers, tall and stooping, came in with Anna Sergeyevna and sat down beside her; he bent his head at every step and seemed to be continually bowing. Most likely this was the husband whom at Yalta, in a rush of bitter feeling, she had called a flunkey. And there really was in his long figure, his side-whiskers, and the small bald patch on his head, something of the flunkey's obsequiousness; his smile was sugary, and in his buttonhole there was some badge of distinction like the number on a waiter.

During the first interval the husband went away to smoke; she remained alone in her stall. Gurov, who was sitting in the stalls, too, went up to her and said in a trembling voice, with a forced smile:

"Good-evening."

She glanced at him and turned pale, then glanced again with horror, unable to believe her eyes, and tightly gripped the fan and the lorgnette in her hands, evidently struggling with herself not to faint. Both were silent. She was sitting, he was standing, frightened by her confusion and not venturing to sit down beside her. The violins and the flute began tuning up. He felt suddenly frightened; it seemed as though all the people in the boxes were looking at them. She got up and went quickly to the door; he followed her, and both walked senselessly along passages, and up and down stairs, and figures in legal, scholastic, and civil service uniforms, all wearing badges, flitted before their eyes. They caught glimpses of ladies, of fur coats hanging on pegs; the draughts blew on them, bringing a smell of stale tobacco. And Gurov, whose heart was beating violently, thought:

"Oh, heavens! Why are these people here and this orchestra! . . ."

And at that instant he recalled how when he had seen Anna Sergeyevna off at the station he had thought that everything was over and they would never meet again. But how far they were still from the end!

On the narrow, gloomy staircase over which was written "To the Amphitheatre," she stopped.

"How you have frightened me!" she said, breathing hard, still pale and overwhelmed. "Oh, how you have frightened me! I am half dead. Why have you come? Why?"

"But do understand, Anna, do understand . . ." he said hastily in a low voice. "I entreat you to understand. . . ."

She looked at him with dread, with entreaty, with love; she looked at him intently, to keep his features more distinctly in her memory.

"I am so unhappy," she went on, not heeding him. "I have thought of nothing but you all the time; I live only in the thought of you. And I wanted to forget, to forget you; but why, oh, why, have you come?"

On the landing above them two schoolboys were smoking and looking down, but that was nothing to Gurov; he drew Anna Sergeyevna to him, and began kissing her face, her cheeks, and her hands.

"What are you doing, what are you doing!" she cried in horror, pushing him away. "We are mad. Go away to-day; go away at once. . . . I beseech you by all that is sacred, I implore you. . . . There are people coming this way!"

Some one was coming up the stairs.

"You must go away," Anna Sergeyevna went on in a whisper. "Do you hear, Dmitri Dmitritch? I will come and see you in Moscow. I have never been happy; I am miserable now, and I never, never shall be happy, never! Don't make me suffer still more! I swear I'll come to Moscow. But now let us part. My precious, good, dear one, we must part!"

She pressed his hand and began rapidly going downstairs, looking round at him, and from her eyes he could see that she really was unhappy. Gurov stood for a little while, listened, then, when all sound had died away, he found his coat and left the theatre.

IV

And Anna Sergeyevna began coming to see him in Moscow. Once in two or three months she left S----, telling her husband that she was going to consult a doctor about an internal complaint—and her husband believed her, and did not believe her. In Moscow she stayed at the Slaviansky Bazaar hotel, and at once sent a man in a red cap to Gurov. Gurov went to see her, and no one in Moscow knew of it.

Once he was going to see her in this way on a winter morning (the messenger had come the evening before when he was out). With him walked his daughter, whom he wanted to take to school: it was on the way. Snow was falling in big wet flakes.

"It's three degrees above freezing-point, and yet it is snowing," said Gurov to his daughter. "The thaw is only on the surface of the earth; there is quite a different temperature at a greater height in the atmosphere."

"And why are there no thunderstorms in the winter, father?"

He explained that, too. He talked, thinking all the while that he was going to see her, and no living soul knew of it, and probably never would know. He had two lives: one, open, seen and known by all who cared to know, full of relative truth and of relative falsehood, exactly like the lives of his friends and acquaintances; and another life running its course in secret. And through some strange, perhaps accidental, conjunction of circumstances, everything that was essential, of interest and of value to him, everything in which he was sincere and did not deceive himself, everything that made the kernel of his life, was hidden from other people; and all that was false in him, the sheath in which he hid himself to conceal the truth—such, for instance, as his work in the bank, his discussions at the club, his "lower race," his presence with his wife at anniversary festivities—all that was open. And he judged of others by himself, not believing in what he saw, and always believing that every man had his real, most interesting life under the cover of secrecy and under the cover of night. All personal life rested on secrecy, and possibly it was partly on that account that civilised man was so nervously anxious that personal privacy should be respected.

After leaving his daughter at school, Gurov went on to the Slaviansky Bazaar. He took off his fur coat below, went upstairs, and softly knocked at the door. Anna Sergeyevna, wearing his favourite grey dress, exhausted by the journey and the suspense, had been expecting him since the evening before. She was pale; she looked at him, and did not smile, and he had hardly come in when she fell on his breast. Their kiss was slow and prolonged, as though they had not met for two years.

"Well, how are you getting on there?" he asked. "What news?"

"Wait; I'll tell you directly. . . . I can't talk."

She could not speak; she was crying. She turned away from him, and pressed her handkerchief to her eyes.

"Let her have her cry out. I'll sit down and wait," he thought, and he sat down in an arm-chair.

Then he rang and asked for tea to be brought him, and while he drank his tea she remained standing at the window with her back to him. She was crying from emotion, from the miserable consciousness that their life was so hard for them; they could only meet in secret, hiding themselves from people, like thieves! Was not their life shattered?

"Come, do stop!" he said.

It was evident to him that this love of theirs would not soon be over, that he could not see the end of it. Anna Sergeyevna grew more and more attached to him. She adored him, and it was unthinkable to say to her that it was bound to have an end some day; besides, she would not have believed it!

He went up to her and took her by the shoulders to say something affectionate and cheering, and at that moment he saw himself in the looking-glass.

His hair was already beginning to turn grey. And it seemed strange to him that he had grown so much older, so much plainer during the last few years. The shoulders on which his hands rested were warm and quivering. He felt compassion for this life, still so warm and lovely, but probably already not far from beginning to fade and wither like his own. Why did she love him so much? He always seemed to women different from what he was, and they loved in him not himself, but the man created by their imagination, whom they had been eagerly seeking all their lives; and afterwards, when they noticed their mistake, they loved him all the same. And not one of them had been happy with him. Time passed, he had made their acquaintance, got on with them, parted, but he had never once loved; it was anything you like, but not love.

And only now when his head was grey he had fallen properly, really in love—for the first time in his life.

Anna Sergeyevna and he loved each other like people very close and akin, like husband and wife, like tender friends; it seemed to them that fate itself had meant them for one another, and they could not understand why he had a wife and she a husband; and it was as though they were a pair of birds of passage, caught and forced to live in different cages. They forgave each other for what they were ashamed of in their past, they forgave everything in the present, and felt that this love of theirs had changed them both.

In moments of depression in the past he had comforted himself with any arguments that came into his mind, but now he no longer cared for arguments; he felt profound compassion, he wanted to be sincere and tender. . . .

"Don't cry, my darling," he said. "You've had your cry; that's enough. . . . Let us talk now, let us think of some plan."

Then they spent a long while taking counsel together, talked of how to avoid the necessity for secrecy, for deception, for living in different towns and not seeing each other for long at a time. How could they be free from this intolerable bondage?

"How? How?" he asked, clutching his head. "How?"

And it seemed as though in a little while the solution would be found, and then a new and splendid life would begin; and it was clear to both of them that they had still a long, long road before them, and that the most complicated and difficult part of it was only just beginning.

A DOCTOR'S VISIT

The Professor received a telegram from the Lyalikovs' factory; he was asked to come as quickly as possible. The daughter of some Madame Lyalikov, apparently the owner of the factory, was ill, and that was all that one could make out of the long, incoherent telegram. And the Professor did not go himself, but sent instead his assistant, Korolyov.

It was two stations from Moscow, and there was a drive of three miles from the station. A carriage with three horses had been sent to the station to meet Korolyov; the coachman wore a hat with a peacock's feather on it, and answered every question in a loud voice like a soldier: "No, sir!" "Certainly, sir!"

It was Saturday evening; the sun was setting, the workpeople were coming in crowds from the factory to the station, and they bowed to the carriage in which Korolyov was driving. And he was charmed with the evening, the farmhouses and villas on the road, and the birch-trees, and the quiet atmosphere all around, when the fields and woods and the sun seemed preparing, like the workpeople now on the eve of the holiday, to rest, and perhaps to pray. . . .

He was born and had grown up in Moscow; he did not know the country, and he had never taken any interest in factories, or been inside one, but he had happened to read about factories, and had been in the houses of manufacturers and had talked to them; and whenever he saw a factory far or near, he always thought how quiet and peaceable it was outside, but within there was always sure to be impenetrable ignorance and dull egoism on the side of the owners, wearisome, unhealthy toil on the side of the workpeople, squabbling, vermin, vodka. And now when the workpeople timidly and respectfully made way for the carriage, in their faces, their caps, their walk, he read physical impurity, drunkenness, nervous exhaustion, bewilderment.

They drove in at the factory gates. On each side he caught glimpses of the little houses of workpeople, of the faces of women, of quilts and linen on the railings. "Look out!" shouted the coachman, not pulling up the horses. It was a wide courtyard without grass, with five immense blocks of buildings with tall chimneys a little distance one from another, warehouses and barracks, and over everything a sort of grey powder as though from dust. Here and there, like oases in the desert, there were pitiful gardens, and the green and red roofs of the houses in which the managers and clerks lived. The coachman suddenly pulled up the horses, and the carriage stopped at the house, which had been newly painted grey; here was a flower garden, with a lilac bush covered with dust, and on the yellow steps at the front door there was a strong smell of paint.

"Please come in, doctor," said women's voices in the passage and the entry, and at the same time he heard sighs and whisperings. "Pray walk in. . . . We've been expecting you so long . . . we're in real trouble. Here, this way."

Madame Lyalikov—a stout elderly lady wearing a black silk dress with fashionable sleeves, but, judging from her face, a simple uneducated woman—looked at the doctor in a flutter, and could not bring herself to hold out her hand to him; she did not dare. Beside her stood a personage with short hair and a pince-nez; she was wearing a blouse of many colours, and was very thin and no longer young. The servants called her Christina Dmitryevna, and Korolyov guessed that this was the governess. Probably, as the person of most education in the house, she had been charged to meet and receive the doctor, for she began immediately, in great haste, stating the causes of the illness, giving trivial and tiresome details, but without saying who was ill or what was the matter.

The doctor and the governess were sitting talking while the lady of the house stood motionless at the door, waiting. From the conversation Korolyov learned that the patient was Madame Lyalikov's only daughter and heiress, a girl of twenty, called Liza; she had been ill for a long time, and had consulted various doctors, and the previous night she had suffered till morning from such violent palpitations of the heart, that no one in the house had slept, and they had been afraid she might die.

"She has been, one may say, ailing from a child," said Christina Dmitryevna in a sing-song voice, continually wiping her lips with her hand. "The doctors say it is nerves; when she was a little girl she was scrofulous, and the doctors drove it inwards, so I think it may be due to that."

They went to see the invalid. Fully grown up, big and tall, but ugly like her mother, with the same little eyes and disproportionate breadth of the lower part of the face, lying with her hair in disorder, muffled up to the chin, she made upon Korolyov at the first minute the impression of a poor, destitute creature, sheltered and cared for here out of charity, and he could hardly believe that this was the heiress of the five huge buildings.

"I am the doctor come to see you," said Korolyov. "Good evening."

He mentioned his name and pressed her hand, a large, cold, ugly hand; she sat up, and, evidently accustomed to doctors, let herself be sounded, without showing the least concern that her shoulders and chest were uncovered.

"I have palpitations of the heart," she said, "It was so awful all night. . . . I almost died of fright! Do give me something."

"I will, I will; don't worry yourself."

Korolyov examined her and shrugged his shoulders.

"The heart is all right," he said; "it's all going on satisfactorily; everything is in good order. Your nerves must have been playing pranks a little, but that's so common. The attack is over by now, one must suppose; lie down and go to sleep."

At that moment a lamp was brought into the bed-room. The patient screwed up her eyes at the light, then suddenly put her hands to her head and broke into sobs. And the impression of a destitute, ugly creature vanished, and Korolyov no longer noticed the little eyes or the heavy development of the lower part of the face. He saw a soft, suffering expression which was intelligent and touching: she seemed to him altogether graceful, feminine, and simple; and he longed to soothe her, not with drugs, not with advice, but with simple, kindly words. Her mother put her arms round her head and hugged her. What despair, what grief was in the old woman's face! She, her mother, had reared her and brought her up, spared nothing, and devoted her whole life to having her daughter taught French, dancing, music: had engaged a dozen teachers for her; had consulted the best doctors, kept a governess. And now she could not make out the reason of these tears, why there was all this misery, she could not understand, and was bewildered; and she had a guilty, agitated, despairing expression, as though she had omitted something very important, had left something undone, had neglected to call in somebody—and whom, she did not know.

"Lizanka, you are crying again . . . again," she said, hugging her daughter to her. "My own, my darling, my child, tell me what it is! Have pity on me! Tell me."

Both wept bitterly. Korolyov sat down on the side of the bed and took Liza's hand.

"Come, give over; it's no use crying," he said kindly. "Why, there is nothing in the world that is worth those tears. Come, we won't cry; that's no good. . . ."

And inwardly he thought:

"It's high time she was married. . . ."

"Our doctor at the factory gave her kalibromati," said the governess, "but I notice it only makes her worse. I should have thought that if she is given anything for the heart it ought to be drops. . . . I forget the name. . . . Convallaria, isn't it?"

And there followed all sorts of details. She interrupted the doctor, preventing his speaking, and there was a look of effort on her face, as though she supposed that, as the woman of most education in the house, she was duty bound to keep up a conversation with the doctor, and on no other subject but medicine.

Korolyov felt bored.

"I find nothing special the matter," he said, addressing the mother as he went out of the bedroom. "If your daughter is being attended by the factory doctor, let him go on attending her. The treatment so far has been perfectly correct, and I see no reason for changing your doctor. Why change? It's such an ordinary trouble; there's nothing seriously wrong."

He spoke deliberately as he put on his gloves, while Madame Lyalikov stood without moving, and looked at him with her tearful eyes.

"I have half an hour to catch the ten o'clock train," he said. "I hope I am not too late."

"And can't you stay?" she asked, and tears trickled down her cheeks again. "I am ashamed to trouble you, but if you would be so good . . . . For God's sake," she went on in an undertone, glancing towards the door, "do stay to-night with us! She is all I have . . . my only daughter. . . . She frightened me last night; I can't get over it. . . . Don't go away, for goodness' sake! . . ."

He wanted to tell her that he had a great deal of work in Moscow, that his family were expecting him home; it was disagreeable to him to spend the evening and the whole night in a strange house quite needlessly; but he looked at her face, heaved a sigh, and began taking off his gloves without a word.

All the lamps and candles were lighted in his honour in the drawing-room and the dining-room. He sat down at the piano and began turning over the music. Then he looked at the pictures on the walls, at the portraits. The pictures, oil-paintings in gold frames, were views of the Crimea—a stormy sea with a ship, a Catholic monk with a wineglass; they were all dull, smooth daubs, with no trace of talent in them. There was not a single good-looking face among the portraits, nothing but broad cheekbones and astonished-looking eyes. Lyalikov, Liza's father, had a low forehead and a self-satisfied expression; his uniform sat like a sack on his bulky plebeian figure; on his breast was a medal and a Red Cross Badge. There was little sign of culture, and the luxury was senseless and haphazard, and was as ill fitting as that uniform. The floors irritated him with their brilliant polish, the lustres on the chandelier irritated him, and he was reminded for some reason of the story of the merchant who used to go to the baths with a medal on his neck. . . .

He heard a whispering in the entry; some one was softly snoring. And suddenly from outside came harsh, abrupt, metallic sounds, such as Korolyov had never heard before, and which he did not understand now; they roused strange, unpleasant echoes in his soul.

"I believe nothing would induce me to remain here to live . . ." he thought, and went back to the music-books again.

"Doctor, please come to supper!" the governess called him in a low voice.

He went into supper. The table was large and laid with a vast number of dishes and wines, but there were only two to supper: himself and Christina Dmitryevna. She drank Madeira, ate rapidly, and talked, looking at him through her pince-nez:

"Our workpeople are very contented. We have performances at the factory every winter; the workpeople act themselves. They have lectures with a magic lantern, a splendid tea-room, and everything they want. They are very much attached to us, and when they heard that Lizanka was worse they had a service sung for her. Though they have no education, they have their feelings, too."

"It looks as though you have no man in the house at all," said Korolyov.

"Not one. Pyotr Nikanoritch died a year and a half ago, and left us alone. And so there are the three of us. In the summer we live here, and in winter we live in Moscow, in Polianka. I have been living with them for eleven years—as one of the family."

At supper they served sterlet, chicken rissoles, and stewed fruit; the wines were expensive French wines.

"Please don't stand on ceremony, doctor," said Christina Dmitryevna, eating and wiping her mouth with her fist, and it was evident she found her life here exceedingly pleasant. "Please have some more."

After supper the doctor was shown to his room, where a bed had been made up for him, but he did not feel sleepy. The room was stuffy and it smelt of paint; he put on his coat and went out.

It was cool in the open air; there was already a glimmer of dawn, and all the five blocks of buildings, with their tall chimneys, barracks, and warehouses, were distinctly outlined against the damp air. As it was a holiday, they were not working, and the windows were dark, and in only one of the buildings was there a furnace burning; two windows were crimson, and fire mixed with smoke came from time to time from the chimney. Far away beyond the yard the frogs were croaking and the nightingales singing.

Looking at the factory buildings and the barracks, where the workpeople were asleep, he thought again what he always thought when he saw a factory. They may have performances for the workpeople, magic lanterns, factory doctors, and improvements of all sorts, but, all the same, the workpeople he had met that day on his way from the station did not look in any way different from those he had known long ago in his childhood, before there were factory performances and improvements. As a doctor accustomed to judging correctly of chronic complaints, the radical cause of which was incomprehensible and incurable, he looked upon factories as something baffling, the cause of which also was obscure and not removable, and all the improvements in the life of the factory hands he looked upon not as superfluous, but as comparable with the treatment of incurable illnesses.

"There is something baffling in it, of course . . ." he thought, looking at the crimson windows. "Fifteen hundred or two thousand workpeople are working without rest in unhealthy surroundings, making bad cotton goods, living on the verge of starvation, and only waking from this nightmare at rare intervals in the tavern; a hundred people act as overseers, and the whole life of that hundred is spent in imposing fines, in abuse, in injustice, and only two or three so-called owners enjoy the profits, though they don't work at all, and despise the wretched cotton. But what are the profits, and how do they enjoy them? Madame Lyalikov and her daughter are unhappy—it makes one wretched to look at them; the only one who enjoys her life is Christina Dmitryevna, a stupid, middle-aged maiden lady in pince-nez. And so it appears that all these five blocks of buildings are at work, and inferior cotton is sold in the Eastern markets, simply that Christina Dmitryevna may eat sterlet and drink Madeira."

Suddenly there came a strange noise, the same sound Korolyov had heard before supper. Some one was striking on a sheet of metal near one of the buildings; he struck a note, and then at once checked the vibrations, so that short, abrupt, discordant sounds were produced, rather like "Dair . . . dair . . . dair. . . ." Then there was half a minute of stillness, and from another building there came sounds equally abrupt and unpleasant, lower bass notes: "Drin . . . drin . . . drin. . ." Eleven times. Evidently it was the watchman striking the hour. Near the third building he heard: "Zhuk . . . zhuk . . . zhuk. . . ." And so near all the buildings, and then behind the barracks and beyond the gates. And in the stillness of the night it seemed as though these sounds were uttered by a monster with crimson eyes—the devil himself, who controlled the owners and the work-people alike, and was deceiving both.

Korolyov went out of the yard into the open country.

"Who goes there?" some one called to him at the gates in an abrupt voice.

"It's just like being in prison," he thought, and made no answer.

Here the nightingales and the frogs could be heard more distinctly, and one could feel it was a night in May. From the station came the noise of a train; somewhere in the distance drowsy cocks were crowing; but, all the same, the night was still, the world was sleeping tranquilly. In a field not far from the factory there could be seen the framework of a house and heaps of building material:

Korolyov sat down on the planks and went on thinking.

"The only person who feels happy here is the governess, and the factory hands are working for her gratification. But that's only apparent: she is only the figurehead. The real person, for whom everything is being done, is the devil."

And he thought about the devil, in whom he did not believe, and he looked round at the two windows where the fires were gleaming. It seemed to him that out of those crimson eyes the devil himself was looking at him—that unknown force that had created the mutual relation of the strong and the weak, that coarse blunder which one could never correct. The strong must hinder the weak from living such was the law of Nature; but only in a newspaper article or in a school book was that intelligible and easily accepted. In the hotchpotch which was everyday life, in the tangle of trivialities out of which human relations were woven, it was no longer a law, but a logical absurdity, when the strong and the weak were both equally victims of their mutual relations, unwillingly submitting to some directing force, unknown, standing outside life, apart from man.

So thought Korolyov, sitting on the planks, and little by little he was possessed by a feeling that this unknown and mysterious force was really close by and looking at him. Meanwhile the east was growing paler, time passed rapidly; when there was not a soul anywhere near, as though everything were dead, the five buildings and their chimneys against the grey background of the dawn had a peculiar look—not the same as by day; one forgot altogether that inside there were steam motors, electricity, telephones, and kept thinking of lake-dwellings, of the Stone Age, feeling the presence of a crude, unconscious force. . . .

And again there came the sound: "Dair . . . dair . . . dair . . . dair . . ." twelve times. Then there was stillness, stillness for half a minute, and at the other end of the yard there rang out.

"Drin . . . drin . . . drin. . . ."

"Horribly disagreeable," thought Korolyov.

"Zhuk . . . zhuk . . ." there resounded from a third place, abruptly, sharply, as though with annoyance—"Zhuk . . . zhuk. . . ."

And it took four minutes to strike twelve. Then there was a hush; and again it seemed as though everything were dead.

Korolyov sat a little longer, then went to the house, but sat up for a good while longer. In the adjoining rooms there was whispering, there was a sound of shuffling slippers and bare feet.

"Is she having another attack?" thought Korolyov.

He went out to have a look at the patient. By now it was quite light in the rooms, and a faint glimmer of sunlight, piercing through the morning mist, quivered on the floor and on the wall of the drawing-room. The door of Liza's room was open, and she was sitting in a low chair beside her bed, with her hair down, wearing a dressing-gown and wrapped in a shawl. The blinds were down on the windows.

"How do you feel?" asked Korolyov.

"Well, thank you."

He touched her pulse, then straightened her hair, that had fallen over her forehead.

"You are not asleep," he said. "It's beautiful weather outside. It's spring. The nightingales are singing, and you sit in the dark and think of something."

She listened and looked into his face; her eyes were sorrowful and intelligent, and it was evident she wanted to say something to him.

"Does this happen to you often?" he said.

She moved her lips, and answered:

"Often, I feel wretched almost every night."

At that moment the watchman in the yard began striking two o'clock.

They heard: "Dair . . . dair . . ." and she shuddered.

"Do those knockings worry you?" he asked.

"I don't know. Everything here worries me," she answered, and pondered. "Everything worries me. I hear sympathy in your voice; it seemed to me as soon as I saw you that I could tell you all about it."

"Tell me, I beg you."

"I want to tell you of my opinion. It seems to me that I have no illness, but that I am weary and frightened, because it is bound to be so and cannot be otherwise. Even the healthiest person can't help being uneasy if, for instance, a robber is moving about under his window. I am constantly being doctored," she went on, looking at her knees, and she gave a shy smile. "I am very grateful, of course, and I do not deny that the treatment is a benefit; but I should like to talk, not with a doctor, but with some intimate friend who would understand me and would convince me that I was right or wrong."

"Have you no friends?" asked Korolyov.

"I am lonely. I have a mother; I love her, but, all the same, I am lonely. That's how it happens to be. . . . Lonely people read a great deal, but say little and hear little. Life for them is mysterious; they are mystics and often see the devil where he is not. Lermontov's Tamara was lonely and she saw the devil."

"Do you read a great deal?"

"Yes. You see, my whole time is free from morning till night. I read by day, and by night my head is empty; instead of thoughts there are shadows in it."

"Do you see anything at night?" asked Korolyov.

"No, but I feel. . . ."

She smiled again, raised her eyes to the doctor, and looked at him so sorrowfully, so intelligently; and it seemed to him that she trusted him, and that she wanted to speak frankly to him, and that she thought the same as he did. But she was silent, perhaps waiting for him to speak.

And he knew what to say to her. It was clear to him that she needed as quickly as possible to give up the five buildings and the million if she had it—to leave that devil that looked out at night; it was clear to him, too, that she thought so herself, and was only waiting for some one she trusted to confirm her.

But he did not know how to say it. How? One is shy of asking men under sentence what they have been sentenced for; and in the same way it is awkward to ask very rich people what they want so much money for, why they make such a poor use of their wealth, why they don't give it up, even when they see in it their unhappiness; and if they begin a conversation about it themselves, it is usually embarrassing, awkward, and long.

"How is one to say it?" Korolyov wondered. "And is it necessary to speak?"

And he said what he meant in a roundabout way:

"You in the position of a factory owner and a wealthy heiress are dissatisfied; you don't believe in your right to it; and here now you can't sleep. That, of course, is better than if you were satisfied, slept soundly, and thought everything was satisfactory. Your sleeplessness does you credit; in any case, it is a good sign. In reality, such a conversation as this between us now would have been unthinkable for our parents. At night they did not talk, but slept sound; we, our generation, sleep badly, are restless, but talk a great deal, and are always trying to settle whether we are right or not. For our children or grandchildren that question— whether they are right or not—will have been settled. Things will be clearer for them than for us. Life will be good in fifty years' time; it's only a pity we shall not last out till then. It would be interesting to have a peep at it."

"What will our children and grandchildren do?" asked Liza.

"I don't know. . . . I suppose they will throw it all up and go away."

"Go where?"

"Where? . . . Why, where they like," said Korolyov; and he laughed.

"There are lots of places a good, intelligent person can go to."

He glanced at his watch.

"The sun has risen, though," he said. "It is time you were asleep. Undress and sleep soundly. Very glad to have made your acquaintance," he went on, pressing her hand. "You are a good, interesting woman. Good-night!"

He went to his room and went to bed.

In the morning when the carriage was brought round they all came out on to the steps to see him off. Liza, pale and exhausted, was in a white dress as though for a holiday, with a flower in her hair; she looked at him, as yesterday, sorrowfully and intelligently, smiled and talked, and all with an expression as though she wanted to tell him something special, important—him alone. They could hear the larks trilling and the church bells pealing. The windows in the factory buildings were sparkling gaily, and, driving across the yard and afterwards along the road to the station, Korolyov thought neither of the workpeople nor of lake dwellings, nor of the devil, but thought of the time, perhaps close at hand, when life would be as bright and joyous as that still Sunday morning; and he thought how pleasant it was on such a morning in the spring to drive with three horses in a good carriage, and to bask in the sunshine.

AN UPHEAVAL

Mashenka Pavletsky, a young girl who had only just finished her studies at a boarding school, returning from a walk to the house of the Kushkins, with whom she was living as a governess, found the household in a terrible turmoil. Mihailo, the porter who opened the door to her, was excited and red as a crab.

Loud voices were heard from upstairs.

"Madame Kushkin is in a fit, most likely, or else she has quarrelled with her husband," thought Mashenka.

In the hall and in the corridor she met maid-servants. One of them was crying. Then Mashenka saw, running out of her room, the master of the house himself, Nikolay Sergeitch, a little man with a flabby face and a bald head, though he was not old. He was red in the face and twitching all over. He passed the governess without noticing her, and throwing up his arms, exclaimed:

"Oh, how horrible it is! How tactless! How stupid! How barbarous! Abominable!"

Mashenka went into her room, and then, for the first time in her life, it was her lot to experience in all its acuteness the feeling that is so familiar to persons in dependent positions, who eat the bread of the rich and powerful, and cannot speak their minds. There was a search going on in her room. The lady of the house, Fedosya Vassilyevna, a stout, broad-shouldered, uncouth woman with thick black eyebrows, a faintly perceptible moustache, and red hands, who was exactly like a plain, illiterate cook in face and manners, was standing, without her cap on, at the table, putting back into Mashenka's workbag balls of wool, scraps of materials, and bits of paper. . . . Evidently the governess's arrival took her by surprise, since, on looking round and seeing the girl's pale and astonished face, she was a little taken aback, and muttered:

"Pardon. I . . . I upset it accidentally. . . . My sleeve caught in it. . ."

And saying something more, Madame Kushkin rustled her long skirts and went out. Mashenka looked round her room with wondering eyes, and, unable to understand it, not knowing what to think, shrugged her shoulders, and turned cold with dismay. What had Fedosya Vassilyevna been looking for in her work-bag? If she really had, as she said, caught her sleeve in it and upset everything, why had Nikolay Sergeitch dashed out of her room so excited and red in the face? Why was one drawer of the table pulled out a little way? The money-box, in which the governess put away ten kopeck pieces and old stamps, was open. They had opened it, but did not know how to shut it, though they had scratched the lock all over. The whatnot with her books on it, the things on the table, the bed—all bore fresh traces of a search. Her linen-basket, too. The linen had been carefully folded, but it was not in the same order as Mashenka had left it when she went out. So the search had been thorough, most thorough. But what was it for? Why? What had happened? Mashenka remembered the excited porter, the general turmoil which was still going on, the weeping servant-girl; had it not all some connection with the search that had just been made in her room? Was not she mixed up in something dreadful? Mashenka turned pale, and feeling cold all over, sank on to her linen-basket.

A maid-servant came into the room.

"Liza, you don't know why they have been rummaging in my room?" the governess asked her.

"Mistress has lost a brooch worth two thousand," said Liza.

"Yes, but why have they been rummaging in my room?"

"They've been searching every one, miss. They've searched all my things, too. They stripped us all naked and searched us. . . . God knows, miss, I never went near her toilet-table, let alone touching the brooch. I shall say the same at the police-station."

"But . . . why have they been rummaging here?" the governess still wondered.

"A brooch has been stolen, I tell you. The mistress has been rummaging in everything with her own hands. She even searched Mihailo, the porter, herself. It's a perfect disgrace! Nikolay Sergeitch simply looks on and cackles like a hen. But you've no need to tremble like that, miss. They found nothing here. You've nothing to be afraid of if you didn't take the brooch."

"But, Liza, it's vile . . . it's insulting," said Mashenka, breathless with indignation. "It's so mean, so low! What right had she to suspect me and to rummage in my things?"

"You are living with strangers, miss," sighed Liza. "Though you are a young lady, still you are . . . as it were . . . a servant. . . . It's not like living with your papa and mamma."

Mashenka threw herself on the bed and sobbed bitterly. Never in her life had she been subjected to such an outrage, never had she been so deeply insulted. . . . She, well-educated, refined, the daughter of a teacher, was suspected of theft; she had been searched like a street-walker! She could not imagine a greater insult. And to this feeling of resentment was added an oppressive dread of what would come next. All sorts of absurd ideas came into her mind. If they could suspect her of theft, then they might arrest her, strip her naked, and search her, then lead her through the street with an escort of soldiers, cast her into a cold, dark cell with mice and woodlice, exactly like the dungeon in which Princess Tarakanov was imprisoned. Who would stand up for her? Her parents lived far away in the provinces; they had not the money to come to her. In the capital she was as solitary as in a desert, without friends or kindred. They could do what they liked with her.

"I will go to all the courts and all the lawyers," Mashenka thought, trembling. "I will explain to them, I will take an oath. . . . They will believe that I could not be a thief!"

Mashenka remembered that under the sheets in her basket she had some sweetmeats, which, following the habits of her schooldays, she had put in her pocket at dinner and carried off to her room. She felt hot all over, and was ashamed at the thought that her little secret was known to the lady of the house; and all this terror, shame, resentment, brought on an attack of palpitation of the heart, which set up a throbbing in her temples, in her heart, and deep down in her stomach.

"Dinner is ready," the servant summoned Mashenka.

"Shall I go, or not?"

Mashenka brushed her hair, wiped her face with a wet towel, and went into the dining-room. There they had already begun dinner. At one end of the table sat Fedosya Vassilyevna with a stupid, solemn, serious face; at the other end Nikolay Sergeitch. At the sides there were the visitors and the children. The dishes were handed by two footmen in swallowtails and white gloves. Every one knew that there was an upset in the house, that Madame Kushkin was in trouble, and every one was silent. Nothing was heard but the sound of munching and the rattle of spoons on the plates.

The lady of the house, herself, was the first to speak.

"What is the third course?" she asked the footman in a weary, injured voice.

"Esturgeon a la russe," answered the footman.

"I ordered that, Fenya," Nikolay Sergeitch hastened to observe. "I wanted some fish. If you don't like it, *ma chere*, don't let them serve it. I just ordered it. . . ."

Fedosya Vassilyevna did not like dishes that she had not ordered herself, and now her eyes filled with tears.

"Come, don't let us agitate ourselves," Mamikov, her household doctor, observed in a honeyed voice, just touching her arm, with a smile as honeyed. "We are nervous enough as it is. Let us forget the brooch! Health is worth more than two thousand roubles!"

"It's not the two thousand I regret," answered the lady, and a big tear rolled down her cheek. "It's the fact itself that revolts me! I cannot put up with thieves in my house. I don't regret it—I regret nothing; but to steal from me is such ingratitude! That's how they repay me for my kindness. . . ."

They all looked into their plates, but Mashenka fancied after the lady's words that every one was looking at her. A lump rose in her throat; she began crying and put her handkerchief to her lips.

"Pardon," she muttered. "I can't help it. My head aches. I'll go away."

And she got up from the table, scraping her chair awkwardly, and went out quickly, still more overcome with confusion.

"It's beyond everything!" said Nikolay Sergeitch, frowning. "What need was there to search her room? How out of place it was!"

"I don't say she took the brooch," said Fedosya Vassilyevna, "but can you answer for her? To tell the truth, I haven't much confidence in these learned paupers."

"It really was unsuitable, Fenya. . . . Excuse me, Fenya, but you've no kind of legal right to make a search."

"I know nothing about your laws. All I know is that I've lost my brooch. And I will find the brooch!" She brought her fork down on the plate with a clatter, and her eyes flashed angrily. "And you eat your dinner, and don't interfere in what doesn't concern you!"

Nikolay Sergeitch dropped his eyes mildly and sighed. Meanwhile Mashenka, reaching her room, flung herself on her bed. She felt now neither alarm nor shame, but she felt an intense longing to go and slap the cheeks of this hard, arrogant, dull-witted, prosperous woman.

Lying on her bed she breathed into her pillow and dreamed of how nice it would be to go and buy the most expensive brooch and fling it into the face of this bullying woman. If only it were God's will that Fedosya Vassilyevna should come to ruin and wander about begging, and should taste all the horrors of poverty and dependence, and that Mashenka, whom she had insulted, might give her alms! Oh, if only she could come in for a big fortune, could buy a carriage, and could drive noisily past the windows so as to be envied by that woman!

But all these were only dreams, in reality there was only one thing left to do—to get away as quickly as possible, not to stay another hour in this place. It was true it was terrible to lose her place, to go back to her parents, who had nothing; but what could she do? Mashenka could not bear the sight of the lady of the house nor of her little room; she felt stifled and wretched here. She was so disgusted with Fedosya Vassilyevna, who was so obsessed by her illnesses and her supposed aristocratic rank, that everything in the world seemed to have become coarse and unattractive because this woman was living in it. Mashenka jumped up from the bed and began packing.

"May I come in?" asked Nikolay Sergeitch at the door; he had come up noiselessly to the door, and spoke in a soft, subdued voice. "May I?"

"Come in."

He came in and stood still near the door. His eyes looked dim and his red little nose was shiny. After dinner he used to drink beer, and the fact was perceptible in his walk, in his feeble, flabby hands.

"What's this?" he asked, pointing to the basket.

"I am packing. Forgive me, Nikolay Sergeitch, but I cannot remain in your house. I feel deeply insulted by this search!"

"I understand. . . . Only you are wrong to go. Why should you? They've searched your things, but you . . . what does it matter to you? You will be none the worse for it."

Mashenka was silent and went on packing. Nikolay Sergeitch pinched his moustache, as though wondering what he should say next, and went on in an ingratiating voice:

"I understand, of course, but you must make allowances. You know my wife is nervous, headstrong; you mustn't judge her too harshly."

Mashenka did not speak.

"If you are so offended," Nikolay Sergeitch went on, "well, if you like, I'm ready to apologise. I ask your pardon."

Mashenka made no answer, but only bent lower over her box. This exhausted, irresolute man was of absolutely no significance in the household. He stood in the pitiful position of a dependent and hanger-on, even with the servants, and his apology meant nothing either.

"H'm! . . . You say nothing! That's not enough for you. In that case, I will apologise for my wife. In my wife's name. . . . She behaved tactlessly, I admit it as a gentleman. . . ."

Nikolay Sergeitch walked about the room, heaved a sigh, and went on:

"Then you want me to have it rankling here, under my heart. . . .

You want my conscience to torment me. . . ."

"I know it's not your fault, Nikolay Sergeitch," said Mashenka, looking him full in the face with her big tear-stained eyes. "Why should you worry yourself?"

"Of course, no. . . . But still, don't you . . . go away. I entreat you."

Mashenka shook her head. Nikolay Sergeitch stopped at the window and drummed on the pane with his finger-tips.

"Such misunderstandings are simply torture to me," he said. "Why, do you want me to go down on my knees to you, or what? Your pride is wounded, and here you've been crying and packing up to go; but I have pride, too, and you do not spare it! Or do you want me to tell you what I would not tell as Confession? Do you? Listen; you want me to tell you what I won't tell the priest on my deathbed?"

Mashenka made no answer.

"I took my wife's brooch," Nikolay Sergeitch said quickly. "Is that enough now? Are you satisfied? Yes, I . . . took it. . . . But, of course, I count on your discretion. . . . For God's sake, not a word, not half a hint to any one!"

Mashenka, amazed and frightened, went on packing; she snatched her things, crumpled them up, and thrust them anyhow into the box and the basket. Now, after this candid avowal on the part of Nikolay Sergeitch, she could not remain another minute, and could not understand how she could have gone on living in the house before.

"And it's nothing to wonder at," Nikolay Sergeitch went on after a pause. "It's an everyday story! I need money, and she . . . won't give it to me. It was my father's money that bought this house and everything, you know! It's all mine, and the brooch belonged to my mother, and . . . it's all mine! And she took it, took possession of everything. . . . I can't go to law with her, you'll admit. . . . I beg you most earnestly, overlook it . . . stay on. Tout comprendre, tout pardonner. Will you stay?"

"No!" said Mashenka resolutely, beginning to tremble. "Let me alone, I entreat you!"

"Well, God bless you!" sighed Nikolay Sergeitch, sitting down on the stool near the box. "I must own I like people who still can feel resentment, contempt, and so on. I could sit here forever and look at your indignant face. . . . So you won't stay, then? I understand. . . . It's bound to be so. . . Yes, of course. . . . It's all right for you, but for me—wo-o-o-o! . . . I can't stir a step out of this cellar. I'd go off to one of our estates, but in every one of them there are some of my wife's rascals. . . stewards, experts, damn them all! They mortgage and remortgage. . . . You mustn't catch fish, must keep off the grass, mustn't break the trees."

"Nikolay Sergeitch!" his wife's voice called from the drawing-room.

"Agnia, call your master!"

"Then you won't stay?" asked Nikolay Sergeitch, getting up quickly and going towards the door. "You might as well stay, really. In the evenings I could come and have a talk with you. Eh? Stay! If you go, there won't be a human face left in the house. It's awful!"

Nikolay Sergeitch's pale, exhausted face besought her, but Mashenka shook her head, and with a wave of his hand he went out.

Half an hour later she was on her way.

IONITCH

I

WHEN visitors to the provincial town S---- complained of the dreariness and monotony of life, the inhabitants of the town, as though defending themselves, declared that it was very nice in S----, that there was a library, a theatre, a club; that they had balls; and, finally, that there were clever, agreeable, and interesting families with whom one could make acquaintance. And they used to point to the family of the Turkins as the most highly cultivated and talented.

This family lived in their own house in the principal street, near the Governor's. Ivan Petrovitch Turkin himself—a stout, handsome, dark man with whiskers—used to get up amateur performances for benevolent objects, and used to take the part of an elderly general and cough very amusingly. He knew a number of anecdotes, charades, proverbs, and was fond of being humorous and witty, and he always wore an expression from which it was impossible to tell whether he were joking or in earnest. His wife, Vera Iosifovna—a thin, nice-looking lady who wore a pince-nez—used to write novels and stories, and was very fond of reading them aloud to her visitors. The daughter, Ekaterina Ivanovna, a young girl, used to play on the piano. In short, every member of the family had a special talent. The Turkins welcomed visitors, and good-humouredly displayed their talents with genuine simplicity. Their stone house was roomy and cool in summer; half of the windows looked into a shady old garden, where nightingales used to sing in the spring. When there were visitors in the house, there was a clatter of knives in the kitchen and a smell of fried onions in the yard—and that was always a sure sign of a plentiful and savoury supper to follow.

And as soon as Dmitri Ionitch Startsev was appointed the district doctor, and took up his abode at Dyalizh, six miles from S----, he, too, was told that as a cultivated man it was essential for him to make the acquaintance of the Turkins. In the winter he was introduced to Ivan Petrovitch in the street; they talked about the weather, about the theatre, about the cholera; an invitation followed. On a holiday in the spring—it was Ascension Day—after seeing his patients, Startsev set off for town in search of a little recreation and to make some purchases. He walked in a leisurely way (he had not yet set up his carriage), humming all the time:

"'Before I'd drunk the tears from life's goblet. . . .'"

In town he dined, went for a walk in the gardens, then Ivan Petrovitch's invitation came into his mind, as it were of itself, and he decided to call on the Turkins and see what sort of people they were.

"How do you do, if you please?" said Ivan Petrovitch, meeting him on the steps. "Delighted, delighted to see such an agreeable visitor. Come along; I will introduce you to my better half. I tell him, Verotchka," he went on, as he presented the doctor to his wife—"I tell him that he has no human right to sit at home in a hospital; he ought to devote his leisure to society. Oughtn't he, darling?"

"Sit here," said Vera Iosifovna, making her visitor sit down beside her. "You can dance attendance on me. My husband is jealous—he is an Othello; but we will try and behave so well that he will notice nothing."

"Ah, you spoilt chicken!" Ivan Petrovitch muttered tenderly, and he kissed her on the forehead. "You have come just in the nick of time," he said, addressing the doctor again. "My better half has written a 'hugeous' novel, and she is going to read it aloud to-day."

"Petit Jean," said Vera Iosifovna to her husband, "dites que l'on nous donne du the."

Startsev was introduced to Ekaterina Ivanovna, a girl of eighteen, very much like her mother, thin and pretty. Her expression was still childish and her figure was soft and slim; and her developed girlish bosom, healthy and beautiful, was suggestive of spring, real spring.

Then they drank tea with jam, honey, and sweetmeats, and with very nice cakes, which melted in the mouth. As the evening came on, other visitors gradually arrived, and Ivan Petrovitch fixed his laughing eyes on each of them and said:

"How do you do, if you please?"

Then they all sat down in the drawing-room with very serious faces, and Vera Iosifovna read her novel. It began like this: "The frost was intense. . . ." The windows were wide open; from the kitchen came the clatter of knives and the smell of fried onions. . . . It was comfortable in the soft deep arm-chair; the lights had such a friendly twinkle in the twilight of the drawing-room, and at the moment on a summer evening when sounds of voices and laughter floated in from the street and whiffs of lilac from the yard, it was difficult to grasp that the frost was intense, and that the setting sun was lighting with its chilly rays a solitary wayfarer on the snowy plain. Vera Iosifovna read how a beautiful young countess founded a school, a hospital, a library, in her village, and fell in love with a wandering artist; she read of what never happens in real life, and yet it was pleasant to listen—it was comfortable, and such agreeable, serene thoughts kept coming into the mind, one had no desire to get up.

"Not badsome . . ." Ivan Petrovitch said softly.

And one of the visitors hearing, with his thoughts far away, said hardly audibly:

"Yes . . . truly. . . ."

One hour passed, another. In the town gardens close by a band was playing and a chorus was singing. When Vera Iosifovna shut her manuscript book, the company was silent for five minutes, listening to "Lutchina" being sung by the chorus, and the song gave what was not in the novel and is in real life.

"Do you publish your stories in magazines?" Startsev asked Vera Iosifovna.

"No," she answered. "I never publish. I write it and put it away in my cupboard. Why publish?" she explained. "We have enough to live on."

And for some reason every one sighed.

"And now, Kitten, you play something," Ivan Petrovitch said to his daughter.

The lid of the piano was raised and the music lying ready was opened. Ekaterina Ivanovna sat down and banged on the piano with both hands, and then banged again with all her might, and then again and again; her shoulders and bosom shook. She obstinately banged on the same notes, and it sounded as if she would not leave off until she had hammered the keys into the piano. The drawing-room was filled with the din; everything was resounding; the floor, the ceiling, the furniture. . . . Ekaterina Ivanovna was playing a difficult passage, interesting simply on account of its difficulty, long and monotonous, and Startsev, listening, pictured stones dropping down a steep hill and going on dropping, and he wished they would leave off dropping; and at the same time Ekaterina Ivanovna, rosy from the violent exercise, strong and vigorous, with a lock of hair falling over her forehead, attracted him very much. After the winter spent at Dyalizh among patients and peasants, to sit in a drawing-room, to watch this young, elegant, and, in all probability, pure creature, and to listen to these noisy, tedious but still cultured sounds, was so pleasant, so novel. . . .

"Well, Kitten, you have played as never before," said Ivan Petrovitch, with tears in his eyes, when his daughter had finished and stood up. "Die, Denis; you won't write anything better."

All flocked round her, congratulated her, expressed astonishment, declared that it was long since they had heard such music, and she listened in silence with a faint smile, and her whole figure was expressive of triumph.

"Splendid, superb!"

"Splendid," said Startsev, too, carried away by the general enthusiasm. "Where have you studied?" he asked Ekaterina Ivanovna. "At the Conservatoire?"

"No, I am only preparing for the Conservatoire, and till now have been working with Madame Zavlovsky."

"Have you finished at the high school here?"

"Oh, no," Vera Iosifovna answered for her, "We have teachers for her at home; there might be bad influences at the high school or a boarding school, you know. While a young girl is growing up, she ought to be under no influence but her mother's."

"All the same, I'm going to the Conservatoire," said Ekaterina Ivanovna.

"No. Kitten loves her mamma. Kitten won't grieve papa and mamma."

"No, I'm going, I'm going," said Ekaterina Ivanovna, with playful caprice and stamping her foot.

And at supper it was Ivan Petrovitch who displayed his talents. Laughing only with his eyes, he told anecdotes, made epigrams, asked ridiculous riddles and answered them himself, talking the whole time in his extraordinary language, evolved in the course of prolonged practice in witticism and evidently now become a habit: "Badsome," "Hugeous," "Thank you most dumbly," and so on.

But that was not all. When the guests, replete and satisfied, trooped into the hall, looking for their coats and sticks, there bustled about them the footman Pavlusha, or, as he was called in the family, Pava—a lad of fourteen with shaven head and chubby cheeks.

"Come, Pava, perform!" Ivan Petrovitch said to him.

Pava struck an attitude, flung up his arm, and said in a tragic tone: "Unhappy woman, die!"

And every one roared with laughter.

"It's entertaining," thought Startsev, as he went out into the street.

He went to a restaurant and drank some beer, then set off to walk home to Dyalizh; he walked all the way singing:

"'Thy voice to me so languid and caressing. . . .'"

On going to bed, he felt not the slightest fatigue after the six miles' walk. On the contrary, he felt as though he could with pleasure have walked another twenty.

"Not badsome," he thought, and laughed as he fell asleep.

II

Startsev kept meaning to go to the Turkins' again, but there was a great deal of work in the hospital, and he was unable to find free time. In this way more than a year passed in work and solitude. But one day a letter in a light blue envelope was brought him from the town.

Vera Iosifovna had been suffering for some time from migraine, but now since Kitten frightened her every day by saying that she was going away to the Conservatoire, the attacks began to be more frequent. All the doctors of the town had been at the Turkins'; at last it was the district doctor's turn. Vera Iosifovna wrote him a touching letter in which she begged him to come and relieve her sufferings. Startsev went, and after that he began to be often, very often at the Turkins'. . . . He really did something for Vera Iosifovna, and she was already telling all her visitors that he was a wonderful and exceptional doctor. But it was not for the sake of her migraine that he visited the Turkins' now. . . .

It was a holiday. Ekaterina Ivanovna finished her long, wearisome exercises on the piano. Then they sat a long time in the dining-room, drinking tea, and Ivan Petrovitch told some amusing story. Then there was a ring and he had to go into the hall to welcome a guest;

Startsev took advantage of the momentary commotion, and whispered to Ekaterina Ivanovna in great agitation:

"For God's sake, I entreat you, don't torment me; let us go into the garden!"

She shrugged her shoulders, as though perplexed and not knowing what he wanted of her, but she got up and went.

"You play the piano for three or four hours," he said, following her; "then you sit with your mother, and there is no possibility of speaking to you. Give me a quarter of an hour at least, I beseech you."

Autumn was approaching, and it was quiet and melancholy in the old garden; the dark leaves lay thick in the walks. It was already beginning to get dark early.

"I haven't seen you for a whole week," Startsev went on, "and if you only knew what suffering it is! Let us sit down. Listen to me."

They had a favourite place in the garden; a seat under an old spreading maple. And now they sat down on this seat.

"What do you want?" said Ekaterina Ivanovna drily, in a matter-of-fact tone.

"I have not seen you for a whole week; I have not heard you for so long. I long passionately, I thirst for your voice. Speak."

She fascinated him by her freshness, the naive expression of her eyes and cheeks. Even in the way her dress hung on her, he saw something extraordinarily charming, touching in its simplicity and naive grace; and at the same time, in spite of this naivete, she seemed to him intelligent and developed beyond her years. He could talk with her about literature, about art, about anything he liked; could complain to her of life, of people, though it sometimes happened in the middle of serious conversation she would laugh inappropriately or run away into the house. Like almost all girls of her neighbourhood, she had read a great deal (as a rule, people read very little in S----, and at the lending library they said if it were not for the girls and the young Jews, they might as well shut up the library). This afforded Startsev infinite delight; he used to ask her eagerly every time what she had been reading the last few days, and listened enthralled while she told him.

"What have you been reading this week since I saw you last?" he asked now. "Do please tell me."

"I have been reading Pisemsky."

"What exactly?"

"'A Thousand Souls,'" answered Kitten. "And what a funny name Pisemsky had—Alexey Feofilaktitch!

"Where are you going?" cried Startsev in horror, as she suddenly got up and walked towards the house. "I must talk to you; I want to explain myself. . . . Stay with me just five minutes, I supplicate you!"

She stopped as though she wanted to say something, then awkwardly thrust a note into his hand, ran home and sat down to the piano again.

"Be in the cemetery," Startsev read, "at eleven o'clock to-night, near the tomb of Demetti."

"Well, that's not at all clever," he thought, coming to himself.

"Why the cemetery? What for?"

It was clear: Kitten was playing a prank. Who would seriously dream of making an appointment at night in the cemetery far out of the town, when it might have been arranged in the street or in the town gardens? And was it in keeping with him—a district doctor, an intelligent, staid man—to be sighing, receiving notes, to hang about cemeteries, to do silly things that even schoolboys think ridiculous nowadays? What would this romance lead to? What would his colleagues say when they heard of it? Such were Startsev's reflections as he wandered round the tables at the club, and at half-past ten he suddenly set off for the cemetery.

By now he had his own pair of horses, and a coachman called Panteleimon, in a velvet waistcoat. The moon was shining. It was still warm, warm as it is in autumn. Dogs were howling in the suburb near the slaughter-house. Startsev left his horses in one of the side-streets at the end of the town, and walked on foot to the cemetery.

"We all have our oddities," he thought. "Kitten is odd, too; and who knows?--perhaps she is not joking, perhaps she will come"; and he abandoned himself to this faint, vain hope, and it intoxicated him.

He walked for half a mile through the fields; the cemetery showed as a dark streak in the distance, like a forest or a big garden. The wall of white stone came into sight, the gate. . . . In the moonlight he could read on the gate: "The hour cometh." Startsev went in at the little gate, and before anything else he saw the white crosses and monuments on both sides of the broad avenue, and the black shadows of them and the poplars; and for a long way round it was all white and black, and the slumbering trees bowed their branches over the white stones. It seemed as though it were lighter here than in the fields; the maple-leaves stood out sharply like paws on the yellow sand of the avenue and on the stones, and the inscriptions on the tombs could be clearly read. For the first moments Startsev was struck now by what he saw for the first time in his life, and what he would probably never see again; a world not like anything else, a world in which the moonlight was as soft and beautiful, as though slumbering here in its cradle, where there was no life, none whatever; but in every dark poplar, in every tomb, there was felt the presence of a mystery that promised a life peaceful, beautiful, eternal. The stones and faded flowers, together with the autumn scent of the leaves, all told of forgiveness, melancholy, and peace.

All was silence around; the stars looked down from the sky in the profound stillness, and Startsev's footsteps sounded loud and out of place, and only when the church clock began striking and he imagined himself dead, buried there for ever, he felt as though some one were looking at him, and for a moment he thought that it was not peace and tranquillity, but stifled despair, the dumb dreariness of non-existence. . . .

Demetti's tomb was in the form of a shrine with an angel at the top. The Italian opera had once visited S---- and one of the singers had died; she had been buried here, and this monument put up to her. No one in the town remembered her, but the lamp at the entrance reflected the moonlight, and looked as though it were burning.

There was no one, and, indeed, who would come here at midnight? But Startsev waited, and as though the moonlight warmed his passion, he waited passionately, and, in imagination, pictured kisses and embraces. He sat near the monument for half an hour, then paced up and down the side avenues, with his hat in his hand, waiting and thinking of the many women and girls buried in these tombs who had been beautiful and fascinating, who had loved, at night burned with passion, yielding themselves to caresses. How wickedly Mother Nature jested at man's expense, after all! How humiliating it was to recognise it!

Startsev thought this, and at the same time he wanted to cry out that he wanted love, that he was eager for it at all costs. To his eyes they were not slabs of marble, but fair white bodies in the moonlight; he saw shapes hiding bashfully in the shadows of the trees, felt their warmth, and the languor was oppressive. . . .

And as though a curtain were lowered, the moon went behind a cloud, and suddenly all was darkness. Startsev could scarcely find the gate—by now it was as dark as it is on an autumn night. Then he wandered about for an hour and a half, looking for the side-street in which he had left his horses.

"I am tired; I can scarcely stand on my legs," he said to Panteleimon.

And settling himself with relief in his carriage, he thought: "Och!

I ought not to get fat!"

III

The following evening he went to the Turkins' to make an offer. But it turned out to be an inconvenient moment, as Ekaterina Ivanovna was in her own room having her hair done by a hair-dresser. She was getting ready to go to a dance at the club.

He had to sit a long time again in the dining-room drinking tea. Ivan Petrovitch, seeing that his visitor was bored and preoccupied, drew some notes out of his waistcoat pocket, read a funny letter from a German steward, saying that all the ironmongery was ruined and the plasticity was peeling off the walls.

"I expect they will give a decent dowry," thought Startsev, listening absent-mindedly.

After a sleepless night, he found himself in a state of stupefaction, as though he had been given something sweet and soporific to drink; there was fog in his soul, but joy and warmth, and at the same time a sort of cold, heavy fragment of his brain was reflecting:

"Stop before it is too late! Is she the match for you? She is spoilt, whimsical, sleeps till two o'clock in the afternoon, while you are a deacon's son, a district doctor. . . ."

"What of it?" he thought. "I don't care."

"Besides, if you marry her," the fragment went on, "then her relations will make you give up the district work and live in the town."

"After all," he thought, "if it must be the town, the town it must be. They will give a dowry; we can establish ourselves suitably."

At last Ekaterina Ivanovna came in, dressed for the ball, with a low neck, looking fresh and pretty; and Startsev admired her so much, and went into such ecstasies, that he could say nothing, but simply stared at her and laughed.

She began saying good-bye, and he—he had no reason for staying now—got up, saying that it was time for him to go home; his patients were waiting for him.

"Well, there's no help for that," said Ivan Petrovitch. "Go, and you might take Kitten to the club on the way."

It was spotting with rain; it was very dark, and they could only tell where the horses were by Panteleimon's husky cough. The hood of the carriage was put up.

"I stand upright; you lie down right; he lies all right," said Ivan Petrovitch as he put his daughter into the carriage.

They drove off.

"I was at the cemetery yesterday," Startsev began. "How ungenerous and merciless it was on your part! . . ."

"You went to the cemetery?"

"Yes, I went there and waited almost till two o'clock. I suffered . . ."

"Well, suffer, if you cannot understand a joke."

Ekaterina Ivanovna, pleased at having so cleverly taken in a man who was in love with her, and at being the object of such intense love, burst out laughing and suddenly uttered a shriek of terror, for, at that very minute, the horses turned sharply in at the gate of the club, and the carriage almost tilted over. Startsev put his arm round Ekaterina Ivanovna's waist; in her fright she nestled up to him, and he could not restrain himself, and passionately kissed her on the lips and on the chin, and hugged her more tightly.

"That's enough," she said drily.

And a minute later she was not in the carriage, and a policeman near the lighted entrance of the club shouted in a detestable voice to Panteleimon:

"What are you stopping for, you crow? Drive on."

Startsev drove home, but soon afterwards returned. Attired in another man's dress suit and a stiff white tie which kept sawing at his neck and trying to slip away from the collar, he was sitting at midnight in the club drawing-room, and was saying with enthusiasm to Ekaterina Ivanovna.

"Ah, how little people know who have never loved! It seems to me that no one has ever yet written of love truly, and I doubt whether this tender, joyful, agonising feeling can be described, and any one who has once experienced it would not attempt to put it into words. What is the use of preliminaries and introductions? What is the use of unnecessary fine words? My love is immeasurable. I beg, I beseech you," Startsev brought out at last, "be my wife!"

"Dmitri Ionitch," said Ekaterina Ivanovna, with a very grave face, after a moment's thought—"Dmitri Ionitch, I am very grateful to you for the honour. I respect you, but . . ." she got up and continued standing, "but, forgive me, I cannot be your wife. Let us talk seriously. Dmitri Ionitch, you know I love art beyond everything in life. I adore music; I love it frantically; I have dedicated my whole life to it. I want to be an artist; I want fame, success, freedom, and you want me to go on living in this town, to go on living this empty, useless life, which has become insufferable to me. To become a wife—oh, no, forgive me! One must strive towards a lofty, glorious goal, and married life would put me in bondage for ever. Dmitri Ionitch" (she faintly smiled as she pronounced his name; she thought of "Alexey Feofilaktitch")--"Dmitri Ionitch, you are a good, clever, honourable man; you are better than any one. . . ." Tears came into her eyes. "I feel for you with my whole heart, but . . . but you will understand. . . ."

And she turned away and went out of the drawing-room to prevent herself from crying.

Startsev's heart left off throbbing uneasily. Going out of the club into the street, he first of all tore off the stiff tie and drew a deep breath. He was a little ashamed and his vanity was wounded— he had not expected a refusal—and could not believe that all his dreams, his hopes and yearnings, had led him up to such a stupid end, just as in some little play at an amateur performance, and he was sorry for his feeling, for that love of his, so sorry that he felt as though he could have burst into sobs or have violently belaboured Panteleimon's broad back with his umbrella.

For three days he could not get on with anything, he could not eat nor sleep; but when the news reached him that Ekaterina Ivanovna had gone away to Moscow to enter the Conservatoire, he grew calmer and lived as before.

Afterwards, remembering sometimes how he had wandered about the cemetery or how he had driven all over the town to get a dress suit, he stretched lazily and said:

"What a lot of trouble, though!"

IV

Four years had passed. Startsev already had a large practice in the town. Every morning he hurriedly saw his patients at Dyalizh, then he drove in to see his town patients. By now he drove, not with a pair, but with a team of three with bells on them, and he returned home late at night. He had grown broader and stouter, and was not very fond of walking, as he was somewhat asthmatic. And Panteleimon had grown stout, too, and the broader he grew, the more mournfully he sighed and complained of his hard luck: he was sick of driving! Startsev used to visit various households and met many people, but did not become intimate with any one. The inhabitants irritated him by their conversation, their views of life, and even their appearance. Experience taught him by degrees that while he played cards or lunched with one of these people, the man was a peaceable, friendly, and even intelligent human being; that as soon as one talked of anything not eatable, for instance, of politics or science, he would be completely at a loss, or would expound a philosophy so stupid and ill-natured that there was nothing else to do but wave one's hand in despair and go away. Even when Startsev tried to talk to liberal citizens, saying, for instance, that humanity, thank God, was progressing, and that one day it would be possible to dispense with passports and capital punishment, the liberal citizen would look at him askance and ask him mistrustfully: "Then any one could murder any one he chose in the open street?" And when, at tea or supper, Startsev observed in company that one should work, and that one ought not to live without working, every one took this as a reproach, and began to get angry and argue aggressively. With all that, the inhabitants did nothing, absolutely nothing, and took no interest in anything, and it was quite impossible to think of anything to say. And Startsev avoided conversation, and confined himself to eating and playing *vint*; and when there was a family festivity in some household and he was invited to a meal, then he sat and ate in silence, looking at his plate.

And everything that was said at the time was uninteresting, unjust, and stupid; he felt irritated and disturbed, but held his tongue, and, because he sat glumly silent and looked at his plate, he was nicknamed in the town "the haughty Pole," though he never had been a Pole.

All such entertainments as theatres and concerts he declined, but he played *vint* every evening for three hours with enjoyment. He had another diversion to which he took imperceptibly, little by little: in the evening he would take out of his pockets the notes he had gained by his practice, and sometimes there were stuffed in his pockets notes—yellow and green, and smelling of scent and vinegar and incense and fish oil—up to the value of seventy roubles; and when they amounted to some hundreds he took them to the Mutual Credit Bank and deposited the money there to his account.

He was only twice at the Turkins' in the course of the four years after Ekaterina Ivanovna had gone away, on each occasion at the invitation of Vera Iosifovna, who was still undergoing treatment for migraine. Every summer Ekaterina Ivanovna came to stay with her parents, but he did not once see her; it somehow never happened.

But now four years had passed. One still, warm morning a letter was brought to the hospital. Vera Iosifovna wrote to Dmitri Ionitch that she was missing him very much, and begged him to come and see them, and to relieve her sufferings; and, by the way, it was her birthday. Below was a postscript: "I join in mother's request.— K."

Startsev considered, and in the evening he went to the Turkins'.

"How do you do, if you please?" Ivan Petrovitch met him, smiling with his eyes only. "Bongjour."

Vera Iosifovna, white-haired and looking much older, shook Startsev's hand, sighed affectedly, and said:

"You don't care to pay attentions to me, doctor. You never come and see us; I am too old for you. But now some one young has come; perhaps she will be more fortunate."

And Kitten? She had grown thinner, paler, had grown handsomer and more graceful; but now she was Ekaterina Ivanovna, not Kitten; she had lost the freshness and look of childish naivete. And in her expression and manners there was something new— guilty and diffident, as though she did not feel herself at home here in the Turkins' house.

"How many summers, how many winters!" she said, giving Startsev her hand, and he could see that her heart was beating with excitement; and looking at him intently and curiously, she went on: "How much stouter you are! You look sunburnt and more manly, but on the whole you have changed very little."

Now, too, he thought her attractive, very attractive, but there was something lacking in her, or else something superfluous—he could not himself have said exactly what it was, but something prevented him from feeling as before. He did not like her pallor, her new expression, her faint smile, her voice, and soon afterwards he disliked her clothes, too, the low chair in which she was sitting; he disliked something in the past when he had almost married her. He thought of his love, of the dreams and the hopes which had troubled him four years before—and he felt awkward.

They had tea with cakes. Then Vera Iosifovna read aloud a novel; she read of things that never happen in real life, and Startsev listened, looked at her handsome grey head, and waited for her to finish.

"People are not stupid because they can't write novels, but because they can't conceal it when they do," he thought.

"Not badsome," said Ivan Petrovitch.

Then Ekaterina Ivanovna played long and noisily on the piano, and when she finished she was profusely thanked and warmly praised.

"It's a good thing I did not marry her," thought Startsev.

She looked at him, and evidently expected him to ask her to go into the garden, but he remained silent.

"Let us have a talk," she said, going up to him. "How are you getting on? What are you doing? How are things? I have been thinking about you all these days," she went on nervously. "I wanted to write to you, wanted to come myself to see you at Dyalizh. I quite made up my mind to go, but afterwards I thought better of it. God knows what your attitude is towards me now; I have been looking forward to seeing you to-day with such emotion. For goodness' sake let us go into the garden."

They went into the garden and sat down on the seat under the old maple, just as they had done four years before. It was dark.

"How are you getting on?" asked Ekaterina Ivanovna.

"Oh, all right; I am jogging along," answered Startsev.

And he could think of nothing more. They were silent.

"I feel so excited!" said Ekaterina Ivanovna, and she hid her face in her hands. "But don't pay attention to it. I am so happy to be at home; I am so glad to see every one. I can't get used to it. So many memories! I thought we should talk without stopping till morning."

Now he saw her face near, her shining eyes, and in the darkness she looked younger than in the room, and even her old childish expression seemed to have come back to her. And indeed she was looking at him with naive curiosity, as though she wanted to get a closer view and understanding of the man who had loved her so ardently, with such tenderness, and so unsuccessfully; her eyes thanked him for that love. And he remembered all that had been, every minute detail; how he had wandered about the cemetery, how he had returned home in the morning exhausted, and he suddenly felt sad and regretted the past. A warmth began glowing in his heart.

"Do you remember how I took you to the dance at the club?" he asked.

"It was dark and rainy then. . ."

The warmth was glowing now in his heart, and he longed to talk, to rail at life. . . .

"Ech!" he said with a sigh. "You ask how I am living. How do we live here? Why, not at all. We grow old, we grow stout, we grow slack. Day after day passes; life slips by without colour, without expressions, without thoughts. . . . In the daytime working for gain, and in the evening the club, the company of card-players, alcoholic, raucous-voiced gentlemen whom I can't endure. What is there nice in it?"

"Well, you have work—a noble object in life. You used to be so fond of talking of your hospital. I was such a queer girl then; I imagined myself such a great pianist. Nowadays all young ladies play the piano, and I played, too, like everybody else, and there was nothing special about me. I am just such a pianist as my mother is an authoress. And of course I didn't understand you then, but afterwards in Moscow I often thought of you. I thought of no one but you. What happiness to be a district doctor; to help the suffering; to be serving the people! What happiness!" Ekaterina Ivanovna repeated with enthusiasm. "When I thought of you in Moscow, you seemed to me so ideal, so lofty. . . ."

Startsev thought of the notes he used to take out of his pockets in the evening with such pleasure, and the glow in his heart was quenched.

He got up to go into the house. She took his arm.

"You are the best man I've known in my life," she went on. "We will see each other and talk, won't we? Promise me. I am not a pianist;

I am not in error about myself now, and I will not play before you or talk of music."

When they had gone into the house, and when Startsev saw in the lamplight her face, and her sad, grateful, searching eyes fixed upon him, he felt uneasy and thought again:

"It's a good thing I did not marry her then."

He began taking leave.

"You have no human right to go before supper," said Ivan Petrovitch as he saw him off. "It's extremely perpendicular on your part. Well, now, perform!" he added, addressing Pava in the hall.

Pava, no longer a boy, but a young man with moustaches, threw himself into an attitude, flung up his arm, and said in a tragic voice:

"Unhappy woman, die!"

All this irritated Startsev. Getting into his carriage, and looking at the dark house and garden which had once been so precious and so dear, he thought of everything at once—Vera Iosifovna's novels and Kitten's noisy playing, and Ivan Petrovitch's jokes and Pava's tragic posturing, and thought if the most talented people in the town were so futile, what must the town be?

Three days later Pava brought a letter from Ekaterina Ivanovna.

"You don't come and see us—why?" she wrote to him. "I am afraid that you have changed towards us. I am afraid, and I am terrified at the very thought of it. Reassure me; come and tell me that everything is well.

"I must talk to you.—Your E. I."

He read this letter, thought a moment, and said to Pava:

"Tell them, my good fellow, that I can't come to-day; I am very busy. Say I will come in three days or so."

But three days passed, a week passed; he still did not go. Happening once to drive past the Turkins' house, he thought he must go in, if only for a moment, but on second thoughts . . . did not go in.

And he never went to the Turkins' again.

V

Several more years have passed. Startsev has grown stouter still, has grown corpulent, breathes heavily, and already walks with his head thrown back. When stout and red in the face, he drives with his bells and his team of three horses, and Panteleimon, also stout and red in the face with his thick beefy neck, sits on the box, holding his arms stiffly out before him as though they were made of wood, and shouts to those he meets: "Keep to the ri-i-ight!" it is an impressive picture; one might think it was not a mortal, but some heathen deity in his chariot. He has an immense practice in the town, no time to breathe, and already has an estate and two houses in the town, and he is looking out for a third more profitable; and when at the Mutual Credit Bank he is told of a house that is for sale, he goes to the house without ceremony, and, marching through all the rooms, regardless of half-dressed women and children who gaze at him in amazement and alarm, he prods at the doors with his stick, and says:

"Is that the study? Is that a bedroom? And what's here?"

And as he does so he breathes heavily and wipes the sweat from his brow.

He has a great deal to do, but still he does not give up his work as district doctor; he is greedy for gain, and he tries to be in all places at once. At Dyalizh and in the town he is called simply "Ionitch": "Where is Ionitch off to?" or "Should not we call in Ionitch to a consultation?"

Probably because his throat is covered with rolls of fat, his voice has changed; it has become thin and sharp. His temper has changed, too: he has grown ill-humoured and irritable. When he sees his patients he is usually out of temper; he impatiently taps the floor with his stick, and shouts in his disagreeable voice:

"Be so good as to confine yourself to answering my questions! Don't talk so much!"

He is solitary. He leads a dreary life; nothing interests him.

During all the years he had lived at Dyalizh his love for Kitten had been his one joy, and probably his last. In the evenings he plays *vint* at the club, and then sits alone at a big table and has supper. Ivan, the oldest and most respectable of the waiters, serves him, hands him Lafitte No. 17, and every one at the club— the members of the committee, the cook and waiters—know what he likes and what he doesn't like and do their very utmost to satisfy him, or else he is sure to fly into a rage and bang on the floor with his stick.

As he eats his supper, he turns round from time to time and puts in his spoke in some conversation:

"What are you talking about? Eh? Whom?"

And when at a neighbouring table there is talk of the Turkins, he asks:

"What Turkins are you speaking of? Do you mean the people whose daughter plays on the piano?"

That is all that can be said about him.

And the Turkins? Ivan Petrovitch has grown no older; he is not changed in the least, and still makes jokes and tells anecdotes as of old. Vera Iosifovna still reads her novels aloud to her visitors with eagerness and touching simplicity. And Kitten plays the piano for four hours every day. She has grown visibly older, is constantly ailing, and every autumn goes to the Crimea with her mother. When Ivan Petrovitch sees them off at the station, he wipes his tears as the train starts, and shouts:

"Good-bye, if you please."

And he waves his handkerchief.

THE HEAD OF THE FAMILY

IT is, as a rule, after losing heavily at cards or after a drinking-bout when an attack of dyspepsia is setting in that Stepan Stepanitch Zhilin wakes up in an exceptionally gloomy frame of mind. He looks sour, rumpled, and dishevelled; there is an expression of displeasure on his grey face, as though he were offended or disgusted by something. He dresses slowly, sips his Vichy water deliberately, and begins walking about the rooms.

"I should like to know what b-b-beast comes in here and does not shut the door!" he grumbles angrily, wrapping his dressing-gown about him and spitting loudly. "Take away that paper! Why is it lying about here? We keep twenty servants, and the place is more untidy than a pot-house. Who was that ringing? Who the devil is that?"

"That's Anfissa, the midwife who brought our Fedya into the world," answers his wife.

"Always hanging about . . . these cadging toadies!"

"There's no making you out, Stepan Stepanitch. You asked her yourself, and now you scold."

"I am not scolding; I am speaking. You might find something to do, my dear, instead of sitting with your hands in your lap trying to pick a quarrel. Upon my word, women are beyond my comprehension! Beyond my comprehension! How can they waste whole days doing nothing? A man works like an ox, like a b-beast, while his wife, the partner of his life, sits like a pretty doll, sits and does nothing but watch for an opportunity to quarrel with her husband by way of diversion. It's time to drop these schoolgirlish ways, my dear. You are not a schoolgirl, not a young lady; you are a wife and mother! You turn away? Aha! It's not agreeable to listen to the bitter truth!"

"It's strange that you only speak the bitter truth when your liver is out of order."

"That's right; get up a scene."

"Have you been out late? Or playing cards?"

"What if I have? Is that anybody's business? Am I obliged to give an account of my doings to any one? It's my own money I lose, I suppose? What I spend as well as what is spent in this house belongs to me—me. Do you hear? To me!"

And so on, all in the same style. But at no other time is Stepan Stepanitch so reasonable, virtuous, stern or just as at dinner, when all his household are sitting about him. It usually begins with the soup. After swallowing the first spoonful Zhilin suddenly frowns and puts down his spoon.

"Damn it all!" he mutters; "I shall have to dine at a restaurant, I suppose."

"What's wrong?" asks his wife anxiously. "Isn't the soup good?"

"One must have the taste of a pig to eat hogwash like that! There's too much salt in it; it smells of dirty rags . . . more like bugs than onions. . . . It's simply revolting, Anfissa Ivanovna," he says, addressing the midwife. "Every day I give no end of money for housekeeping. . . . I deny myself everything, and this is what they provide for my dinner! I suppose they want me to give up the office and go into the kitchen to do the cooking myself."

"The soup is very good to-day," the governess ventures timidly.

"Oh, you think so?" says Zhilin, looking at her angrily from under his eyelids. "Every one to his taste, of course. It must be confessed our tastes are very different, Varvara Vassilyevna. You, for instance, are satisfied with the behaviour of this boy" (Zhilin with a tragic gesture points to his son Fedya); "you are delighted with him, while I . . . I am disgusted. Yes!"

Fedya, a boy of seven with a pale, sickly face, leaves off eating and drops his eyes. His face grows paler still.

"Yes, you are delighted, and I am disgusted. Which of us is right, I cannot say, but I venture to think as his father, I know my own son better than you do. Look how he is sitting! Is that the way decently brought up children sit? Sit properly."

Fedya tilts his chin up, cranes his neck, and fancies that he is holding himself better. Tears come into his eyes.

"Eat your dinner! Hold your spoon properly! You wait. I'll show you, you horrid boy! Don't dare to whimper! Look straight at me!"

Fedya tries to look straight at him, but his face is quivering and his eyes fill with tears.

"A-ah! . . . you cry? You are naughty and then you cry? Go and stand in the corner, you beast!"

"But . . . let him have his dinner first," his wife intervenes.

"No dinner for him! Such bla . . . such rascals don't deserve dinner!"

Fedya, wincing and quivering all over, creeps down from his chair and goes into the corner.

"You won't get off with that!" his parent persists. "If nobody else cares to look after your bringing up, so be it; I must begin. . . . I won't let you be naughty and cry at dinner, my lad! Idiot! You must do your duty! Do you understand? Do your duty! Your father works and you must work, too! No one must eat the bread of idleness! You must be a man! A m-man!"

"For God's sake, leave off," says his wife in French. "Don't nag at us before outsiders, at least. . . . The old woman is all ears; and now, thanks to her, all the town will hear of it."

"I am not afraid of outsiders," answers Zhilin in Russian. "Anfissa Ivanovna sees that I am speaking the truth. Why, do you think I ought to be pleased with the boy? Do you know what he costs me? Do you know, you nasty boy, what you cost me? Or do you imagine that I coin money, that I get it for nothing? Don't howl! Hold your tongue! Do you hear what I say? Do you want me to whip you, you young ruffian?"

Fedya wails aloud and begins to sob.

"This is insufferable," says his mother, getting up from the table and flinging down her dinner-napkin. "You never let us have dinner in peace! Your bread sticks in my throat."

And putting her handkerchief to her eyes, she walks out of the dining-room.

"Now she is offended," grumbles Zhilin, with a forced smile. "She's been spoilt. . . . That's how it is, Anfissa Ivanovna; no one likes to hear the truth nowadays. . . . It's all my fault, it seems."

Several minutes of silence follow. Zhilin looks round at the plates, and noticing that no one has yet touched their soup, heaves a deep sigh, and stares at the flushed and uneasy face of the governess.

"Why don't you eat, Varvara Vassilyevna?" he asks. "Offended, I suppose? I see. . . . You don't like to be told the truth. You must forgive me, it's my nature; I can't be a hypocrite. . . . I always blurt out the plain truth" (a sigh). "But I notice that my presence is unwelcome. No one can eat or talk while I am here. . . . Well, you should have told me, and I would have gone away. . . . I will go."

Zhilin gets up and walks with dignity to the door. As he passes the weeping Fedya he stops.

"After all that has passed here, you are free," he says to Fedya, throwing back his head with dignity. "I won't meddle in your bringing up again. I wash my hands of it! I humbly apologise that as a father, from a sincere desire for your welfare, I have disturbed you and your mentors. At the same time, once for all I disclaim all responsibility for your future. . . ."

Fedya wails and sobs more loudly than ever. Zhilin turns with dignity to the door and departs to his bedroom.

When he wakes from his after-dinner nap he begins to feel the stings of conscience. He is ashamed to face his wife, his son, Anfissa Ivanovna, and even feels very wretched when he recalls the scene at dinner, but his amour-propre is too much for him; he has not the manliness to be frank, and he goes on sulking and grumbling.

Waking up next morning, he feels in excellent spirits, and whistles gaily as he washes. Going into the dining-room to breakfast, he finds there Fedya, who, at the sight of his father, gets up and looks at him helplessly.

"Well, young man?" Zhilin greets him good-humouredly, sitting down to the table. "What have you got to tell me, young man? Are you all right? Well, come, chubby; give your father a kiss."

With a pale, grave face Fedya goes up to his father and touches his cheek with his quivering lips, then walks away and sits down in his place without a word.

THE BLACK MONK

I

Andrey Vassilitch Kovrin, who held a master's degree at the University, had exhausted himself, and had upset his nerves. He did not send for a doctor, but casually, over a bottle of wine, he spoke to a friend who was a doctor, and the latter advised him to spend the spring and summer in the country. Very opportunely a long letter came from Tanya Pesotsky, who asked him to come and stay with them at Borissovka. And he made up his mind that he really must go.

To begin with—that was in April—he went to his own home, Kovrinka, and there spent three weeks in solitude; then, as soon as the roads were in good condition, he set off, driving in a carriage, to visit Pesotsky, his former guardian, who had brought him up, and was a horticulturist well known all over Russia. The distance from Kovrinka to Borissovka was reckoned only a little over fifty miles. To drive along a soft road in May in a comfortable carriage with springs was a real pleasure.

Pesotsky had an immense house with columns and lions, off which the stucco was peeling, and with a footman in swallow-tails at the entrance. The old park, laid out in the English style, gloomy and severe, stretched for almost three-quarters of a mile to the river, and there ended in a steep, precipitous clay bank, where pines grew with bare roots that looked like shaggy paws; the water shone below with an unfriendly gleam, and the peewits flew up with a plaintive cry, and there one always felt that one must sit down and write a ballad. But near the house itself, in the courtyard and orchard, which together with the nurseries covered ninety acres, it was all life and gaiety even in bad weather. Such marvellous roses, lilies, camellias; such tulips of all possible shades, from glistening white to sooty black—such a wealth of flowers, in fact, Kovrin had never seen anywhere as at Pesotsky's. It was only the beginning of spring, and the real glory of the flower-beds was still hidden away in the hot-houses. But even the flowers along the avenues, and here and there in the flower-beds, were enough to make one feel, as one walked about the garden, as though one were in a realm of tender colours, especially in the early morning when the dew was glistening on every petal.

What was the decorative part of the garden, and what Pesotsky contemptuously spoke of as rubbish, had at one time in his childhood given Kovrin an impression of fairyland.

Every sort of caprice, of elaborate monstrosity and mockery at Nature was here. There were espaliers of fruit-trees, a pear-tree in the shape of a pyramidal poplar, spherical oaks and lime-trees, an apple-tree in the shape of an umbrella, plum-trees trained into arches, crests, candelabra, and even into the number 1862--the year when Pesotsky first took up horticulture. One came across, too, lovely, graceful trees with strong, straight stems like palms, and it was only by looking intently that one could recognise these trees as gooseberries or currants. But what made the garden most cheerful and gave it a lively air, was the continual coming and going in it, from early morning till evening; people with wheelbarrows, shovels, and watering-cans swarmed round the trees and bushes, in the avenues and the flower-beds, like ants. . . .

Kovrin arrived at Pesotsky's at ten o'clock in the evening. He found Tanya and her father, Yegor Semyonitch, in great anxiety. The clear starlight sky and the thermometer foretold a frost towards morning, and meanwhile Ivan Karlovitch, the gardener, had gone to the town, and they had no one to rely upon. At supper they talked of nothing but the morning frost, and it was settled that Tanya should not go to bed, and between twelve and one should walk through the garden, and see that everything was done properly, and Yegor Semyonitch should get up at three o'clock or even earlier.

Kovrin sat with Tanya all the evening, and after midnight went out with her into the garden. It was cold. There was a strong smell of burning already in the garden. In the big orchard, which was called the commercial garden, and which brought Yegor Semyonitch several thousand clear profit, a thick, black, acrid smoke was creeping over the ground and, curling around the trees, was saving those thousands from the frost. Here the trees were arranged as on a chessboard, in straight and regular rows like ranks of soldiers, and this severe pedantic regularity, and the fact that all the trees were of the same size, and had tops and trunks all exactly alike, made them look monotonous and even dreary. Kovrin and Tanya walked along the rows where fires of dung, straw, and all sorts of refuse were smouldering, and from time to time they were met by labourers who wandered in the smoke like shadows. The only trees in flower were the cherries, plums, and certain sorts of apples, but the whole garden was plunged in smoke, and it was only near the nurseries that Kovrin could breathe freely.

"Even as a child I used to sneeze from the smoke here," he said, shrugging his shoulders, "but to this day I don't understand how smoke can keep off frost."

"Smoke takes the place of clouds when there are none . . ." answered Tanya.

"And what do you want clouds for?"

"In overcast and cloudy weather there is no frost."

"You don't say so."

He laughed and took her arm. Her broad, very earnest face, chilled with the frost, with her delicate black eyebrows, the turned-up collar of her coat, which prevented her moving her head freely, and the whole of her thin, graceful figure, with her skirts tucked up on account of the dew, touched him.

"Good heavens! she is grown up," he said. "When I went away from here last, five years ago, you were still a child. You were such a thin, longlegged creature, with your hair hanging on your shoulders; you used to wear short frocks, and I used to tease you, calling you a heron. . . . What time does!"

"Yes, five years!" sighed Tanya. "Much water has flowed since then. Tell me, Andryusha, honestly," she began eagerly, looking him in the face: "do you feel strange with us now? But why do I ask you? You are a man, you live your own interesting life, you are somebody . . . . To grow apart is so natural! But however that may be, Andryusha, I want you to think of us as your people. We have a right to that."

"I do, Tanya."

"On your word of honour?"

"Yes, on my word of honour."

"You were surprised this evening that we have so many of your photographs. You know my father adores you. Sometimes it seems to me that he loves you more than he does me. He is proud of you. You are a clever, extraordinary man, you have made a brilliant career for yourself, and he is persuaded that you have turned out like this because he brought you up. I don't try to prevent him from thinking so. Let him."

Dawn was already beginning, and that was especially perceptible from the distinctness with which the coils of smoke and the tops of the trees began to stand out in the air.

"It's time we were asleep, though," said Tanya, "and it's cold, too." She took his arm. "Thank you for coming, Andryusha. We have only uninteresting acquaintances, and not many of them. We have only the garden, the garden, the garden, and nothing else. Standards, half-standards," she laughed. "Aports, Reinettes, Borovinkas, budded stocks, grafted stocks. . . . All, all our life has gone into the garden. I never even dream of anything but apples and pears. Of course, it is very nice and useful, but sometimes one longs for something else for variety. I remember that when you used to come to us for the summer holidays, or simply a visit, it always seemed to be fresher and brighter in the house, as though the covers had been taken off the lustres and the furniture. I was only a little girl then, but yet I understood it."

She talked a long while and with great feeling. For some reason the idea came into his head that in the course of the summer he might grow fond of this little, weak, talkative creature, might be carried away and fall in love; in their position it was so possible and natural! This thought touched and amused him; he bent down to her sweet, preoccupied face and hummed softly:

"'Onyegin, I won't conceal it;

I madly love Tatiana. . . .'"

By the time they reached the house, Yegor Semyonitch had got up. Kovrin did not feel sleepy; he talked to the old man and went to the garden with him. Yegor Semyonitch was a tall, broad-shouldered, corpulent man, and he suffered from asthma, yet he walked so fast that it was hard work to hurry after him. He had an extremely preoccupied air; he was always hurrying somewhere, with an expression that suggested that if he were one minute late all would be ruined!

"Here is a business, brother . . ." he began, standing still to take breath. "On the surface of the ground, as you see, is frost; but if you raise the thermometer on a stick fourteen feet above the ground, there it is warm. . . . Why is that?"

"I really don't know," said Kovrin, and he laughed.

"H'm! . . . One can't know everything, of course. . . . However large the intellect may be, you can't find room for everything in it. I suppose you still go in chiefly for philosophy?"

"Yes, I lecture in psychology; I am working at philosophy in general."

"And it does not bore you?"

"On the contrary, it's all I live for."

"Well, God bless you! . . ." said Yegor Semyonitch, meditatively stroking his grey whiskers. "God bless you! . . . I am delighted about you . . . delighted, my boy. . . ."

But suddenly he listened, and, with a terrible face, ran off and quickly disappeared behind the trees in a cloud of smoke.

"Who tied this horse to an apple-tree?" Kovrin heard his despairing, heart-rending cry. "Who is the low scoundrel who has dared to tie this horse to an apple-tree? My God, my God! They have ruined everything; they have spoilt everything; they have done everything filthy, horrible, and abominable. The orchard's done for, the orchard's ruined. My God!"

When he came back to Kovrin, his face looked exhausted and mortified.

"What is one to do with these accursed people?" he said in a tearful voice, flinging up his hands. "Styopka was carting dung at night, and tied the horse to an apple-tree! He twisted the reins round it, the rascal, as tightly as he could, so that the bark is rubbed off in three places. What do you think of that! I spoke to him and he stands like a post and only blinks his eyes. Hanging is too good for him."

Growing calmer, he embraced Kovrin and kissed him on the cheek.

"Well, God bless you! . . . God bless you! . . ." he muttered. "I am very glad you have come. Unutterably glad. . . . Thank you."

Then, with the same rapid step and preoccupied face, he made the round of the whole garden, and showed his former ward all his greenhouses and hot-houses, his covered-in garden, and two apiaries which he called the marvel of our century.

While they were walking the sun rose, flooding the garden with brilliant light. It grew warm. Foreseeing a long, bright, cheerful day, Kovrin recollected that it was only the beginning of May, and that he had before him a whole summer as bright, cheerful, and long; and suddenly there stirred in his bosom a joyous, youthful feeling, such as he used to experience in his childhood, running about in that garden. And he hugged the old man and kissed him affectionately. Both of them, feeling touched, went indoors and drank tea out of old-fashioned china cups, with cream and satisfying krendels made with milk and eggs; and these trifles reminded Kovrin again of his childhood and boyhood. The delightful present was blended with the impressions of the past that stirred within him; there was a tightness at his heart; yet he was happy.

He waited till Tanya was awake and had coffee with her, went for a walk, then went to his room and sat down to work. He read attentively, making notes, and from time to time raised his eyes to look out at the open windows or at the fresh, still dewy flowers in the vases on the table; and again he dropped his eyes to his book, and it seemed to him as though every vein in his body was quivering and fluttering with pleasure.

II

In the country he led just as nervous and restless a life as in town. He read and wrote a great deal, he studied Italian, and when he was out for a walk, thought with pleasure that he would soon sit down to work again. He slept so little that every one wondered at him; if he accidentally dozed for half an hour in the daytime, he would lie awake all night, and, after a sleepless night, would feel cheerful and vigorous as though nothing had happened.

He talked a great deal, drank wine, and smoked expensive cigars. Very often, almost every day, young ladies of neighbouring families would come to the Pesotskys', and would sing and play the piano with Tanya; sometimes a young neighbour who was a good violinist would come, too. Kovrin listened with eagerness to the music and singing, and was exhausted by it, and this showed itself by his eyes closing and his head falling to one side.

One day he was sitting on the balcony after evening tea, reading. At the same time, in the drawing-room, Tanya taking soprano, one of the young ladies a contralto, and the young man with his violin, were practising a well-known serenade of Braga's. Kovrin listened to the words—they were Russian—and could not understand their meaning. At last, leaving his book and listening attentively, he understood: a maiden, full of sick fancies, heard one night in her garden mysterious sounds, so strange and lovely that she was obliged to recognise them as a holy harmony which is unintelligible to us mortals, and so flies back to heaven. Kovrin's eyes began to close. He got up, and in exhaustion walked up and down the drawing-room, and then the dining-room. When the singing was over he took Tanya's arm, and with her went out on the balcony.

"I have been all day thinking of a legend," he said. "I don't remember whether I have read it somewhere or heard it, but it is a strange and almost grotesque legend. To begin with, it is somewhat obscure. A thousand years ago a monk, dressed in black, wandered about the desert, somewhere in Syria or Arabia. . . . Some miles from where he was, some fisherman saw another black monk, who was moving slowly over the surface of a lake. This second monk was a mirage. Now forget all the laws of optics, which the legend does not recognise, and listen to the rest. From that mirage there was cast another mirage, then from that other a third, so that the image of the black monk began to be repeated endlessly from one layer of the atmosphere to another. So that he was seen at one time in Africa, at another in Spain, then in Italy, then in the Far North. . . . Then he passed out of the atmosphere of the earth, and now he is wandering all over the universe, still never coming into conditions in which he might disappear. Possibly he may be seen now in Mars or in some star of the Southern Cross. But, my dear, the real point on which the whole legend hangs lies in the fact that, exactly a thousand years from the day when the monk walked in the desert, the mirage will return to the atmosphere of the earth again and will appear to men. And it seems that the thousand years is almost up . . . . According to the legend, we may look out for the black monk to-day or to-morrow."

"A queer mirage," said Tanya, who did not like the legend.

"But the most wonderful part of it all," laughed Kovrin, "is that I simply cannot recall where I got this legend from. Have I read it somewhere? Have I heard it? Or perhaps I dreamed of the black monk. I swear I don't remember. But the legend interests me. I have been thinking about it all day."

Letting Tanya go back to her visitors, he went out of the house, and, lost in meditation, walked by the flower-beds. The sun was already setting. The flowers, having just been watered, gave forth a damp, irritating fragrance. Indoors they began singing again, and in the distance the violin had the effect of a human voice. Kovrin, racking his brains to remember where he had read or heard the legend, turned slowly towards the park, and unconsciously went as far as the river. By a little path that ran along the steep bank, between the bare roots, he went down to the water, disturbed the peewits there and frightened two ducks. The last rays of the setting sun still threw light here and there on the gloomy pines, but it was quite dark on the surface of the river. Kovrin crossed to the other side by the narrow bridge. Before him lay a wide field covered with young rye not yet in blossom. There was no living habitation, no living soul in the distance, and it seemed as though the little path, if one went along it, would take one to the unknown, mysterious place where the sun had just gone down, and where the evening glow was flaming in immensity and splendour.

"How open, how free, how still it is here!" thought Kovrin, walking along the path. "And it feels as though all the world were watching me, hiding and waiting for me to understand it. . . ."

But then waves began running across the rye, and a light evening breeze softly touched his uncovered head. A minute later there was another gust of wind, but stronger—the rye began rustling, and he heard behind him the hollow murmur of the pines. Kovrin stood still in amazement. From the horizon there rose up to the sky, like a whirlwind or a waterspout, a tall black column. Its outline was indistinct, but from the first instant it could be seen that it was not standing still, but moving with fearful rapidity, moving straight towards Kovrin, and the nearer it came the smaller and the more distinct it was. Kovrin moved aside into the rye to make way for it, and only just had time to do so.

A monk, dressed in black, with a grey head and black eyebrows, his arms crossed over his breast, floated by him. . . . His bare feet did not touch the earth. After he had floated twenty feet beyond him, he looked round at Kovrin, and nodded to him with a friendly but sly smile. But what a pale, fearfully pale, thin face! Beginning to grow larger again, he flew across the river, collided noiselessly with the clay bank and pines, and passing through them, vanished like smoke.

"Why, you see," muttered Kovrin, "there must be truth in the legend."

Without trying to explain to himself the strange apparition, glad that he had succeeded in seeing so near and so distinctly, not only the monk's black garments, but even his face and eyes, agreeably excited, he went back to the house.

In the park and in the garden people were moving about quietly, in the house they were playing—so he alone had seen the monk. He had an intense desire to tell Tanya and Yegor Semyonitch, but he reflected that they would certainly think his words the ravings of delirium, and that would frighten them; he had better say nothing.

He laughed aloud, sang, and danced the mazurka; he was in high spirits, and all of them, the visitors and Tanya, thought he had a peculiar look, radiant and inspired, and that he was very interesting.

III

After supper, when the visitors had gone, he went to his room and lay down on the sofa: he wanted to think about the monk. But a minute later Tanya came in.

"Here, Andryusha; read father's articles," she said, giving him a bundle of pamphlets and proofs. "They are splendid articles. He writes capitally."

"Capitally, indeed!" said Yegor Semyonitch, following her and smiling constrainedly; he was ashamed. "Don't listen to her, please; don't read them! Though, if you want to go to sleep, read them by all means; they are a fine soporific."

"I think they are splendid articles," said Tanya, with deep conviction.
"You read them, Andryusha, and persuade father to write oftener.
He could write a complete manual of horticulture."
Yegor Semyonitch gave a forced laugh, blushed, and began uttering the phrases usually made us of by an embarrassed author. At last he began to give way.

"In that case, begin with Gaucher's article and these Russian articles," he muttered, turning over the pamphlets with a trembling hand, "or else you won't understand. Before you read my objections, you must know what I am objecting to. But it's all nonsense . . . tiresome stuff. Besides, I believe it's bedtime."

Tanya went away. Yegor Semyonitch sat down on the sofa by Kovrin and heaved a deep sigh.

"Yes, my boy . . ." he began after a pause. "That's how it is, my dear lecturer. Here I write articles, and take part in exhibitions, and receive medals. . . . Pesotsky, they say, has apples the size of a head, and Pesotsky, they say, has made his fortune with his garden. In short, 'Kotcheby is rich and glorious.' But one asks oneself: what is it all for? The garden is certainly fine, a model. It's not really a garden, but a regular institution, which is of the greatest public importance because it marks, so to say, a new era in Russian agriculture and Russian industry. But, what's it for? What's the object of it?"

"The fact speaks for itself."

"I do not mean in that sense. I meant to ask: what will happen to the garden when I die? In the condition in which you see it now, it would not be maintained for one month without me. The whole secret of success lies not in its being a big garden or a great number of labourers being employed in it, but in the fact that I love the work. Do you understand? I love it perhaps more than myself.

Look at me; I do everything myself. I work from morning to night:

I do all the grafting myself, the pruning myself, the planting myself. I do it all myself: when any one helps me I am jealous and irritable till I am rude. The whole secret lies in loving it— that is, in the sharp eye of the master; yes, and in the master's hands, and in the feeling that makes one, when one goes anywhere for an hour's visit, sit, ill at ease, with one's heart far away, afraid that something may have happened in the garden. But when I die, who will look after it? Who will work? The gardener? The labourers? Yes? But I will tell you, my dear fellow, the worst enemy in the garden is not a hare, not a cockchafer, and not the frost, but any outside person."

"And Tanya?" asked Kovrin, laughing. "She can't be more harmful than a hare? She loves the work and understands it."

"Yes, she loves it and understands it. If after my death the garden goes to her and she is the mistress, of course nothing better could be wished. But if, which God forbid, she should marry," Yegor Semyonitch whispered, and looked with a frightened look at Kovrin, "that's just it. If she marries and children come, she will have no time to think about the garden. What I fear most is: she will marry some fine gentleman, and he will be greedy, and he will let the garden to people who will run it for profit, and everything will go to the devil the very first year! In our work females are the scourge of God!"

Yegor Semyonitch sighed and paused for a while.

"Perhaps it is egoism, but I tell you frankly: I don't want Tanya to get married. I am afraid of it! There is one young dandy comes to see us, bringing his violin and scraping on it; I know Tanya will not marry him, I know it quite well; but I can't bear to see him! Altogether, my boy, I am very queer. I know that."

Yegor Semyonitch got up and walked about the room in excitement, and it was evident that he wanted to say something very important, but could not bring himself to it.

"I am very fond of you, and so I am going to speak to you openly," he decided at last, thrusting his hands into his pockets. "I deal plainly with certain delicate questions, and say exactly what I think, and I cannot endure so-called hidden thoughts. I will speak plainly: you are the only man to whom I should not be afraid to marry my daughter. You are a clever man with a good heart, and would not let my beloved work go to ruin; and the chief reason is that I love you as a son, and I am proud of you. If Tanya and you could get up a romance somehow, then—well! I should be very glad and even happy. I tell you this plainly, without mincing matters, like an honest man."

Kovrin laughed. Yegor Semyonitch opened the door to go out, and stood in the doorway.

"If Tanya and you had a son, I would make a horticulturist of him," he said, after a moment's thought. "However, this is idle dreaming. Goodnight."

Left alone, Kovrin settled himself more comfortably on the sofa and took up the articles. The title of one was "On Intercropping"; of another, "A few Words on the Remarks of Monsieur Z. concerning the Trenching of the Soil for a New Garden"; a third, "Additional Matter concerning Grafting with a Dormant Bud"; and they were all of the same sort. But what a restless, jerky tone! What nervous, almost hysterical passion! Here was an article, one would have thought, with most peaceable and impersonal contents: the subject of it was the Russian Antonovsky Apple. But Yegor Semyonitch began it with "Audiatur altera pars," and finished it with "Sapienti sat"; and between these two quotations a perfect torrent of venomous phrases directed "at the learned ignorance of our recognised horticultural authorities, who observe Nature from the height of their university chairs," or at Monsieur Gaucher, "whose success has been the work of the vulgar and the dilettanti." "And then followed an inappropriate, affected, and insincere regret that peasants who stole fruit and broke the branches could not nowadays be flogged.

"It is beautiful, charming, healthy work, but even in this there is strife and passion," thought Kovrin, "I suppose that everywhere and in all careers men of ideas are nervous, and marked by exaggerated sensitiveness. Most likely it must be so."

He thought of Tanya, who was so pleased with Yegor Semyonitch's articles. Small, pale, and so thin that her shoulder-blades stuck out, her eyes, wide and open, dark and intelligent, had an intent gaze, as though looking for something. She walked like her father with a little hurried step. She talked a great deal and was fond of arguing, accompanying every phrase, however insignificant, with expressive mimicry and gesticulation. No doubt she was nervous in the extreme.

Kovrin went on reading the articles, but he understood nothing of them, and flung them aside. The same pleasant excitement with which he had earlier in the evening danced the mazurka and listened to the music was now mastering him again and rousing a multitude of thoughts. He got up and began walking about the room, thinking about the black monk. It occurred to him that if this strange, supernatural monk had appeared to him only, that meant that he was ill and had reached the point of having hallucinations. This reflection frightened him, but not for long.

"But I am all right, and I am doing no harm to any one; so there is no harm in my hallucinations," he thought; and he felt happy again.

He sat down on the sofa and clasped his hands round his head. Restraining the unaccountable joy which filled his whole being, he then paced up and down again, and sat down to his work. But the thought that he read in the book did not satisfy him. He wanted something gigantic, unfathomable, stupendous. Towards morning he undressed and reluctantly went to bed: he ought to sleep.

When he heard the footsteps of Yegor Semyonitch going out into the garden, Kovrin rang the bell and asked the footman to bring him some wine. He drank several glasses of Lafitte, then wrapped himself up, head and all; his consciousness grew clouded and he fell asleep.

IV

Yegor Semyonitch and Tanya often quarrelled and said nasty things to each other.

They quarrelled about something that morning. Tanya burst out crying and went to her room. She would not come down to dinner nor to tea. At first Yegor Semyonitch went about looking sulky and dignified, as though to give every one to understand that for him the claims of justice and good order were more important than anything else in the world; but he could not keep it up for long, and soon sank into depression. He walked about the park dejectedly, continually sighing: "Oh, my God! My God!" and at dinner did not eat a morsel. At last, guilty and conscience-stricken, he knocked at the locked door and called timidly:

"Tanya! Tanya!"

And from behind the door came a faint voice, weak with crying but still determined:

"Leave me alone, if you please."

The depression of the master and mistress was reflected in the whole household, even in the labourers working in the garden. Kovrin was absorbed in his interesting work, but at last he, too, felt dreary and uncomfortable. To dissipate the general ill-humour in some way, he made up his mind to intervene, and towards evening he knocked at Tanya's door. He was admitted.

"Fie, fie, for shame!" he began playfully, looking with surprise at Tanya's tear-stained, woebegone face, flushed in patches with crying. "Is it really so serious? Fie, fie!"

"But if you knew how he tortures me!" she said, and floods of scalding tears streamed from her big eyes. "He torments me to death," she went on, wringing her hands. "I said nothing to him . . . nothing . . . I only said that there was no need to keep . . . too many labourers . . . if we could hire them by the day when we wanted them. You know . . . you know the labourers have been doing nothing for a whole week. . . . I . . . I . . . only said that, and he shouted and . . . said . . . a lot of horrible insulting things to me. What for?"

"There, there," said Kovrin, smoothing her hair. "You've quarrelled with each other, you've cried, and that's enough. You must not be angry for long—that's wrong . . . all the more as he loves you beyond everything."

"He has . . . has spoiled my whole life," Tanya went on, sobbing. "I hear nothing but abuse and . . . insults. He thinks I am of no use in the house. Well! He is right. I shall go away to-morrow; I shall become a telegraph clerk. . . . I don't care. . . ."

"Come, come, come. . . . You mustn't cry, Tanya. You mustn't, dear . . . . You are both hot-tempered and irritable, and you are both to blame. Come along; I will reconcile you."

Kovrin talked affectionately and persuasively, while she went on crying, twitching her shoulders and wringing her hands, as though some terrible misfortune had really befallen her. He felt all the sorrier for her because her grief was not a serious one, yet she suffered extremely. What trivialities were enough to make this little creature miserable for a whole day, perhaps for her whole life! Comforting Tanya, Kovrin thought that, apart from this girl and her father, he might hunt the world over and would not find people who would love him as one of themselves, as one of their kindred. If it had not been for those two he might very likely, having lost his father and mother in early childhood, never to the day of his death have known what was meant by genuine affection and that naive, uncritical love which is only lavished on very close blood relations; and he felt that the nerves of this weeping, shaking girl responded to his half-sick, overstrained nerves like iron to a magnet. He never could have loved a healthy, strong, rosy-cheeked woman, but pale, weak, unhappy Tanya attracted him.

And he liked stroking her hair and her shoulders, pressing her hand and wiping away her tears. . . . At last she left off crying. She went on for a long time complaining of her father and her hard, insufferable life in that house, entreating Kovrin to put himself in her place; then she began, little by little, smiling, and sighing that God had given her such a bad temper. At last, laughing aloud, she called herself a fool, and ran out of the room.

When a little later Kovrin went into the garden, Yegor Semyonitch and Tanya were walking side by side along an avenue as though nothing had happened, and both were eating rye bread with salt on it, as both were hungry.

V

Glad that he had been so successful in the part of peacemaker, Kovrin went into the park. Sitting on a garden seat, thinking, he heard the rattle of a carriage and a feminine laugh—visitors were arriving. When the shades of evening began falling on the garden, the sounds of the violin and singing voices reached him indistinctly, and that reminded him of the black monk. Where, in what land or in what planet, was that optical absurdity moving now?

Hardly had he recalled the legend and pictured in his imagination the dark apparition he had seen in the rye-field, when, from behind a pine-tree exactly opposite, there came out noiselessly, without the slightest rustle, a man of medium height with uncovered grey head, all in black, and barefooted like a beggar, and his black eyebrows stood out conspicuously on his pale, death-like face. Nodding his head graciously, this beggar or pilgrim came noiselessly to the seat and sat down, and Kovrin recognised him as the black monk.

For a minute they looked at one another, Kovrin with amazement, and the monk with friendliness, and, just as before, a little slyness, as though he were thinking something to himself.

"But you are a mirage," said Kovrin. "Why are you here and sitting still? That does not fit in with the legend."

"That does not matter," the monk answered in a low voice, not immediately turning his face towards him. "The legend, the mirage, and I are all the products of your excited imagination. I am a phantom."

"Then you don't exist?" said Kovrin.

"You can think as you like," said the monk, with a faint smile. "I exist in your imagination, and your imagination is part of nature, so I exist in nature."

"You have a very old, wise, and extremely expressive face, as though you really had lived more than a thousand years," said Kovrin. "I did not know that my imagination was capable of creating such phenomena. But why do you look at me with such enthusiasm? Do you like me?"

"Yes, you are one of those few who are justly called the chosen of God. You do the service of eternal truth. Your thoughts, your designs, the marvellous studies you are engaged in, and all your life, bear the Divine, the heavenly stamp, seeing that they are consecrated to the rational and the beautiful—that is, to what is eternal."

"You said 'eternal truth.' . . . But is eternal truth of use to man and within his reach, if there is no eternal life?"

"There is eternal life," said the monk.

"Do you believe in the immortality of man?"

"Yes, of course. A grand, brilliant future is in store for you men. And the more there are like you on earth, the sooner will this future be realised. Without you who serve the higher principle and live in full understanding and freedom, mankind would be of little account; developing in a natural way, it would have to wait a long time for the end of its earthly history. You will lead it some thousands of years earlier into the kingdom of eternal truth—and therein lies your supreme service. You are the incarnation of the blessing of God, which rests upon men."

"And what is the object of eternal life?" asked Kovrin.

"As of all life—enjoyment. True enjoyment lies in knowledge, and eternal life provides innumerable and inexhaustible sources of knowledge, and in that sense it has been said: 'In My Father's house there are many mansions.'"

"If only you knew how pleasant it is to hear you!" said Kovrin, rubbing his hands with satisfaction.

"I am very glad."

"But I know that when you go away I shall be worried by the question of your reality. You are a phantom, an hallucination. So I am mentally deranged, not normal?"

"What if you are? Why trouble yourself? You are ill because you have overworked and exhausted yourself, and that means that you have sacrificed your health to the idea, and the time is near at hand when you will give up life itself to it. What could be better? That is the goal towards which all divinely endowed, noble natures strive."

"If I know I am mentally affected, can I trust myself?"

"And are you sure that the men of genius, whom all men trust, did not see phantoms, too? The learned say now that genius is allied to madness. My friend, healthy and normal people are only the common herd. Reflections upon the neurasthenia of the age, nervous exhaustion and degeneracy, et cetera, can only seriously agitate those who place the object of life in the present—that is, the common herd."

"The Romans used to say: *Mens sana in corpore sano.*"

"Not everything the Greeks and the Romans said is true. Exaltation, enthusiasm, ecstasy—all that distinguishes prophets, poets, martyrs for the idea, from the common folk—is repellent to the animal side of man—that is, his physical health. I repeat, if you want to be healthy and normal, go to the common herd."

"Strange that you repeat what often comes into my mind," said Kovrin. "It is as though you had seen and overheard my secret thoughts. But don't let us talk about me. What do you mean by 'eternal truth'?"

The monk did not answer. Kovrin looked at him and could not distinguish his face. His features grew blurred and misty. Then the monk's head and arms disappeared; his body seemed merged into the seat and the evening twilight, and he vanished altogether.

"The hallucination is over," said Kovrin; and he laughed. "It's a pity."

He went back to the house, light-hearted and happy. The little the monk had said to him had flattered, not his vanity, but his whole soul, his whole being. To be one of the chosen, to serve eternal truth, to stand in the ranks of those who could make mankind worthy of the kingdom of God some thousands of years sooner—that is, to free men from some thousands of years of unnecessary struggle, sin, and suffering; to sacrifice to the idea everything—youth, strength, health; to be ready to die for the common weal—what an exalted, what a happy lot! He recalled his past—pure, chaste, laborious; he remembered what he had learned himself and what he had taught to others, and decided that there was no exaggeration in the monk's words.

Tanya came to meet him in the park: she was by now wearing a different dress.

"Are you here?" she said. "And we have been looking and looking for you. . . . But what is the matter with you?" she asked in wonder, glancing at his radiant, ecstatic face and eyes full of tears. "How strange you are, Andryusha!"

"I am pleased, Tanya," said Kovrin, laying his hand on her shoulders. "I am more than pleased: I am happy. Tanya, darling Tanya, you are an extraordinary, nice creature. Dear Tanya, I am so glad, I am so glad!"

He kissed both her hands ardently, and went on:

"I have just passed through an exalted, wonderful, unearthly moment. But I can't tell you all about it or you would call me mad and not believe me. Let us talk of you. Dear, delightful Tanya! I love you, and am used to loving you. To have you near me, to meet you a dozen times a day, has become a necessity of my existence; I don't know how I shall get on without you when I go back home."

"Oh," laughed Tanya, "you will forget about us in two days. We are humble people and you are a great man."

"No; let us talk in earnest!" he said. "I shall take you with me, Tanya. Yes? Will you come with me? Will you be mine?"

"Come," said Tanya, and tried to laugh again, but the laugh would not come, and patches of colour came into her face.

She began breathing quickly and walked very quickly, but not to the house, but further into the park.

"I was not thinking of it . . . I was not thinking of it," she said, wringing her hands in despair.

And Kovrin followed her and went on talking, with the same radiant, enthusiastic face:

"I want a love that will dominate me altogether; and that love only you, Tanya, can give me. I am happy! I am happy!"

She was overwhelmed, and huddling and shrinking together, seemed ten years older all at once, while he thought her beautiful and expressed his rapture aloud:

"How lovely she is!"

VI

Learning from Kovrin that not only a romance had been got up, but that there would even be a wedding, Yegor Semyonitch spent a long time in pacing from one corner of the room to the other, trying to conceal his agitation. His hands began trembling, his neck swelled and turned purple, he ordered his racing droshky and drove off somewhere. Tanya, seeing how he lashed the horse, and seeing how he pulled his cap over his ears, understood what he was feeling, shut herself up in her room, and cried the whole day.

In the hot-houses the peaches and plums were already ripe; the packing and sending off of these tender and fragile goods to Moscow took a great deal of care, work, and trouble. Owing to the fact that the summer was very hot and dry, it was necessary to water every tree, and a great deal of time and labour was spent on doing it. Numbers of caterpillars made their appearance, which, to Kovrin's disgust, the labourers and even Yegor Semyonitch and Tanya squashed with their fingers. In spite of all that, they had already to book autumn orders for fruit and trees, and to carry on a great deal of correspondence. And at the very busiest time, when no one seemed to have a free moment, the work of the fields carried off more than half their labourers from the garden. Yegor Semyonitch, sunburnt, exhausted, ill-humoured, galloped from the fields to the garden and back again; cried that he was being torn to pieces, and that he should put a bullet through his brains.

Then came the fuss and worry of the trousseau, to which the Pesotskys attached a good deal of importance. Every one's head was in a whirl from the snipping of the scissors, the rattle of the sewing-machine, the smell of hot irons, and the caprices of the dressmaker, a huffy and nervous lady. And, as ill-luck would have it, visitors came every day, who had to be entertained, fed, and even put up for the night. But all this hard labour passed unnoticed as though in a fog. Tanya felt that love and happiness had taken her unawares, though she had, since she was fourteen, for some reason been convinced that Kovrin would marry her and no one else. She was bewildered, could not grasp it, could not believe herself. . . . At one minute such joy would swoop down upon her that she longed to fly away to the clouds and there pray to God, at another moment she would remember that in August she would have to part from her home and leave her father; or, goodness knows why, the idea would occur to her that she was worthless—insignificant and unworthy of a great man like Kovrin— and she would go to her room, lock herself in, and cry bitterly for several hours. When there were visitors, she would suddenly fancy that Kovrin looked extraordinarily handsome, and that all the women were in love with him and envying her, and her soul was filled with pride and rapture, as though she had vanquished the whole world; but he had only to smile politely at any young lady for her to be trembling with jealousy, to retreat to her room—and tears again. These new sensations mastered her completely; she helped her father mechanically, without noticing peaches, caterpillars or labourers, or how rapidly the time was passing.

It was almost the same with Yegor Semyonitch. He worked from morning till night, was always in a hurry, was irritable, and flew into rages, but all of this was in a sort of spellbound dream. It seemed as though there were two men in him: one was the real Yegor Semyonitch, who was moved to indignation, and clutched his head in despair when he heard of some irregularity from Ivan Karlovitch the gardener; and another— not the real one—who seemed as though he were half drunk, would interrupt a business conversation at half a word, touch the gardener on the shoulder, and begin muttering:

"Say what you like, there is a great deal in blood. His mother was a wonderful woman, most high-minded and intelligent. It was a pleasure to look at her good, candid, pure face; it was like the face of an angel. She drew splendidly, wrote verses, spoke five foreign languages, sang. . . . Poor thing! she died of consumption. The Kingdom of Heaven be hers."

The unreal Yegor Semyonitch sighed, and after a pause went on:

"When he was a boy and growing up in my house, he had the same angelic face, good and candid. The way he looks and talks and moves is as soft and elegant as his mother's. And his intellect! We were always struck with his intelligence. To be sure, it's not for nothing he's a Master of Arts! It's not for nothing! And wait a bit, Ivan Karlovitch, what will he be in ten years' time? He will be far above us!"

But at this point the real Yegor Semyonitch, suddenly coming to himself, would make a terrible face, would clutch his head and cry:

"The devils! They have spoilt everything! They have ruined everything! They have spoilt everything! The garden's done for, the garden's ruined!"

Kovrin, meanwhile, worked with the same ardour as before, and did not notice the general commotion. Love only added fuel to the flames. After every talk with Tanya he went to his room, happy and triumphant, took up his book or his manuscript with the same passion with which he had just kissed Tanya and told her of his love. What the black monk had told him of the chosen of God, of eternal truth, of the brilliant future of mankind and so on, gave peculiar and extraordinary significance to his work, and filled his soul with pride and the consciousness of his own exalted consequence. Once or twice a week, in the park or in the house, he met the black monk and had long conversations with him, but this did not alarm him, but, on the contrary, delighted him, as he was now firmly persuaded that such apparitions only visited the elect few who rise up above their fellows and devote themselves to the service of the idea.

One day the monk appeared at dinner-time and sat in the dining-room window. Kovrin was delighted, and very adroitly began a conversation with Yegor Semyonitch and Tanya of what might be of interest to the monk; the black-robed visitor listened and nodded his head graciously, and Yegor Semyonitch and Tanya listened, too, and smiled gaily without suspecting that Kovrin was not talking to them but to his hallucination.

Imperceptibly the fast of the Assumption was approaching, and soon after came the wedding, which, at Yegor Semyonitch's urgent desire, was celebrated with "a flourish"—that is, with senseless festivities that lasted for two whole days and nights. Three thousand roubles' worth of food and drink was consumed, but the music of the wretched hired band, the noisy toasts, the scurrying to and fro of the footmen, the uproar and crowding, prevented them from appreciating the taste of the expensive wines and wonderful delicacies ordered from Moscow.

VII

One long winter night Kovrin was lying in bed, reading a French novel. Poor Tanya, who had headaches in the evenings from living in town, to which she was not accustomed, had been asleep a long while, and, from time to time, articulated some incoherent phrase in her restless dreams.

It struck three o'clock. Kovrin put out the light and lay down to sleep, lay for a long time with his eyes closed, but could not get to sleep because, as he fancied, the room was very hot and Tanya talked in her sleep. At half-past four he lighted the candle again, and this time he saw the black monk sitting in an arm-chair near the bed.

"Good-morning," said the monk, and after a brief pause he asked:

"What are you thinking of now?"

"Of fame," answered Kovrin. "In the French novel I have just been reading, there is a description of a young *savant*, who does silly things and pines away through worrying about fame. I can't understand such anxiety."

"Because you are wise. Your attitude towards fame is one of indifference, as towards a toy which no longer interests you."

"Yes, that is true."

"Renown does not allure you now. What is there flattering, amusing, or edifying in their carving your name on a tombstone, then time rubbing off the inscription together with the gilding? Moreover, happily there are too many of you for the weak memory of mankind to be able to retain your names."

"Of course," assented Kovrin. "Besides, why should they be remembered? But let us talk of something else. Of happiness, for instance. What is happiness?"

When the clock struck five, he was sitting on the bed, dangling his feet to the carpet, talking to the monk:

"In ancient times a happy man grew at last frightened of his happiness --it was so great!--and to propitiate the gods he brought as a sacrifice his favourite ring. Do you know, I, too, like Polykrates, begin to be uneasy of my happiness. It seems strange to me that from morning to night I feel nothing but joy; it fills my whole being and smothers all other feelings. I don't know what sadness, grief, or boredom is. Here I am not asleep; I suffer from sleeplessness, but I am not dull. I say it in earnest; I begin to feel perplexed."

"But why?" the monk asked in wonder. "Is joy a supernatural feeling? Ought it not to be the normal state of man? The more highly a man is developed on the intellectual and moral side, the more independent he is, the more pleasure life gives him. Socrates, Diogenes, and Marcus Aurelius, were joyful, not sorrowful. And the Apostle tells us: 'Rejoice continually'; 'Rejoice and be glad.'"

"But will the gods be suddenly wrathful?" Kovrin jested; and he laughed. "If they take from me comfort and make me go cold and hungry, it won't be very much to my taste."

Meanwhile Tanya woke up and looked with amazement and horror at her husband. He was talking, addressing the arm-chair, laughing and gesticulating; his eyes were gleaming, and there was something strange in his laugh.

"Andryusha, whom are you talking to?" she asked, clutching the hand he stretched out to the monk. "Andryusha! Whom?"

"Oh! Whom?" said Kovrin in confusion. "Why, to him. . . . He is sitting here," he said, pointing to the black monk.

"There is no one here . . . no one! Andryusha, you are ill!"

Tanya put her arm round her husband and held him tight, as though protecting him from the apparition, and put her hand over his eyes.

"You are ill!" she sobbed, trembling all over. "Forgive me, my precious, my dear one, but I have noticed for a long time that your mind is clouded in some way. . . . You are mentally ill, Andryusha . . . ."

Her trembling infected him, too. He glanced once more at the arm-chair, which was now empty, felt a sudden weakness in his arms and legs, was frightened, and began dressing.

"It's nothing, Tanya; it's nothing," he muttered, shivering. "I really am not quite well . . . it's time to admit that."

"I have noticed it for a long time . . . and father has noticed it," she said, trying to suppress her sobs. "You talk to yourself, smile somehow strangely . . . and can't sleep. Oh, my God, my God, save us!" she said in terror. "But don't be frightened, Andryusha; for God's sake don't be frightened. . . ."

She began dressing, too. Only now, looking at her, Kovrin realised the danger of his position—realised the meaning of the black monk and his conversations with him. It was clear to him now that he was mad.

Neither of them knew why they dressed and went into the dining-room:

she in front and he following her. There they found Yegor Semyonitch standing in his dressing-gown and with a candle in his hand. He was staying with them, and had been awakened by Tanya's sobs.

"Don't be frightened, Andryusha," Tanya was saying, shivering as though in a fever; "don't be frightened. . . . Father, it will all pass over . . . it will all pass over. . . ."

Kovrin was too much agitated to speak. He wanted to say to his father-in-law in a playful tone: "Congratulate me; it appears I have gone out of my mind"; but he could only move his lips and smile bitterly.

At nine o'clock in the morning they put on his jacket and fur coat, wrapped him up in a shawl, and took him in a carriage to a doctor.

VIII

Summer had come again, and the doctor advised their going into the country. Kovrin had recovered; he had left off seeing the black monk, and he had only to get up his strength. Staying at his father-in-law's, he drank a great deal of milk, worked for only two hours out of the twenty-four, and neither smoked nor drank wine.

On the evening before Elijah's Day they had an evening service in the house. When the deacon was handing the priest the censer the immense old room smelt like a graveyard, and Kovrin felt bored. He went out into the garden. Without noticing the gorgeous flowers, he walked about the garden, sat down on a seat, then strolled about the park; reaching the river, he went down and then stood lost in thought, looking at the water. The sullen pines with their shaggy roots, which had seen him a year before so young, so joyful and confident, were not whispering now, but standing mute and motionless, as though they did not recognise him. And, indeed, his head was closely cropped, his beautiful long hair was gone, his step was lagging, his face was fuller and paler than last summer.

He crossed by the footbridge to the other side. Where the year before there had been rye the oats stood, reaped, and lay in rows. The sun had set and there was a broad stretch of glowing red on the horizon, a sign of windy weather next day. It was still. Looking in the direction from which the year before the black monk had first appeared, Kovrin stood for twenty minutes, till the evening glow had begun to fade. . .

When, listless and dissatisfied, he returned home the service was over. Yegor Semyonitch and Tanya were sitting on the steps of the verandah, drinking tea. They were talking of something, but, seeing Kovrin, ceased at once, and he concluded from their faces that their talk had been about him.

"I believe it is time for you to have your milk," Tanya said to her husband.

"No, it is not time yet . . ." he said, sitting down on the bottom step. "Drink it yourself; I don't want it."

Tanya exchanged a troubled glance with her father, and said in a guilty voice:

"You notice yourself that milk does you good."

"Yes, a great deal of good!" Kovrin laughed. "I congratulate you:

I have gained a pound in weight since Friday." He pressed his head tightly in his hands and said miserably: "Why, why have you cured me? Preparations of bromide, idleness, hot baths, supervision, cowardly consternation at every mouthful, at every step—all this will reduce me at last to idiocy. I went out of my mind, I had megalomania; but then I was cheerful, confident, and even happy; I was interesting and original. Now I have become more sensible and stolid, but I am just like every one else: I am—mediocrity; I am weary of life. . . . Oh, how cruelly you have treated me! . . . I saw hallucinations, but what harm did that do to any one? I ask, what harm did that do any one?"

"Goodness knows what you are saying!" sighed Yegor Semyonitch. "It's positively wearisome to listen to it."

"Then don't listen."

The presence of other people, especially Yegor Semyonitch, irritated Kovrin now; he answered him drily, coldly, and even rudely, never looked at him but with irony and hatred, while Yegor Semyonitch was overcome with confusion and cleared his throat guiltily, though he was not conscious of any fault in himself. At a loss to understand why their charming and affectionate relations had changed so abruptly, Tanya huddled up to her father and looked anxiously in his face; she wanted to understand and could not understand, and all that was clear to her was that their relations were growing worse and worse every day, that of late her father had begun to look much older, and her husband had grown irritable, capricious, quarrelsome and uninteresting. She could not laugh or sing; at dinner she ate nothing; did not sleep for nights together, expecting something awful, and was so worn out that on one occasion she lay in a dead faint from dinner-time till evening. During the service she thought her father was crying, and now while the three of them were sitting together on the terrace she made an effort not to think of it.

"How fortunate Buddha, Mahomed, and Shakespeare were that their kind relations and doctors did not cure them of their ecstasy and their inspiration," said Kovrin. "If

Mahomed had taken bromide for his nerves, had worked only two hours out of the twenty-four, and had drunk milk, that remarkable man would have left no more trace after him than his dog. Doctors and kind relations will succeed in stupefying mankind, in making mediocrity pass for genius and in bringing civilisation to ruin. If only you knew," Kovrin said with annoyance, "how grateful I am to you."

He felt intense irritation, and to avoid saying too much, he got up quickly and went into the house. It was still, and the fragrance of the tobacco plant and the marvel of Peru floated in at the open window. The moonlight lay in green patches on the floor and on the piano in the big dark dining-room. Kovrin remembered the raptures of the previous summer when there had been the same scent of the marvel of Peru and the moon had shone in at the window. To bring back the mood of last year he went quickly to his study, lighted a strong cigar, and told the footman to bring him some wine. But the cigar left a bitter and disgusting taste in his mouth, and the wine had not the same flavour as it had the year before. And so great is the effect of giving up a habit, the cigar and the two gulps of wine made him giddy, and brought on palpitations of the heart, so that he was obliged to take bromide.

Before going to bed, Tanya said to him:

"Father adores you. You are cross with him about something, and it is killing him. Look at him; he is ageing, not from day to day, but from hour to hour. I entreat you, Andryusha, for God's sake, for the sake of your dead father, for the sake of my peace of mind, be affectionate to him."

"I can't, I don't want to."

"But why?" asked Tanya, beginning to tremble all over. "Explain why."

"Because he is antipathetic to me, that's all," said Kovrin carelessly; and he shrugged his shoulders. "But we won't talk about him: he is your father."

"I can't understand, I can't," said Tanya, pressing her hands to her temples and staring at a fixed point. "Something incomprehensible, awful, is going on in the house. You have changed, grown unlike yourself. . . . You, clever, extraordinary man as you are, are irritated over trifles, meddle in paltry nonsense. . . . Such trivial things excite you, that sometimes one is simply amazed and can't believe that it is you. Come, come, don't be angry, don't be angry," she went on, kissing his hands, frightened of her own words. "You are clever, kind, noble. You will be just to father. He is so good."

"He is not good; he is just good-natured. Burlesque old uncles like your father, with well-fed, good-natured faces, extraordinarily hospitable and queer, at one time used to touch me and amuse me in novels and in farces and in life; now I dislike them. They are egoists to the marrow of their bones. What disgusts me most of all is their being so well-fed, and that purely bovine, purely hoggish optimism of a full stomach."

Tanya sat down on the bed and laid her head on the pillow.

"This is torture," she said, and from her voice it was evident that she was utterly exhausted, and that it was hard for her to speak. "Not one moment of peace since the winter. . . . Why, it's awful!

My God! I am wretched."

"Oh, of course, I am Herod, and you and your father are the innocents.

Of course."

His face seemed to Tanya ugly and unpleasant. Hatred and an ironical expression did not suit him. And, indeed, she had noticed before that there was something lacking in his face, as though ever since his hair had been cut his face had changed, too. She wanted to say something wounding to him, but immediately she caught herself in this antagonistic feeling, she was frightened and went out of the bedroom.

IX

Kovrin received a professorship at the University. The inaugural address was fixed for the second of December, and a notice to that effect was hung up in the corridor at the University. But on the day appointed he informed the students' inspector, by telegram, that he was prevented by illness from giving the lecture.

He had haemorrhage from the throat. He was often spitting blood, but it happened two or three times a month that there was a considerable loss of blood, and then he grew extremely weak and sank into a drowsy condition. This illness did not particularly frighten him, as he knew that his mother had lived for ten years or longer suffering from the same disease, and the doctors assured him that there was no danger, and had only advised him to avoid excitement, to lead a regular life, and to speak as little as possible.

In January again his lecture did not take place owing to the same reason, and in February it was too late to begin the course. It had to be postponed to the following year.

By now he was living not with Tanya, but with another woman, who was two years older than he was, and who looked after him as though he were a baby. He was in a calm and tranquil state of mind; he readily gave in to her, and when Varvara Nikolaevna—that was the name of his friend—decided to take him to the Crimea, he agreed, though he had a presentiment that no good would come of the trip.

They reached Sevastopol in the evening and stopped at an hotel to rest and go on the next day to Yalta. They were both exhausted by the journey. Varvara Nikolaevna had some tea, went to bed and was soon asleep. But Kovrin did not go to bed. An hour before starting for the station, he had received a letter from Tanya, and had not brought himself to open it, and now it was lying in his coat pocket, and the thought of it excited him disagreeably. At the bottom of his heart he genuinely considered now that his marriage to Tanya had been a mistake. He was glad that their separation was final, and the thought of that woman who in the end had turned into a living relic, still walking about though everything seemed dead in her except her big, staring, intelligent eyes—the thought of her roused in him nothing but pity and disgust with himself. The handwriting on the envelope reminded him how cruel and unjust he had been two years before, how he had worked off his anger at his spiritual emptiness, his boredom, his loneliness, and his dissatisfaction with life by revenging himself on people in no way to blame. He remembered, also, how he had torn up his dissertation and all the articles he had written during his illness, and how he had thrown them out of window, and the bits of paper had fluttered in the wind and caught on the trees and flowers. In every line of them he saw strange, utterly groundless pretension, shallow defiance, arrogance, megalomania; and they made him feel as though he were reading a description of his vices. But when the last manuscript had been torn up and sent flying out of window, he felt, for some reason, suddenly bitter and angry; he went to his wife and said a great many unpleasant things to her. My God, how he had tormented her! One day, wanting to cause her pain, he told her that her father had played a very unattractive part in their romance, that he had asked him to marry her. Yegor Semyonitch accidentally overheard this, ran into the room, and, in his despair, could not utter a word, could only stamp and make a strange, bellowing sound as though he had lost the power of speech, and Tanya, looking at her father, had uttered a heart-rending shriek and had fallen into a swoon. It was hideous.

All this came back into his memory as he looked at the familiar writing. Kovrin went out on to the balcony; it was still warm weather and there was a smell of the sea. The wonderful bay reflected the moonshine and the lights, and was of a colour for which it was difficult to find a name. It was a soft and tender blending of dark blue and green; in places the water was like blue vitriol, and in places it seemed as though the moonlight were liquefied and filling the bay instead of water. And what harmony of colours, what an atmosphere of peace, calm, and sublimity!

In the lower storey under the balcony the windows were probably open, for women's voices and laughter could be heard distinctly. Apparently there was an evening party.

Kovrin made an effort, tore open the envelope, and, going back into his room, read:

"My father is just dead. I owe that to you, for you have killed him. Our garden is being ruined; strangers are managing it already that is, the very thing is happening that poor father dreaded.

That, too, I owe to you. I hate you with my whole soul, and I hope you may soon perish. Oh, how wretched I am! Insufferable anguish is burning my soul. . . . My curses on you. I took you for an extraordinary man, a genius; I loved you, and you have turned out a madman. . . ."

Kovrin could read no more, he tore up the letter and threw it away. He was overcome by an uneasiness that was akin to terror. Varvara Nikolaevna was asleep behind the screen, and he could hear her breathing. From the lower storey came the sounds of laughter and women's voices, but he felt as though in the whole hotel there were no living soul but him. Because Tanya, unhappy, broken by sorrow, had cursed him in her letter and hoped for his perdition, he felt eerie and kept glancing hurriedly at the door, as though he were afraid that the uncomprehended force which two years before had wrought such havoc in his life and in the life of those near him might come into the room and master him once more.

He knew by experience that when his nerves were out of hand the best thing for him to do was to work. He must sit down to the table and force himself, at all costs, to concentrate his mind on some one thought. He took from his red portfolio a manuscript containing a sketch of a small work of the nature of a compilation, which he had planned in case he should find it dull in the Crimea without work. He sat down to the table and began working at this plan, and it seemed to him that his calm, peaceful, indifferent mood was coming back. The manuscript with the sketch even led him to meditation on the vanity of the world. He thought how much life exacts for the worthless or very commonplace blessings it can give a man. For instance, to gain, before forty, a university chair, to be an ordinary professor, to expound ordinary and second-hand thoughts in dull, heavy, insipid language—in fact, to gain the position of a mediocre learned man, he, Kovrin, had had to study for fifteen years, to work day and night, to endure a terrible mental illness, to experience an unhappy marriage, and to do a great number of stupid and unjust things which it would have been pleasant not to remember. Kovrin recognised clearly, now, that he was a mediocrity, and readily resigned himself to it, as he considered that every man ought to be satisfied with what he is.

The plan of the volume would have soothed him completely, but the torn letter showed white on the floor and prevented him from concentrating his attention. He got up from the table, picked up the pieces of the letter and threw them out of window, but there was a light wind blowing from the sea, and the bits of paper were scattered on the windowsill. Again he was overcome by uneasiness akin to terror, and he felt as though in the whole hotel there were no living soul but himself. . . . He went out on the balcony. The bay, like a living thing, looked at him with its multitude of light blue, dark blue, turquoise and fiery eyes, and seemed beckoning to him. And it really was hot and oppressive, and it would not have been amiss to have a bathe.

Suddenly in the lower storey under the balcony a violin began playing, and two soft feminine voices began singing. It was something familiar. The song was about a maiden, full of sick fancies, who heard one night in her garden mysterious sounds, so strange and lovely that she was obliged to recognise them as a holy harmony which is unintelligible to us mortals, and so flies back to heaven . . . . Kovrin caught his breath and there was a pang of sadness at his heart, and a thrill of the sweet, exquisite delight he had so long forgotten began to stir in his breast.

A tall black column, like a whirlwind or a waterspout, appeared on the further side of the bay. It moved with fearful rapidity across the bay, towards the hotel, growing smaller and darker as it came, and Kovrin only just had time to get out of the way to let it pass . . . . The monk with bare grey head, black eyebrows, barefoot, his arms crossed over his breast, floated by him, and stood still in the middle of the room.

"Why did you not believe me?" he asked reproachfully, looking affectionately at Kovrin. "If you had believed me then, that you were a genius, you would not have spent these two years so gloomily and so wretchedly."

Kovrin already believed that he was one of God's chosen and a genius; he vividly recalled his conversations with the monk in the past and tried to speak, but the blood flowed from his throat on to his breast, and not knowing what he was doing, he passed his hands over his breast, and his cuffs were soaked with blood. He tried to call Varvara Nikolaevna, who was asleep behind the screen; he made an effort and said:

"Tanya!"

He fell on the floor, and propping himself on his arms, called again:

"Tanya!"

He called Tanya, called to the great garden with the gorgeous flowers sprinkled with dew, called to the park, the pines with their shaggy roots, the rye-field, his marvellous learning, his youth, courage, joy—called to life, which was so lovely. He saw on the floor near his face a great pool of blood, and was too weak to utter a word, but an unspeakable, infinite happiness flooded his whole being. Below, under the balcony, they were playing the serenade, and the black monk whispered to him that he was a genius, and that he was dying only because his frail human body had lost its balance and could no longer serve as the mortal garb of genius.

When Varvara Nikolaevna woke up and came out from behind the screen, Kovrin was dead, and a blissful smile was set upon his face.

VOLODYA

At five o'clock one Sunday afternoon in summer, Volodya, a plain, shy, sickly-looking lad of seventeen, was sitting in the arbour of the Shumihins' country villa, feeling dreary. His despondent thought flowed in three directions. In the first place, he had next day, Monday, an examination in mathematics; he knew that if he did not get through the written examination on the morrow, he would be expelled, for he had already been two years in the sixth form and had two and three-quarter marks for algebra in his annual report. In the second place, his presence at the villa of the Shumihins, a wealthy family with aristocratic pretensions, was a continual source of mortification to his *amour-propre*. It seemed to him that Madame Shumihin looked upon him and his maman as poor relations and dependents, that they laughed at his *maman* and did not respect her. He had on one occasion accidently overheard Madame Shumihin, in the verandah, telling her cousin Anna Fyodorovna that his *maman* still tried to look young and got herself up, that she never paid her losses at cards, and had a partiality for other people's shoes and tobacco. Every day Volodya besought his *maman* not to go to the Shumihins', and drew a picture of the humiliating part she played with these gentlefolk. He tried to persuade her, said rude things, but she—a frivolous, pampered woman, who had run through two fortunes, her own and her husband's, in her time, and always gravitated towards acquaintances of high rank—did not understand him, and twice a week Volodya had to accompany her to the villa he hated.

In the third place, the youth could not for one instant get rid of a strange, unpleasant feeling which was absolutely new to him. . . . It seemed to him that he was in love with Anna Fyodorovna, the Shumihins' cousin, who was staying with them. She was a vivacious, loud-voiced, laughter-loving, healthy, and vigorous lady of thirty, with rosy cheeks, plump shoulders, a plump round chin and a continual smile on her thin lips. She was neither young nor beautiful—

Volodya knew that perfectly well; but for some reason he could not help thinking of her, looking at her while she shrugged her plump shoulders and moved her flat back as she played croquet, or after prolonged laughter and running up and down stairs, sank into a low chair, and, half closing her eyes and gasping for breath, pretended that she was stifling and could not breathe. She was married. Her husband, a staid and dignified architect, came once a week to the villa, slept soundly, and returned to town. Volodya's strange feeling had begun with his conceiving an unaccountable hatred for the architect, and feeling relieved every time he went back to town.

Now, sitting in the arbour, thinking of his examination next day, and of his *maman*, at whom they laughed, he felt an intense desire to see Nyuta (that was what the Shumihins called Anna Fyodorovna), to hear her laughter and the rustle of her dress. . . . This desire was not like the pure, poetic love of which he read in novels and about which he dreamed every night when he went to bed; it was strange, incomprehensible; he was ashamed of it, and afraid of it as of something very wrong and impure, something which it was disagreeable to confess even to himself.

"It's not love," he said to himself. "One can't fall in love with women of thirty who are married. It is only a little intrigue . . . . Yes, an intrigue. . . ."

Pondering on the "intrigue," he thought of his uncontrollable shyness, his lack of moustache, his freckles, his narrow eyes, and put himself in his imagination side by side with Nyuta, and the juxtaposition seemed to him impossible; then he made haste to imagine himself bold, handsome, witty, dressed in the latest fashion.

When his dreams were at their height, as he sat huddled together and looking at the ground in a dark corner of the arbour, he heard the sound of light footsteps. Some one was coming slowly along the avenue. Soon the steps stopped and something white gleamed in the entrance.

"Is there any one here?" asked a woman's voice.

Volodya recognised the voice, and raised his head in a fright.

"Who is here?" asked Nyuta, going into the arbour. "Ah, it is you, Volodya? What are you doing here? Thinking? And how can you go on thinking, thinking, thinking? . . . That's the way to go out of your mind!"

Volodya got up and looked in a dazed way at Nyuta. She had only just come back from bathing. Over her shoulder there was hanging a sheet and a rough towel, and from under the white silk kerchief on her head he could see the wet hair sticking to her forehead. There was the cool damp smell of the bath-house and of almond soap still hanging about her. She was out of breath from running quickly. The top button of her blouse was undone, so that the boy saw her throat and bosom.

"Why don't you say something?" said Nyuta, looking Volodya up and down. "It's not polite to be silent when a lady talks to you. What a clumsy seal you are though, Volodya! You always sit, saying nothing, thinking like some philosopher. There's not a spark of life or fire in you! You are really horrid! . . . At your age you ought to be living, skipping, and jumping, chattering, flirting, falling in love."

Volodya looked at the sheet that was held by a plump white hand, and thought. . . .

"He's mute," said Nyuta, with wonder; "it is strange, really. . . . Listen! Be a man! Come, you might smile at least! Phew, the horrid philosopher!" she laughed. "But do you know, Volodya, why you are such a clumsy seal? Because you don't devote yourself to the ladies. Why don't you? It's true there are no girls here, but there is nothing to prevent your flirting with the married ladies! Why don't you flirt with me, for instance?"

Volodya listened and scratched his forehead in acute and painful irresolution.

"It's only very proud people who are silent and love solitude," Nyuta went on, pulling his hand away from his forehead. "You are proud, Volodya. Why do you look at me like that from under your brows? Look me straight in the face, if you please! Yes, now then, clumsy seal!"

Volodya made up his mind to speak. Wanting to smile, he twitched his lower lip, blinked, and again put his hand to his forehead.

"I . . . I love you," he said.

Nyuta raised her eyebrows in surprise, and laughed.

"What do I hear?" she sang, as prima-donnas sing at the opera when they hear something awful. "What? What did you say? Say it again, say it again. . . ."

"I . . . I love you!" repeated Volodya.

And without his will's having any part in his action, without reflection or understanding, he took half a step towards Nyuta and clutched her by the arm.

Everything was dark before his eyes, and tears came into them. The whole world was turned into one big, rough towel which smelt of the bathhouse.

"Bravo, bravo!" he heard a merry laugh. "Why don't you speak? I want you to speak! Well?"

Seeing that he was not prevented from holding her arm, Volodya glanced at Nyuta's laughing face, and clumsily, awkwardly, put both arms round her waist, his hands meeting behind her back. He held her round the waist with both arms, while, putting her hands up to her head, showing the dimples in her elbows, she set her hair straight under the kerchief and said in a calm voice:

"You must be tactful, polite, charming, and you can only become that under feminine influence. But what a wicked, angry face you have! You must talk, laugh. . . . Yes, Volodya, don't be surly; you are young and will have plenty of time for philosophising. Come, let go of me; I am going. Let go."

Without effort she released her waist, and, humming something, walked out of the arbour. Volodya was left alone. He smoothed his hair, smiled, and walked three times to and fro across the arbour, then he sat down on the bench and smiled again. He felt insufferably ashamed, so much so that he wondered that human shame could reach such a pitch of acuteness and intensity. Shame made him smile, gesticulate, and whisper some disconnected words.

He was ashamed that he had been treated like a small boy, ashamed of his shyness, and, most of all, that he had had the audacity to put his arms round the waist of a respectable married woman, though, as it seemed to him, he had neither through age nor by external quality, nor by social position any right to do so.

He jumped up, went out of the arbour, and, without looking round, walked into the recesses of the garden furthest from the house.

"Ah! only to get away from here as soon as possible," he thought, clutching his head. "My God! as soon as possible."

The train by which Volodya was to go back with his *maman* was at eight-forty. There were three hours before the train started, but he would with pleasure have gone to the station at once without waiting for his *maman*.

At eight o'clock he went to the house. His whole figure was expressive of determination: what would be, would be! He made up his mind to go in boldly, to look them straight in the face, to speak in a loud voice, regardless of everything.

He crossed the terrace, the big hall and the drawing-room, and there stopped to take breath. He could hear them in the dining-room, drinking tea. Madame Shumihin, *maman*, and Nyuta were talking and laughing about something.

Volodya listened.

"I assure you!" said Nyuta. "I could not believe my eyes! When he began declaring his passion and—just imagine!--put his arms round my waist, I should not have recognised him. And you know he has a way with him! When he told me he was in love with me, there was something brutal in his face, like a Circassian."

"Really!" gasped *maman*, going off into a peal of laughter. "Really!

How he does remind me of his father!"

Volodya ran back and dashed out into the open air.

"How could they talk of it aloud!" he wondered in agony, clasping his hands and looking up to the sky in horror. "They talk aloud in cold blood . . . and *maman* laughed! . . . *Maman!* My God, why didst Thou give me such a mother? Why?"

But he had to go to the house, come what might. He walked three times up and down the avenue, grew a little calmer, and went into the house.

"Why didn't you come in in time for tea?" Madame Shumihin asked sternly.

"I am sorry, it's . . . it's time for me to go," he muttered, not raising his eyes. "Maman, it's eight o'clock!"

"You go alone, my dear," said his *maman* languidly. "I am staying the night with Lili. Goodbye, my dear. . . . Let me make the sign of the cross over you."

She made the sign of the cross over her son, and said in French, turning to Nyuta:

"He's rather like Lermontov . . . isn't he?"

Saying good-bye after a fashion, without looking any one in the face, Volodya went out of the dining-room. Ten minutes later he was walking along the road to the station, and was glad of it. Now he felt neither frightened nor ashamed; he breathed freely and easily.

About half a mile from the station, he sat down on a stone by the side of the road, and gazed at the sun, which was half hidden behind a barrow. There were lights already here and there at the station, and one green light glimmered dimly, but the train was not yet in sight. It was pleasant to Volodya to sit still without moving, and to watch the evening coming little by little. The darkness of the arbour, the footsteps, the smell of the bath-house, the laughter, and the waist—all these rose with amazing vividness before his imagination, and all this was no longer so terrible and important as before.

"It's of no consequence. . . . She did not pull her hand away, and laughed when I held her by the waist," he thought. "So she must have liked it. If she had disliked it she would have been angry. . . ."

And now Volodya felt sorry that he had not had more boldness there in the arbour. He felt sorry that he was so stupidly going away, and he was by now persuaded that if the same thing happened again he would be bolder and look at it more simply.

And it would not be difficult for the opportunity to occur again. They used to stroll about for a long time after supper at the Shumihins'. If Volodya went for a walk with Nyuta in the dark garden, there would be an opportunity!

"I will go back," he thought, "and will go by the morning train to-morrow. . . . I will say I have missed the train."

And he turned back. . . . Madame Shumihin, *Maman*, Nyuta, and one of the nieces were sitting on the verandah, playing *vint*. When Volodya told them the lie that he had missed the train, they were uneasy that he might be late for the examination day, and advised him to get up early. All the while they were playing he sat on one side, greedily watching Nyuta and waiting. . . . He already had a plan prepared in his mind: he would go up to Nyuta in the dark, would take her by the hand, then would embrace her; there would be no need to say anything, as both of them would understand without words.

But after supper the ladies did not go for a walk in the garden, but went on playing cards. They played till one o'clock at night, and then broke up to go to bed.

"How stupid it all is!" Volodya thought with vexation as he got into bed. "But never mind; I'll wait till to-morrow . . . to-morrow in the arbour. It doesn't matter. . . ."

He did not attempt to go to sleep, but sat in bed, hugging his knees and thinking. All thought of the examination was hateful to him. He had already made up his mind that they would expel him, and that there was nothing terrible about his being expelled. On the contrary, it was a good thing—a very good thing, in fact. Next day he would be as free as a bird; he would put on ordinary clothes instead of his school uniform, would smoke openly, come out here, and make love to Nyuta when he liked; and he would not be a schoolboy but "a young man." And as for the rest of it, what is called a career, a future, that was clear; Volodya would go into the army or the telegraph service, or he would go into a chemist's shop and work his way up till he was a dispenser. . . . There were lots of callings. An hour or two passed, and he was still sitting and thinking. . . .

Towards three o'clock, when it was beginning to get light, the door creaked cautiously and his *maman* came into the room.

"Aren't you asleep?" she asked, yawning. "Go to sleep; I have only come in for a minute. . . . I am only fetching the drops. . . ."

"What for?"

"Poor Lili has got spasms again. Go to sleep, my child, your examination's to-morrow. . . ."

She took a bottle of something out of the cupboard, went to the window, read the label, and went away.

"Marya Leontyevna, those are not the drops!" Volodya heard a woman's voice, a minute later. "That's convallaria, and Lili wants morphine. Is your son asleep? Ask him to look for it. . . ."

It was Nyuta's voice. Volodya turned cold. He hurriedly put on his trousers, flung his coat over his shoulders, and went to the door.

"Do you understand? Morphine," Nyuta explained in a whisper. "There must be a label in Latin. Wake Volodya; he will find it."

Maman opened the door and Volodya caught sight of Nyuta. She was wearing the same loose wrapper in which she had gone to bathe. Her hair hung loose and disordered on her shoulders, her face looked sleepy and dark in the half-light. . . .

"Why, Volodya is not asleep," she said. "Volodya, look in the cupboard for the morphine, there's a dear! What a nuisance Lili is! She has always something the matter."

Maman muttered something, yawned, and went away.

"Look for it," said Nyuta. "Why are you standing still?"

Volodya went to the cupboard, knelt down, and began looking through the bottles and boxes of medicine. His hands were trembling, and he had a feeling in his chest and stomach as though cold waves were running all over his inside. He felt suffocated and giddy from the smell of ether, carbolic acid, and various drugs, which he quite unnecessarily snatched up with his trembling fingers and spilled in so doing.

"I believe *maman* has gone," he thought. "That's a good thing . . . a good thing. . . ."

"Will you be quick?" said Nyuta, drawling.

"In a minute. . . . Here, I believe this is morphine," said Volodya, reading on one of the labels the word "morph . . ." "Here it is!"

Nyuta was standing in the doorway in such a way that one foot was in his room and one was in the passage. She was tidying her hair, which was difficult to put in order because it was so thick and long, and looked absent-mindedly at Volodya. In her loose wrap, with her sleepy face and her hair down, in the dim light that came into the white sky not yet lit by the sun, she seemed to Volodya captivating, magnificent. . . . Fascinated, trembling all over, and remembering with relish how he had held that exquisite body in his arms in the arbour, he handed her the bottle and said:

"How wonderful you are!"

"What?"

She came into the room.

"What?" she asked, smiling.

He was silent and looked at her, then, just as in the arbour, he took her hand, and she looked at him with a smile and waited for what would happen next.

"I love you," he whispered.

She left off smiling, thought a minute, and said:

"Wait a little; I think somebody is coming. Oh, these schoolboys!" she said in an undertone, going to the door and peeping out into the passage. "No, there is no one to be seen. . . ."

She came back.

Then it seemed to Volodya that the room, Nyuta, the sunrise and himself—all melted together in one sensation of acute, extraordinary, incredible bliss, for which one might give up one's whole life and face eternal torments. . . . But half a minute passed and all that vanished. Volodya saw only a fat, plain face, distorted by an expression of repulsion, and he himself suddenly felt a loathing for what had happened.

"I must go away, though," said Nyuta, looking at Volodya with disgust. "What a wretched, ugly . . . fie, ugly duckling!"

How unseemly her long hair, her loose wrap, her steps, her voice seemed to Volodya now! . . .

"'Ugly duckling' . . ." he thought after she had gone away. "I really am ugly . . . everything is ugly."

The sun was rising, the birds were singing loudly; he could hear the gardener walking in the garden and the creaking of his wheelbarrow . . . and soon afterwards he heard the lowing of the cows and the sounds of the shepherd's pipe. The sunlight and the sounds told him that somewhere in this world there is a pure, refined, poetical life. But where was it? Volodya had never heard a word of it from his *maman* or any of the people round about him.

When the footman came to wake him for the morning train, he pretended to be asleep. . . .

"Bother it! Damn it all!" he thought.

He got up between ten and eleven.

Combing his hair before the looking-glass, and looking at his ugly face, pale from his sleepless night, he thought:

"It's perfectly true . . . an ugly duckling!"

When *maman* saw him and was horrified that he was not at his examination, Volodya said:

"I overslept myself, *maman*. . . . But don't worry, I will get a medical certificate."

Madame Shumihin and Nyuta waked up at one o'clock. Volodya heard Madame Shumihin open her window with a bang, heard Nyuta go off into a peal of laughter in reply to her coarse voice. He saw the door open and a string of nieces and other toadies (among the latter was his *maman*) file into lunch, caught a glimpse of Nyuta's freshly washed laughing face, and, beside her, the black brows and beard of her husband the architect, who had just arrived.

Nyuta was wearing a Little Russian dress which did not suit her at all, and made her look clumsy; the architect was making dull and vulgar jokes. The rissoles served at lunch had too much onion in them—so it seemed to Volodya. It also seemed to him that Nyuta laughed loudly on purpose, and kept glancing in his direction to give him to understand that the memory of the night did not trouble her in the least, and that she was not aware of the presence at table of the "ugly duckling."

At four o'clock Volodya drove to the station with his *maman*. Foul memories, the sleepless night, the prospect of expulsion from school, the stings of conscience—all roused in him now an oppressive, gloomy anger. He looked at *maman*'s sharp profile, at her little nose, and at the raincoat which was a present from Nyuta, and muttered:

"Why do you powder? It's not becoming at your age! You make yourself up, don't pay your debts at cards, smoke other people's tobacco . . . . It's hateful! I don't love you . . . I don't love you!"

He was insulting her, and she moved her little eyes about in alarm, flung up her hands, and whispered in horror:

"What are you saying, my dear! Good gracious! the coachman will hear! Be quiet or the coachman will hear! He can overhear everything."

"I don't love you . . . I don't love you!" he went on breathlessly. "You've no soul and no morals. . . . Don't dare to wear that raincoat! Do you hear? Or else I will tear it into rags. . . ."

"Control yourself, my child," *maman* wept; "the coachman can hear!"

"And where is my father's fortune? Where is your money? You have wasted it all. I am not ashamed of being poor, but I am ashamed of having such a mother. . . . When my schoolfellows ask questions about you, I always blush."

In the train they had to pass two stations before they reached the town. Volodya spent all the time on the little platform between two carriages and shivered all over. He did not want to go into the compartment because there the mother he hated was sitting. He hated himself, hated the ticket collectors, the smoke from the engine, the cold to which he attributed his shivering. And the heavier the weight on his heart, the more strongly he felt that somewhere in the world, among some people, there was a pure, honourable, warm, refined life, full of love, affection, gaiety, and serenity. . . . He felt this and was so intensely miserable that one of the passengers, after looking in his face attentively, actually asked:

"You have the toothache, I suppose?"

In the town *maman* and Volodya lived with Marya Petrovna, a lady of noble rank, who had a large flat and let rooms to boarders. *Maman* had two rooms, one with windows and two pictures in gold frames hanging on the walls, in which her bed stood and in which she lived, and a little dark room opening out of it in which Volodya lived. Here there was a sofa on which he slept, and, except that sofa, there was no other furniture; the rest of the room was entirely filled up with wicker baskets full of clothes, cardboard hat-boxes, and all sorts of rubbish, which *maman* preserved for some reason or other. Volodya prepared his lessons either in his mother's room or in the "general room," as the large room in which the boarders assembled at dinner-time and in the evening was called.

On reaching home he lay down on his sofa and put the quilt over him to stop his shivering. The cardboard hat-boxes, the wicker baskets, and the other rubbish, reminded him that he had not a room of his own, that he had no refuge in which he could get away from his mother, from her visitors, and from the voices that were floating up from the "general room." The satchel and the books lying about in the corners reminded him of the examination he had missed. . . . For some reason there came into his mind, quite inappropriately, Mentone, where he had lived with his father when he was seven years old; he thought of Biarritz and two little English girls with whom he ran about on the sand. . . . He tried to recall to his memory the colour of the sky, the sea, the height of the waves, and his mood at the time, but he could not succeed. The English girls flitted before his imagination as though they were living; all the rest was a medley of images that floated away in confusion. . . .

"No; it's cold here," thought Volodya. He got up, put on his overcoat, and went into the "general room."

There they were drinking tea. There were three people at the samovar:

maman; an old lady with tortoiseshell pince-nez, who gave music lessons; and Avgustin Mihalitch, an elderly and very stout Frenchman, who was employed at a perfumery factory.

"I have had no dinner to-day," said *maman*. "I ought to send the maid to buy some bread."

"Dunyasha!" shouted the Frenchman.

It appeared that the maid had been sent out somewhere by the lady of the house.

"Oh, that's of no consequence," said the Frenchman, with a broad smile. "I will go for some bread myself at once. Oh, it's nothing."

He laid his strong, pungent cigar in a conspicuous place, put on his hat and went out. After he had gone away *maman* began telling the music teacher how she had been staying at the Shumihins', and how warmly they welcomed her.

"Lili Shumihin is a relation of mine, you know," she said. "Her late husband, General Shumihin, was a cousin of my husband. And she was a Baroness Kolb by birth. . . ."

"Maman, that's false!" said Volodya irritably. "Why tell lies?"

He knew perfectly well that what his mother said was true; in what she was saying about General Shumihin and about Baroness Kolb there was not a word of lying, but nevertheless he felt that she was lying. There was a suggestion of falsehood in her manner of speaking, in the expression of her face, in her eyes, in everything.

"You are lying," repeated Volodya; and he brought his fist down on the table with such force that all the crockery shook and *maman*'s tea was spilt over. "Why do you talk about generals and baronesses? It's all lies!"

The music teacher was disconcerted, and coughed into her handkerchief, affecting to sneeze, and *maman* began to cry.

"Where can I go?" thought Volodya.

He had been in the street already; he was ashamed to go to his schoolfellows. Again, quite incongruously, he remembered the two little English girls. . . . He paced up and down the "general room," and went into Avgustin Mihalitch's room. Here there was a strong smell of ethereal oils and glycerine soap. On the table, in the window, and even on the chairs, there were a number of bottles, glasses, and wineglasses containing fluids of various colours. Volodya took up from the table a newspaper, opened it and read the title *Figaro*. . . There was a strong and pleasant scent about the paper. Then he took a revolver from the table. . . .

"There, there! Don't take any notice of it." The music teacher was comforting *maman* in the next room. "He is young! Young people of his age never restrain themselves. One must resign oneself to that."

"No, Yevgenya Andreyevna; he's too spoilt," said *maman* in a singsong voice. "He has no one in authority over him, and I am weak and can do nothing. Oh, I am unhappy!"

Volodya put the muzzle of the revolver to his mouth, felt something like a trigger or spring, and pressed it with his finger. . . . Then felt something else projecting, and once more pressed it. Taking the muzzle out of his mouth, he wiped it with the lapel of his coat, looked at the lock. He had never in his life taken a weapon in his hand before. . . .

"I believe one ought to raise this . . ." he reflected. "Yes, it seems so."

Avgustin Mihalitch went into the "general room," and with a laugh began telling them about something. Volodya put the muzzle in his mouth again, pressed it with his teeth, and pressed something with his fingers. There was a sound of a shot. . . . Something hit Volodya in the back of his head with terrible violence, and he fell on the table with his face downwards among the bottles and glasses. Then he saw his father, as in Mentone, in a top-hat with a wide black band on it, wearing mourning for some lady, suddenly seize him by both hands, and they fell headlong into a very deep, dark pit.

Then everything was blurred and vanished.

AN ANONYMOUS STORY

I

THROUGH causes which it is not the time to go into in detail, I had to enter the service of a Petersburg official called Orlov, in the capacity of a footman. He was about five and thirty, and was called Georgy Ivanitch.

I entered this Orlov's service on account of his father, a prominent political man, whom I looked upon as a serious enemy of my cause. I reckoned that, living with the son, I should—from the conversations I should hear, and from the letters and papers I should find on the table—learn every detail of the father's plans and intentions.

As a rule at eleven o'clock in the morning the electric bell rang in my footman's quarters to let me know that my master was awake. When I went into the bedroom with his polished shoes and brushed clothes, Georgy Ivanitch would be sitting in his bed with a face that looked, not drowsy, but rather exhausted by sleep, and he would gaze off in one direction without any sign of satisfaction at having waked. I helped him to dress, and he let me do it with an air of reluctance without speaking or noticing my presence; then with his head wet with washing, smelling of fresh scent, he used to go into the dining-room to drink his coffee. He used to sit at the table, sipping his coffee and glancing through the newspapers, while the maid Polya and I stood respectfully at the door gazing at him. Two grown-up persons had to stand watching with the gravest attention a third drinking coffee and munching rusks. It was probably ludicrous and grotesque, but I saw nothing humiliating in having to stand near the door, though I was quite as well born and well educated as Orlov himself.

I was in the first stage of consumption, and was suffering from something else, possibly even more serious than consumption. I don't know whether it was the effect of my illness or of an incipient change in my philosophy of life of which I was not conscious at the time, but I was, day by day, more possessed by a passionate, irritating longing for ordinary everyday life. I yearned for mental tranquillity, health, fresh air, good food. I was becoming a dreamer, and, like a dreamer, I did not know exactly what I wanted. Sometimes I felt inclined to go into a monastery, to sit there for days together by the window and gaze at the trees and the fields; sometimes I fancied I would buy fifteen acres of land and settle down as a country gentleman; sometimes I inwardly vowed to take up science and become a professor at some provincial university. I was a retired navy lieutenant; I dreamed of the sea, of our squadron, and of the corvette in which I had made the cruise round the world. I longed to experience again the indescribable feeling when, walking in the tropical forest or looking at the sunset in the Bay of Bengal, one is thrilled with ecstasy and at the same time homesick. I dreamed of mountains, women, music, and, with the curiosity of a child, I looked into people's faces, listened to their voices. And when I stood at the door and watched Orlov sipping his coffee, I felt not a footman, but a man interested in everything in the world, even in Orlov.

In appearance Orlov was a typical Petersburger, with narrow shoulders, a long waist, sunken temples, eyes of an indefinite colour, and scanty, dingy-coloured hair, beard and moustaches. His face had a stale, unpleasant look, though it was studiously cared for. It was particularly unpleasant when he was asleep or lost in thought. It is not worth while describing a quite ordinary appearance; besides, Petersburg is not Spain, and a man's appearance is not of much consequence even in love affairs, and is only of value to a handsome footman or coachman. I have spoken of Orlov's face and hair only because there was something in his appearance worth mentioning. When Orlov took a newspaper or book, whatever it might be, or met people, whoever they be, an ironical smile began to come into his eyes, and his whole countenance assumed an expression of light mockery in which there was no malice. Before reading or hearing anything he always had his irony in readiness, as a savage has his shield. It was an habitual irony, like some old liquor brewed years ago, and now it came into his face probably without any participation of his will, as it were by reflex action. But of that later.

Soon after midday he took his portfolio, full of papers, and drove to his office. He dined away from home and returned after eight o'clock. I used to light the lamp and candles in his study, and he would sit down in a low chair with his legs stretched out on another chair, and, reclining in that position, would begin reading. Almost every day he brought in new books with him or received parcels of them from the shops, and there were heaps of books in three languages, to say nothing of Russian, which he had read and thrown away, in the corners of my room and under my bed. He read with extraordinary rapidity. They say: "Tell me what you read, and I'll tell you who you are." That may be true, but it was absolutely impossible to judge of Orlov by what he read. It was a regular hotchpotch. Philosophy, French novels, political economy, finance, new poets, and publications of the firm Posrednik and he read it all with the same rapidity and with the same ironical expression in his eyes.

After ten o'clock he carefully dressed, often in evening dress, very rarely in his *kammer-junker*'s uniform, and went out, returning in the morning.

Our relations were quiet and peaceful, and we never had any misunderstanding. As a rule he did not notice my presence, and when he talked to me there was no expression of irony on his face—he evidently did not look upon me as a human being.

I only once saw him angry. One day—it was a week after I had entered his service— he came back from some dinner at nine o'clock; his face looked ill-humoured and exhausted. When I followed him into his study to light the candles, he said to me:

"There's a nasty smell in the flat."

"No, the air is fresh," I answered.

"I tell you, there's a bad smell," he answered irritably.

"I open the movable panes every day."

"Don't argue, blockhead!" he shouted.

I was offended, and was on the point of answering, and goodness knows how it would have ended if Polya, who knew her master better than I did, had not intervened.

"There really is a disagreeable smell," she said, raising her eyebrows. "What can it be from? Stepan, open the pane in the drawing-room, and light the fire."

With much bustle and many exclamations, she went through all the rooms, rustling her skirts and squeezing the sprayer with a hissing sound. And Orlov was still out of humour; he was obviously restraining himself not to vent his ill-temper aloud. He was sitting at the table and rapidly writing a letter. After writing a few lines he snorted angrily and tore it up, then he began writing again.

"Damn them all!" he muttered. "They expect me to have an abnormal memory!"

At last the letter was written; he got up from the table and said, turning to me:

"Go to Znamensky Street and deliver this letter to Zinaida Fyodorovna Krasnovsky in person. But first ask the porter whether her husband --that is, Mr. Krasnovsky—has returned yet. If he has returned, don't deliver the letter, but come back. Wait a minute! . . . If she asks whether I have any one here, tell her that there have been two gentlemen here since eight o'clock, writing something."

I drove to Znamensky Street. The porter told me that Mr. Krasnovsky had not yet come in, and I made my way up to the third storey. The door was opened by a tall, stout, drab-coloured flunkey with black whiskers, who in a sleepy, churlish, and apathetic voice, such as only flunkeys use in addressing other flunkeys, asked me what I wanted. Before I had time to answer, a lady dressed in black came hurriedly into the hall. She screwed up her eyes and looked at me.

"Is Zinaida Fyodorovna at home?" I asked.

"That is me," said the lady.

"A letter from Georgy Ivanitch."

She tore the letter open impatiently, and holding it in both hands, so that I saw her sparkling diamond rings, she began reading. I made out a pale face with soft lines, a prominent chin, and long dark lashes. From her appearance I should not have judged the lady to be more than five and twenty.

"Give him my thanks and my greetings," she said when she had finished the letter. "Is there any one with Georgy Ivanitch?" she asked softly, joyfully, and as though ashamed of her mistrust.

"Two gentlemen," I answered. "They're writing something."

"Give him my greetings and thanks," she repeated, bending her head sideways, and, reading the letter as she walked, she went noiselessly out. I saw few women at that time, and this lady of whom I had a passing glimpse made an impression on me. As I walked home I recalled her face and the delicate fragrance about her, and fell to dreaming. By the time I got home Orlov had gone out.

II

And so my relations with my employer were quiet and peaceful, but still the unclean and degrading element which I so dreaded on becoming a footman was conspicuous and made itself felt every day. I did not get on with Polya. She was a well-fed and pampered hussy who adored Orlov because he was a gentleman and despised me because I was a footman. Probably, from the point of view of a real flunkey or cook, she was fascinating, with her red cheeks, her turned-up nose, her coquettish glances, and the plumpness, one might almost say fatness, of her person. She powdered her face, coloured her lips and eyebrows, laced herself in, and wore a bustle, and a bangle made of coins. She walked with little ripping steps; as she walked she swayed, or, as they say, wriggled her shoulders and back. The rustle of her skirts, the creaking of her stays, the jingle her bangle and the vulgar smell of lip salve, toilet vinegar, and scent stolen from her master, aroused me whilst I was doing the rooms with her in the morning a sensation as though I were taking part with her in some abomination.

Either because I did not steal as she did, or because I displayed no desire to become her lover, which she probably looked upon as an insult, or perhaps because she felt that I was a man of a different order, she hated me from the first day. My inexperience, my appearance --so unlike a flunkey—and my illness, seemed to her pitiful and excited her disgust. I had a bad cough at that time, and sometimes at night I prevented her from sleeping, as our rooms were only divided by a wooden partition, and every morning she said to me:

"Again you didn't let me sleep. You ought to be in hospital instead of in service."

She so genuinely believed that I was hardly a human being, but something infinitely below her, that, like the Roman matrons who were not ashamed to bathe before their slaves, she sometimes went about in my presence in nothing but her chemise.

Once when I was in a happy, dreamy mood, I asked her at dinner (we had soup and roast meat sent in from a restaurant every day)

"Polya, do you believe in God?"

"Why, of course!"

"Then," I went on, "you believe there will be a day of judgment, and that we shall have to answer to God for every evil action?"

She gave me no reply, but simply made a contemptuous grimace, and, looking that time at her cold eyes and over-fed expression, I realised that for her complete and finished personality no God, no conscience, no laws existed, and that if I had had to set fire to the house, to murder or to rob, I could not have hired a better accomplice.

In my novel surroundings I felt very uncomfortable for the first week at Orlov's before I got used to being addressed as "thou," and being constantly obliged to tell lies (saying "My master is not at home" when he was). In my flunkey's swallow-tail I felt as though I were in armour. But I grew accustomed to it in time. Like a genuine footman, I waited at table, tidied the rooms, ran and drove about on errands of all sorts. When Orlov did not want to keep an appointment with Zinaida Fyodorovna, or when he forgot that he had promised to go and see her, I drove to Znamensky Street, put a letter into her hands and told a lie. And the result of it all was quite different from what I had expected when I became a footman. Every day of this new life of mine was wasted for me and my cause, as Orlov never spoke of his father, nor did his visitors, and all I could learn of the stateman's doings was, as before, what I could glean from the newspapers or from correspondence with my comrades. The hundreds of notes and papers I used to find in the study and read had not the remotest connection with what I was looking for. Orlov was absolutely uninterested in his father's political work, and looked as though he had never heard of it, or as though his father had long been dead.

III

Every Thursday we had visitors.

I ordered a piece of roast beef from the restaurant and telephoned to Eliseyev's to send us caviare, cheese, oysters, and so on. I bought playing-cards. Polya was busy all day getting ready the tea-things and the dinner service. To tell the truth, this spurt of activity came as a pleasant change in our idle life, and Thursdays were for us the most interesting days.

Only three visitors used to come. The most important and perhaps the most interesting was the one called Pekarsky—a tall, lean man of five and forty, with a long hooked nose, with a big black beard, and a bald patch on his head. His eyes were large and prominent, and his expression was grave and thoughtful like that of a Greek philosopher. He was on the board of management of some railway, and also had some post in a bank; he was a consulting lawyer in some important Government institution, and had business relations with a large number of private persons as a trustee, chairman of committees, and so on. He was of quite a low grade in the service, and modestly spoke of himself as a lawyer, but he had a vast influence. A note or card from him was enough to make a celebrated doctor, a director of a railway, or a great dignitary see any one without waiting; and it was said that through his protection one might obtain even a post of the Fourth Class, and get any sort of unpleasant business hushed up. He was looked upon as a very intelligent man, but his was a strange, peculiar intelligence. He was able to multiply 213 by 373 in his head instantaneously, or turn English pounds into German marks without help of pencil or paper; he understood finance and railway business thoroughly, and the machinery of Russian administration had no secrets for him; he was a most skilful pleader in civil suits, and it was not easy to get the better of him at law. But that exceptional intelligence could not grasp many things which are understood even by some stupid people. For instance, he was absolutely unable to understand why people are depressed, why they weep, shoot themselves, and even kill others; why they fret about things that do not affect them personally, and why they laugh when they read Gogol or Shtchedrin . . . . Everything abstract, everything belonging to the domain of thought and feeling, was to him boring and incomprehensible, like music to one who has no ear. He looked at people simply from the business point of view, and divided them into competent and incompetent. No other classification existed for him. Honesty and rectitude were only signs of competence. Drinking, gambling, and debauchery were permissible, but must not be allowed to interfere with business. Believing in God was rather stupid, but religion ought be safeguarded, as the common people must have some principle to restrain them, otherwise they would not work. Punishment is only necessary as deterrent. There was no need to go away for holidays, as it was just as nice in town. And so on. He was a widower and had no children, but lived on a large scale, as though he had a family, and paid thousand roubles a year for his flat.

The second visitor, Kukushkin, an actual civil councillor though a young man, was short, and was conspicuous for his extremely unpleasant appearance, which was due to the disproportion between his fat, puffy body and his lean little face. His lips were puckered up suavely, and his little trimmed moustaches looked as though they had been fixed on with glue. He was a man with the manners of a lizard. He did not walk, but, as it were, crept along with tiny steps, squirming and sniggering, and when he laughed he showed his teeth. He was a clerk on special commissions, and did nothing, though he received a good salary, especially in the summer, when special and lucrative jobs were found for him. He was a man of personal ambition, not only to the marrow of his bones, but more fundamentally—to the last drop of his blood; but even in his ambitions he was petty and did not rely on himself, but was building his career on the chance favour flung him by his superiors. For the sake of obtaining some foreign decoration, or for the sake of having his name mentioned in the newspapers as having been present at some special service in the company of other great personages, he was ready to submit to any kind of humiliation, to beg, to flatter, to promise. He flattered Orlov and Pekarsky from cowardice, because he thought they were powerful; he flattered Polya and me because we were in the service of a powerful man. Whenever I took off his fur coat he tittered and asked me: "Stepan, are you married?" and then unseemly vulgarities followed—by way of showing me special attention. Kukushkin flattered Orlov's weaknesses, humoured his corrupted and blasé ways; to please him he affected malicious raillery and atheism, in his company criticised persons before whom in other places he would slavishly grovel. When at supper they talked of love and women, he pretended to be a subtle and perverse voluptuary. As a rule, one may say, Petersburg rakes are fond of talking of their abnormal tastes. Some young actual civil councillor is perfectly satisfied with the embraces of his cook or of some unhappy street-walker on the Nevsky Prospect, but to listen to him you would think he was contaminated by all the vices of East and West combined, that he was an honourary member of a dozen iniquitous secret societies and was already marked by the police. Kukushkin lied about himself in an unconscionable way, and they did not exactly disbelieve him, but paid little heed to his incredible stories.

The third guest was Gruzin, the son of a worthy and learned general; a man of Orlov's age, with long hair, short-sighted eyes, and gold spectacles. I remember his long white fingers, that looked like a pianist's; and, indeed, there was something of a musician, of a virtuoso, about his whole figure. The first violins in orchestras look just like that. He used to cough, suffered from migraine, and seemed invalidish and delicate. Probably at home he was dressed and undressed like a baby. He had finished at the College of Jurisprudence, and had at first served in the Department of Justice, then he was transferred to the Senate; he left that, and through patronage had received a post in the Department of Crown Estates, and had soon afterwards given that up. In my time he was serving in Orlov's department; he was his head-clerk, but he said that he should soon exchange into the Department of Justice again. He took his duties and his shifting about from one post to another with exceptional levity, and when people talked before him seriously of grades in the service, decorations, salaries, he smiled good-naturedly and repeated Prutkov's aphorism: "It's only in the Government service you learn the truth." He had a little wife with a wrinkled face, who was very jealous of him, and five weedy-looking children. He was unfaithful to his wife, he was only fond of his children when he saw them, and on the whole was rather indifferent to his family, and made fun of them. He and his family existed on credit, borrowing wherever they could at every opportunity, even from his superiors in the office and porters in people's houses. His was a flabby nature; he was so lazy that he did not care what became of himself, and drifted along heedless where or why he was going. He went where he was taken. If he was taken to some low haunt, he went; if wine was set before him, he drank—if it were not put before him, he abstained; if wives were abused in his presence, he abused his wife, declaring she had ruined his life—when wives were praised, he praised his and said quite sincerely: "I am very fond of her, poor thing!" He had no fur coat and always wore a rug which smelt of the nursery. When at supper he rolled balls of bread and drank a great deal of red wine, absorbed in thought, strange to say, I used to feel almost certain that there was something in him of which perhaps he had a vague sense, though in the bustle and vulgarity of his daily life he had not time to understand and appreciate it. He played a little on the piano. Sometimes he would sit down at the piano, play a chord or two, and begin singing softly:

"What does the coming day bring to me?"

But at once, as though afraid, he would get up and walk from the piano.

The visitors usually arrived about ten o'clock. They played cards in Orlov's study, and Polya and I handed them tea. It was only on these occasions that I could gauge the full sweetness of a flunkey's life. Standing for four or five hours at the door, watching that no one's glass should be empty, changing the ash-trays, running to the table to pick up the chalk or a card when it was dropped, and, above all, standing, waiting, being attentive without venturing to speak, to cough, to smile—is harder, I assure you, is harder than the hardest of field labour. I have stood on watch at sea for four hours at a stretch on stormy winter nights, and to my thinking it is an infinitely easier duty.

They used to play cards till two, sometimes till three o'clock at night, and then, stretching, they would go into the dining-room to supper, or, as Orlov said, for a snack of something. At supper there was conversation. It usually began by Orlov's speaking with laughing eyes of some acquaintance, of some book he had lately been reading, of a new appointment or Government scheme. Kukushkin, always ingratiating, would fall into his tone, and what followed was to me, in my mood at that time, a revolting exhibition. The irony of Orlov and his friends knew no bounds, and spared no one and nothing. If they spoke of religion, it was with irony; they spoke of philosophy, of the significance and object of life—irony again, if any one began about the peasantry, it was with irony.

There is in Petersburg a species of men whose specialty it is to jeer at every aspect of life; they cannot even pass by a starving man or a suicide without saying something vulgar. But Orlov and his friends did not jeer or make jokes, they talked ironically. They used to say that there was no God, and personality was completely lost at death; the immortals only existed in the French Academy. Real good did not and could not possibly exist, as its existence was conditional upon human perfection, which was a logical absurdity. Russia was a country as poor and dull as Persia. The intellectual class was hopeless; in Pekarsky's opinion the overwhelming majority in it were incompetent persons, good for nothing. The people were drunken, lazy, thievish, and degenerate. We had no science, our literature was uncouth, our commerce rested on swindling—"No selling without cheating." And everything was in that style, and everything was a subject for laughter.

Towards the end of supper the wine made them more good-humoured, and they passed to more lively conversation. They laughed over Gruzin's family life, over Kukushkin's conquests, or at Pekarsky, who had, they said, in his account book one page headed *Charity* and another *Physiological Necessities*. They said that no wife was faithful; that there was no wife from whom one could not, with practice, obtain caresses without leaving her drawing-room while her husband was sitting in his study close by; that girls in their teens were perverted and knew everything. Orlov had preserved a letter of a schoolgirl of fourteen: on her way home from school she had "hooked an officer on the Nevsky," who had, it appears, taken her home with him, and had only let her go late in the evening; and she hastened to write about this to her school friend to share her joy with her. They maintained that there was not and never had been such a thing as moral purity, and that evidently it was unnecessary; mankind had so far done very well without it. The harm done by so-called vice was undoubtedly exaggerated. Vices which are punished by our legal code had not prevented Diogenes from being a philosopher and a teacher. Caesar and Cicero were profligates and at the same time great men. Cato in his old age married a young girl, and yet he was regarded as a great ascetic and a pillar of morality.

At three or four o'clock the party broke up or they went off together out of town, or to Officers' Street, to the house of a certain Varvara Ossipovna, while I retired to my quarters, and was kept awake a long while by coughing and headache.

IV

Three weeks after I entered Orlov's service—it was Sunday morning, I remember—somebody rang the bell. It was not yet eleven, and Orlov was still asleep. I went to open the door. You can imagine my astonishment when I found a lady in a veil standing at the door on the landing.

"Is Georgy Ivanitch up?" she asked.

From her voice I recognised Zinaida Fyodorovna, to whom I had taken letters in Znamensky Street. I don't remember whether I had time or self-possession to answer her—I was taken aback at seeing her. And, indeed, she did not need my answer. In a flash she had darted by me, and, filling the hall with the fragrance of her perfume, which I remember to this day, she went on, and her footsteps died away. For at least half an hour afterwards I heard nothing. But again some one rang. This time it was a smartly dressed girl, who looked like a maid in a wealthy family, accompanied by our house porter. Both were out of breath, carrying two trunks and a dress-basket.

"These are for Zinaida Fyodorovna," said the girl.

And she went down without saying another word. All this was mysterious, and made Polya, who had a deep admiration for the pranks of her betters, smile slyly to herself; she looked as though she would like to say, "So that's what we're up to," and she walked about the whole time on tiptoe. At last we heard footsteps; Zinaida Fyodorovna came quickly into the hall, and seeing me at the door of my room, said:

"Stepan, take Georgy Ivanitch his things."

When I went in to Orlov with his clothes and his boots, he was sitting on the bed with his feet on the bearskin rug. There was an air of embarrassment about his whole figure. He did not notice me, and my menial opinion did not interest him; he was evidently perturbed and embarrassed before himself, before his inner eye. He dressed, washed, and used his combs and brushes silently and deliberately, as though allowing himself time to think over his position and to reflect, and even from his back one could see he was troubled and dissatisfied with himself.

They drank coffee together. Zinaida Fyodorovna poured out coffee for herself and for Orlov, then she put her elbows on the table and laughed.

"I still can't believe it," she said. "When one has been a long while on one's travels and reaches a hotel at last, it's difficult to believe that one hasn't to go on. It is pleasant to breathe freely."

With the expression of a child who very much wants to be mischievous, she sighed with relief and laughed again.

"You will excuse me," said Orlov, nodding towards the coffee. "Reading at breakfast is a habit I can't get over. But I can do two things at once—read and listen."

"Read away. . . . You shall keep your habits and your freedom. But why do you look so solemn? Are you always like that in the morning, or is it only to-day? Aren't you glad?"

"Yes, I am. But I must own I am a little overwhelmed."

"Why? You had plenty of time to prepare yourself for my descent upon you. I've been threatening to come every day."

"Yes, but I didn't expect you to carry out your threat to-day."

"I didn't expect it myself, but that's all the better. It's all the better, my dear. It's best to have an aching tooth out and have done with it."

"Yes, of course."

"Oh, my dear," she said, closing her eyes, "all is well that ends well; but before this happy ending, what suffering there has been! My laughing means nothing; I am glad, I am happy, but I feel more like crying than laughing. Yesterday I had to fight a regular battle," she went on in French. "God alone knows how wretched I was. But I laugh because I can't believe in it. I keep fancying that my sitting here drinking coffee with you is not real, but a dream."

Then, still speaking French, she described how she had broken with her husband the day before and her eyes were alternately full of tears and of laughter while she gazed with rapture at Orlov. She told him her husband had long suspected her, but had avoided explanations; they had frequent quarrels, and usually at the most heated moment he would suddenly subside into silence and depart to his study for fear that in his exasperation he might give utterance to his suspicions or she might herself begin to speak openly. And she had felt guilty, worthless, incapable of taking a bold and serious step, and that had made her hate herself and her husband more every day, and she had suffered the torments of hell. But the day before, when during a quarrel he had cried out in a tearful voice, "My God, when will it end?" and had walked off to his study, she had run after him like a cat after a mouse, and, preventing him from shutting the door, she had cried that she hated him with her whole soul. Then he let her come into the study and she had told him everything, had confessed that she loved some one else, that that some one else was her real, most lawful husband, and that she thought it her true duty to go away to him that very day, whatever might happen, if she were to be shot for it.

"There's a very romantic streak in you," Orlov interrupted, keeping his eyes fixed on the newspaper.

She laughed and went on talking without touching her coffee. Her cheeks glowed and she was a little embarrassed by it, and she looked in confusion at Polya and me. From what she went on to say I learnt that her husband had answered her with threats, reproaches, and finally tears, and that it would have been more accurate to say that she, and not he, had been the attacking party.

"Yes, my dear, so long as I was worked up, everything went all right," she told Orlov; "but as night came on, my spirits sank. You don't believe in God, *George*, but I do believe a little, and I fear retribution. God requires of us patience, magnanimity, self-sacrifice, and here I am refusing to be patient and want to remodel my life to suit myself. Is that right? What if from the point of view of God it's wrong? At two o'clock in the night my husband came to me and said: 'You dare not go away. I'll fetch you back through the police and make a scandal.' And soon afterwards I saw him like a shadow at my door. 'Have mercy on me! Your elopement may injure me in the service.' Those words had a coarse effect upon me and made me feel stiff all over. I felt as though the retribution were beginning already; I began crying and trembling with terror. I felt as though the ceiling would fall upon me, that I should be dragged off to the police-station at once, that you would grow cold to me—all sorts of things, in fact! I thought I would go into a nunnery or become a nurse, and give up all thought of happiness, but then I remembered that you loved me, and that I had no right to dispose of myself without your knowledge; and everything in my mind was in a tangle—I was in despair and did not know what to do or think. But the sun rose and I grew happier. As soon as it was morning I dashed off to you. Ah, what I've been through, dear one! I haven't slept for two nights!"

She was tired out and excited. She was sleepy, and at the same time she wanted to talk endlessly, to laugh and to cry, and to go to a restaurant to lunch that she might feel her freedom.

"You have a cosy flat, but I am afraid it may be small for the two of us," she said, walking rapidly through all the rooms when they had finished breakfast. "What room will you give me? I like this one because it is next to your study."

At one o'clock she changed her dress in the room next to the study, which from that time she called hers, and she went off with Orlov to lunch. They dined, too, at a restaurant, and spent the long interval between lunch and dinner in shopping. Till late at night I was opening the door to messengers and errand-boys from the shops. They bought, among other things, a splendid pier-glass, a dressing-table, a bedstead, and a gorgeous tea service which we did not need. They bought a regular collection of copper saucepans, which we set in a row on the shelf in our cold, empty kitchen. As we were unpacking the tea service Polya's eyes gleamed, and she looked at me two or three times with hatred and fear that I, not she, would be the first to steal one of these charming cups. A lady's writing-table, very expensive and inconvenient, came too. It was evident that Zinaida Fyodorovna contemplated settling with us for good, and meant to make the flat her home.

She came back with Orlov between nine and ten. Full of proud consciousness that she had done something bold and out of the common, passionately in love, and, as she imagined, passionately loved, exhausted, looking forward to a sweet sound sleep, Zinaida Fyodorovna was revelling in her new life. She squeezed her hands together in the excess of her joy, declared that everything was delightful, and swore that she would love Orlov for ever; and these vows, and the naive, almost childish confidence that she too was deeply loved and would be loved forever, made her at least five years younger. She talked charming nonsense and laughed at herself.

"There's no other blessing greater than freedom!" she said, forcing herself to say something serious and edifying. "How absurd it is when you think of it! We attach no value to our own opinion even when it is wise, but tremble before the opinion of all sorts of stupid people. Up to the last minute I was afraid of what other people would say, but as soon as I followed my own instinct and made up my mind to go my own way, my eyes were opened, I overcame my silly fears, and now I am happy and wish every one could be as happy!"

But her thoughts immediately took another turn, and she began talking of another flat, of wallpapers, horses, a trip to Switzerland and Italy. Orlov was tired by the restaurants and the shops, and was still suffering from the same uneasiness that I had noticed in the morning. He smiled, but more from politeness than pleasure, and when she spoke of anything seriously, he agreed ironically: "Oh, yes."

"Stepan, make haste and find us a good cook," she said to me.

"There's no need to be in a hurry over the kitchen arrangements," said Orlov, looking at me coldly. "We must first move into another flat."

We had never had cooking done at home nor kept horses, because, as he said, "he did not like disorder about him," and only put up with having Polya and me in his flat from necessity. The so-called domestic hearth with its everyday joys and its petty cares offended his taste as vulgarity; to be with child, or to have children and talk about them, was bad form, like a petty bourgeois. And I began to feel very curious to see how these two creatures would get on together in one flat—she, domestic and home-loving with her copper saucepans and her dreams of a good cook and horses; and he, fond of saying to his friends that a decent and orderly man's flat ought, like a warship, to have nothing in it superfluous—no women, no children, no rags, no kitchen utensils.

V

Then I will tell you what happened the following Thursday. That day Zinaida Fyodorovna dined at Content's or Donon's. Orlov returned home alone, and Zinaida Fyodorovna, as I learnt afterwards, went to the Petersburg Side to spend with her old governess the time visitors were with us. Orlov did not care to show her to his friends. I realised that at breakfast, when he began assuring her that for the sake of her peace of mind it was essential to give up his Thursday evenings.

As usual the visitors arrived at almost the same time.

"Is your mistress at home, too?" Kukushkin asked me in a whisper.

"No, sir," I answered.

He went in with a sly, oily look in his eyes, smiling mysteriously, rubbing his hands, which were cold from the frost.

"I have the honour to congratulate you," he said to Orlov, shaking all over with ingratiating, obsequious laughter. "May you increase and multiply like the cedars of Lebanon."

The visitors went into the bedroom, and were extremely jocose on the subject of a pair of feminine slippers, the rug that had been put down between the two beds, and a grey dressing-jacket that hung at the foot of the bedstead. They were amused that the obstinate man who despised all the common place details of love had been caught in feminine snares in such a simple and ordinary way.

"He who pointed the finger of scorn is bowing the knee in homage," Kukushkin repeated several times. He had, I may say in parenthesis, an unpleasant habit of adorning his conversation with texts in Church Slavonic. "Sh-sh!" he said as they went from the bedroom into the room next to the study. "Sh-sh! Here Gretchen is dreaming of her Faust."

He went off into a peal of laughter as though he had said something very amusing. I watched Gruzin, expecting that his musical soul would not endure this laughter, but I was mistaken. His thin, good-natured face beamed with pleasure. When they sat down to play cards, he, lisping and choking with laughter, said that all that "dear *George*" wanted to complete his domestic felicity was a cherry-wood pipe and a guitar. Pekarsky laughed sedately, but from his serious expression one could see that Orlov's new love affair was distasteful to him. He did not understand what had happened exactly.

"But how about the husband?" he asked in perplexity, after they had played three rubbers.

"I don't know," answered Orlov.

Pekarsky combed his big beard with his fingers and sank into thought, and he did not speak again till supper-time. When they were seated at supper, he began deliberately, drawling every word:

"Altogether, excuse my saying so, I don't understand either of you. You might love each other and break the seventh commandment to your heart's content—that I understand. Yes, that's comprehensible. But why make the husband a party to your secrets? Was there any need for that?"

"But does it make any difference?"

"Hm! . . . ." Pekarsky mused. "Well, then, let me tell you this, my friend," he went on, evidently thinking hard: "if I ever marry again and you take it into your head to seduce my wife, please do it so that I don't notice it. It's much more honest to deceive a man than to break up his family life and injure his reputation. I understand. You both imagine that in living together openly you are doing something exceptionally honourable and advanced, but I can't agree with that . . . what shall I call it? . . . romantic attitude?"

Orlov made no reply. He was out of humour and disinclined to talk. Pekarsky, still perplexed, drummed on the table with his fingers, thought a little, and said:

"I don't understand you, all the same. You are not a student and she is not a dressmaker. You are both of you people with means. I should have thought you might have arranged a separate flat for her."

"No, I couldn't. Read Turgenev."

"Why should I read him? I have read him already."

"Turgenev teaches us in his novels that every exalted, noble-minded girl should follow the man she loves to the ends of the earth, and should serve his idea," said Orlov, screwing up his eyes ironically. "The ends of the earth are poetic license; the earth and all its ends can be reduced to the flat of the man she loves. . . . And so not to live in the same flat with the woman who loves you is to deny her her exalted vocation and to refuse to share her ideals. Yes, my dear fellow, Turgenev wrote, and I have to suffer for it."

"What Turgenev has got to do with it I don't understand," said Gruzin softly, and he shrugged his shoulders. "Do you remember, *George*, how in 'Three Meetings' he is walking late in the evening somewhere in Italy, and suddenly hears, 'Vieni pensando a me segretamente,'" Gruzin hummed. "It's fine."

"But she hasn't come to settle with you by force," said Pekarsky.

"It was your own wish."

"What next! Far from wishing it, I never imagined that this would ever happen. When she said she was coming to live with me, I thought it was a charming joke on her part."

Everybody laughed.

"I couldn't have wished for such a thing," said Orlov in the tone of a man compelled to justify himself. "I am not a Turgenev hero, and if I ever wanted to free Bulgaria I shouldn't need a lady's company. I look upon love primarily as a necessity of my physical nature, degrading and antagonistic to my spirit; it must either be satisfied with discretion or renounced altogether, otherwise it will bring into one's life elements as unclean as itself. For it to be an enjoyment and not a torment, I will try to make it beautiful and to surround it with a mass of illusions. I should never go and see a woman unless I were sure beforehand that she would be beautiful and fascinating; and I should never go unless I were in the mood. And it is only in that way that we succeed in deceiving one another, and fancying that we are in love and happy. But can I wish for copper saucepans and untidy hair, or like to be seen myself when I am unwashed or out of humour? Zinaida Fyodorovna in the simplicity of her heart wants me to love what I have been shunning all my life.

She wants my flat to smell of cooking and washing up; she wants all the fuss of moving into another flat, of driving about with her own horses; she wants to count over my linen and to look after my health; she wants to meddle in my personal life at every instant, and to watch over every step; and at the same time she assures me genuinely that my habits and my freedom will be untouched. She is persuaded that, like a young couple, we shall very soon go for a honeymoon that is, she wants to be with me all the time in trains and hotels, while I like to read on the journey and cannot endure talking in trains."

"You should give her a talking to," said Pekarsky.

"What! Do you suppose she would understand me? Why, we think so differently. In her opinion, to leave one's papa and mamma or one's husband for the sake of the man one loves is the height of civic virtue, while I look upon it as childish. To fall in love and run away with a man to her means beginning a new life, while to my mind it means nothing at all. Love and man constitute the chief interest of her life, and possibly it is the philosophy of the unconscious at work in her. Try and make her believe that love is only a simple physical need, like the need of food or clothes; that it doesn't mean the end of the world if wives and husbands are unsatisfactory; that a man may be a profligate and a libertine, and yet a man of honour and a genius; and that, on the other hand, one may abstain from the pleasures of love and at the same time be a stupid, vicious animal! The civilised man of to-day, even among the lower classes for instance, the French workman—spends ten *sous* on dinner, five *sous* on his wine, and five or ten *sous* on woman, and devotes his brain and nerves entirely to his work. But Zinaida Fyodorovna assigns to love not so many *sous*, but her whole soul. I might give her a talking to, but she would raise a wail in answer, and declare in all sincerity that I had ruined her, that she had nothing left to live for."

"Don't say anything to her," said Pekarsky, "but simply take a separate flat for her, that's all."

"That's easy to say."

There was a brief silence.

"But she is charming," said Kukushkin. "She is exquisite. Such women imagine that they will be in love for ever, and abandon themselves with tragic intensity."

"But one must keep a head on one's shoulders," said Orlov; "one must be reasonable. All experience gained from everyday life and handed down in innumerable novels and plays, uniformly confirms the fact that adultery and cohabitation of any sort between decent people never lasts longer than two or at most three years, however great the love may have been at the beginning. That she ought to know. And so all this business of moving, of saucepans, hopes of eternal love and harmony, are nothing but a desire to delude herself and me. She is charming and exquisite—who denies it? But she has turned my life upside down; what I have regarded as trivial and nonsensical till now she has forced me to raise to the level of a serious problem; I serve an idol whom I have never looked upon as God. She is charming—exquisite, but for some reason now when I am going home, I feel uneasy, as though I expected to meet with something inconvenient at home, such as workmen pulling the stove to pieces and blocking up the place with heaps of bricks. In fact, I am no longer giving up to love a *sous*, but part of my peace of mind and my nerves. And that's bad."

"And she doesn't hear this villain!" sighed Kukushkin. "My dear sir," he said theatrically, "I will relieve you from the burdensome obligation to love that adorable creature! I will wrest Zinaida Fyodorovna from you!"

"You may . . ." said Orlov carelessly.

For half a minute Kukushkin laughed a shrill little laugh, shaking all over, then he said:

"Look out; I am in earnest! Don't you play the Othello afterwards!"

They all began talking of Kukushkin's indefatigable energy in love affairs, how irresistible he was to women, and what a danger he was to husbands; and how the devil would roast him in the other world for his immorality in this. He screwed up his eyes and remained silent, and when the names of ladies of their acquaintance were mentioned, he held up his little finger—as though to say they mustn't give away other people's secrets.

Orlov suddenly looked at his watch.

His friends understood, and began to take their leave. I remember that Gruzin, who was a little drunk, was wearisomely long in getting off. He put on his coat, which was cut like children's coats in poor families, pulled up the collar, and began telling some long-winded story; then, seeing he was not listened to, he flung the rug that smelt of the nursery over one shoulder, and with a guilty and imploring face begged me to find his hat.

"George, my angel," he said tenderly. "Do as I ask you, dear boy; come out of town with us!"

"You can go, but I can't. I am in the position of a married man now."

"She is a dear, she won't be angry. My dear chief, come along! It's glorious weather; there's snow and frost. . . . Upon my word, you want shaking up a bit; you are out of humour. I don't know what the devil is the matter with you. . . ."

Orlov stretched, yawned, and looked at Pekarsky.

"Are you going?" he said, hesitating.

"I don't know. Perhaps."

"Shall I get drunk? All right, I'll come," said Orlov after some hesitation. "Wait a minute; I'll get some money."

He went into the study, and Gruzin slouched in, too, dragging his rug after him. A minute later both came back into the hall. Gruzin, a little drunk and very pleased, was crumpling a ten-rouble note in his hands.

"We'll settle up to-morrow," he said. "And she is kind, she won't be cross. . . . She is my Lisotchka's godmother; I am fond of her, poor thing! Ah, my dear fellow!" he laughed joyfully, and pressing his forehead on Pekarsky's back. "Ah, Pekarsky, my dear soul! Advocatissimus—as dry as a biscuit, but you bet he is fond of women. . . ."

"Fat ones," said Orlov, putting on his fur coat. "But let us get off, or we shall be meeting her on the doorstep."

"'Vieni pensando a me segretamente,'" hummed Gruzin.

At last they drove off: Orlov did not sleep at home, and returned next day at dinner-time.

VI

Zinaida Fyodorovna had lost her gold watch, a present from her father. This loss surprised and alarmed her. She spent half a day going through the rooms, looking helplessly on all the tables and on all the windows. But the watch had disappeared completely.

Only three days afterwards Zinaida Fyodorovna, on coming in, left her purse in the hall. Luckily for me, on that occasion it was not I but Polya who helped her off with her coat. When the purse was missed, it could not be found in the hall.

"Strange," said Zinaida Fyodorovna in bewilderment. "I distinctly remember taking it out of my pocket to pay the cabman . . . and then I put it here near the looking-glass. It's very odd!"

I had not stolen it, but I felt as though I had stolen it and had been caught in the theft. Tears actually came into my eyes. When they were seated at dinner, Zinaida Fyodorovna said to Orlov in French:

"There seem to be spirits in the flat. I lost my purse in the hall to-day, and now, lo and behold, it is on my table. But it's not quite a disinterested trick of the spirits. They took out a gold coin and twenty roubles in notes."

"You are always losing something; first it's your watch and then it's your money . . ." said Orlov. "Why is it nothing of the sort ever happens to me?"

A minute later Zinaida Fyodorovna had forgotten the trick played by the spirits, and was telling with a laugh how the week before she had ordered some notepaper and had forgotten to give her new address, and the shop had sent the paper to her old home at her husband's, who had to pay twelve roubles for it. And suddenly she turned her eyes on Polya and looked at her intently. She blushed as she did so, and was so confused that she began talking of something else.

When I took in the coffee to the study, Orlov was standing with his back to the fire and she was sitting in an arm-chair facing him.

"I am not in a bad temper at all," she was saying in French. "But I have been putting things together, and now I see it clearly. I can give you the day and the hour when she stole my watch. And the purse? There can be no doubt about it. Oh!" she laughed as she took the coffee from me. "Now I understand why I am always losing my handkerchiefs and gloves. Whatever you say, I shall dismiss the magpie to-morrow and send Stepan for my Sofya. She is not a thief and has not got such a repulsive appearance."

"You are out of humour. To-morrow you will feel differently, and will realise that you can't discharge people simply because you suspect them."

"It's not suspicion; it's certainty," said Zinaida Fyodorovna. "So long as I suspected that unhappy-faced, poor-looking valet of yours, I said nothing. It's too bad of you not to believe me, *George.*"

"If we think differently about anything, it doesn't follow that I don't believe you. You may be right," said Orlov, turning round and flinging his cigarette-end into the fire, "but there is no need to be excited about it, anyway. In fact, I must say, I never expected my humble establishment would cause you so much serious worry and agitation. You've lost a gold coin: never mind—you may have a hundred of mine; but to change my habits, to pick up a new housemaid, to wait till she is used to the place—all that's a tedious, tiring business and does not suit me. Our present maid certainly is fat, and has, perhaps, a weakness for gloves and handkerchiefs, but she is perfectly well behaved, well trained, and does not shriek when Kukushkin pinches her."

"You mean that you can't part with her? . . . Why don't you say so?"

"Are you jealous?"

"Yes, I am," said Zinaida Fyodorovna, decidedly.

"Thank you."

"Yes, I am jealous," she repeated, and tears glistened in her eyes. "No, it's something worse . . . which I find it difficult to find a name for." She pressed her hands on her temples, and went on impulsively. "You men are so disgusting! It's horrible!"

"I see nothing horrible about it."

"I've not seen it; I don't know; but they say that you men begin with housemaids as boys, and get so used to it that you feel no repugnance. I don't know, I don't know, but I have actually read . . . George, of course you are right," she said, going up to Orlov and changing to a caressing and imploring tone. "I really am out of humour to-day. But, you must understand, I can't help it. She disgusts me and I am afraid of her. It makes me miserable to see her."

"Surely you can rise above such paltriness?" said Orlov, shrugging his shoulders in perplexity, and walking away from the fire. "Nothing could be simpler: take no notice of her, and then she won't disgust you, and you won't need to make a regular tragedy out of a trifle."

I went out of the study, and I don't know what answer Orlov received. Whatever it was, Polya remained. After that Zinaida Fyodorovna never applied to her for anything, and evidently tried to dispense with her services. When Polya handed her anything or even passed by her, jingling her bangle and rustling her skirts, she shuddered.

I believe that if Gruzin or Pekarsky had asked Orlov to dismiss Polya he would have done so without the slightest hesitation, without troubling about any explanations. He was easily persuaded, like all indifferent people. But in his relations with Zinaida Fyodorovna he displayed for some reason, even in trifles, an obstinacy which sometimes was almost irrational. I knew beforehand that if Zinaida Fyodorovna liked anything, it would be certain not to please Orlov. When on coming in from shopping she made haste to show him with pride some new purchase, he would glance at it and say coldly that the more unnecessary objects they had in the flat, the less airy it would be. It sometimes happened that after putting on his dress clothes to go out somewhere, and after saying good-bye to Zinaida Fyodorovna, he would suddenly change his mind and remain at home from sheer perversity. I used to think that he remained at home then simply in order to feel injured.

"Why are you staying?" said Zinaida Fyodorovna, with a show of vexation, though at the same time she was radiant with delight. "Why do you? You are not accustomed to spending your evenings at home, and I don't want you to alter your habits on my account. Do go out as usual, if you don't want me to feel guilty."

"No one is blaming you," said Orlov.

With the air of a victim he stretched himself in his easy-chair in the study, and shading his eyes with his hand, took up a book. But soon the book dropped from his hand, he turned heavily in his chair, and again screened his eyes as though from the sun. Now he felt annoyed that he had not gone out.

"May I come in?" Zinaida Fyodorovna would say, coming irresolutely into the study. "Are you reading? I felt dull by myself, and have come just for a minute . . . to have a peep at you."

I remember one evening she went in like that, irresolutely and inappropriately, and sank on the rug at Orlov's feet, and from her soft, timid movements one could see that she did not understand his mood and was afraid.

"You are always reading . . ." she said cajolingly, evidently wishing to flatter him. "Do you know, *George*, what is one of the secrets of your success? You are very clever and well-read. What book have you there?"

Orlov answered. A silence followed for some minutes which seemed to me very long. I was standing in the drawing-room, from which I could watch them, and was afraid of coughing.

"There is something I wanted to tell you," said Zinaida Fyodorovna, and she laughed; "shall I? Very likely you'll laugh and say that I flatter myself. You know I want, I want horribly to believe that you are staying at home to-night for my sake . . . that we might spend the evening together. Yes? May I think so?"

"Do," he said, screening his eyes. "The really happy man is he who thinks not only of what is, but of what is not."

"That was a long sentence which I did not quite understand. You mean happy people live in their imagination. Yes, that's true. I love to sit in your study in the evening and let my thoughts carry me far, far away. . . . It's pleasant sometimes to dream. Let us dream aloud, *George*."

"I've never been at a girls' boarding-school; I never learnt the art."

"You are out of humour?" said Zinaida Fyodorovna, taking Orlov's hand. "Tell me why. When you are like that, I'm afraid. I don't know whether your head aches or whether you are angry with me. . . ."

Again there was a silence lasting several long minutes.

"Why have you changed?" she said softly. "Why are you never so tender or so gay as you used to be at Znamensky Street? I've been with you almost a month, but it seems to me as though we had not yet begun to live, and have not yet talked of anything as we ought to. You always answer me with jokes or else with a long cold lecture like a teacher. And there is something cold in your jokes. . . . Why have you given up talking to me seriously?"

"I always talk seriously."

"Well, then, let us talk. For God's sake, *George*. . . . Shall we?"

"Certainly, but about what?"

"Let us talk of our life, of our future," said Zinaida Fyodorovna dreamily. "I keep making plans for our life, plans and plans—and I enjoy doing it so! *George*, I'll begin with the question, when are you going to give up your post?"

"What for?" asked Orlov, taking his hand from his forehead.

"With your views you cannot remain in the service. You are out of place there."

"My views?" Orlov repeated. "My views? In conviction and temperament I am an ordinary official, one of Shtchedrin's heroes. You take me for something different, I venture to assure you."

"Joking again, *George*!"

"Not in the least. The service does not satisfy me, perhaps; but, anyway, it is better for me than anything else. I am used to it, and in it I meet men of my own sort; I am in my place there and find it tolerable."

"You hate the service and it revolts you."

"Indeed? If I resign my post, take to dreaming aloud and letting myself be carried away into another world, do you suppose that that world would be less hateful to me than the service?"

"You are ready to libel yourself in order to contradict me." Zinaida Fyodorovna was offended and got up. "I am sorry I began this talk."

"Why are you angry? I am not angry with you for not being an official.

Every one lives as he likes best."

"Why, do you live as you like best? Are you free? To spend your life writing documents that are opposed to your own ideas," Zinaida Fyodorovna went on, clasping her hands in despair: "to submit to authority, congratulate your superiors at the New Year, and then cards and nothing but cards: worst of all, to be working for a system which must be distasteful to you—no, *George*, no! You should not make such horrid jokes. It's dreadful. You are a man of ideas, and you ought to be working for your ideas and nothing else."

"You really take me for quite a different person from what I am," sighed Orlov.

"Say simply that you don't want to talk to me. You dislike me, that's all," said Zinaida Fyodorovna through her tears.

"Look here, my dear," said Orlov admonishingly, sitting up in his chair. "You were pleased to observe yourself that I am a clever, well-read man, and to teach one who knows does nothing but harm. I know very well all the ideas, great and small, which you mean when you call me a man of ideas. So if I prefer the service and cards to those ideas, you may be sure I have good grounds for it. That's one thing. Secondly, you have, so far as I know, never been in the service, and can only have drawn your ideas of Government service from anecdotes and indifferent novels. So it would not be amiss for us to make a compact, once for all, not to talk of things we know already or of things about which we are not competent to speak."

"Why do you speak to me like that?" said Zinaida Fyodorovna, stepping back as though in horror. "What for? *George*, for God's sake, think what you are saying!"

Her voice quivered and broke; she was evidently trying to restrain her tears, but she suddenly broke into sobs.

"George, my darling, I am perishing!" she said in French, dropping down before Orlov, and laying her head on his knees. "I am miserable, I am exhausted. I can't bear it, I can't bear it. . . . In my childhood my hateful, depraved stepmother, then my husband, now you . . . you! . . . You meet my mad love with coldness and irony. . . . And that horrible, insolent servant," she went on, sobbing. "Yes, yes, I see: I am not your wife nor your friend, but a woman you don't respect because she has become your mistress. . . . I shall kill myself!"

I had not expected that her words and her tears would make such an impression on Orlov. He flushed, moved uneasily in his chair, and instead of irony, his face wore a look of stupid, schoolboyish dismay.

"My darling, you misunderstood me," he muttered helplessly, touching her hair and her shoulders. "Forgive me, I entreat you. I was unjust and I hate myself."

"I insult you with my whining and complaints. You are a true, generous . . . rare man—I am conscious of it every minute; but I've been horribly depressed for the last few days. . ."

Zinaida Fyodorovna impulsively embraced Orlov and kissed him on the cheek.

"Only please don't cry," he said.

"No, no. . . . I've had my cry, and now I am better."

"As for the servant, she shall be gone to-morrow," he said, still moving uneasily in his chair.

"No, she must stay, *George!* Do you hear? I am not afraid of her now. . . . One must rise above trifles and not imagine silly things. You are right! You are a wonderful, rare person!"

She soon left off crying. With tears glistening on her eyelashes, sitting on Orlov's knee, she told him in a low voice something touching, something like a reminiscence of childhood and youth. She stroked his face, kissed him, and carefully examined his hands with the rings on them and the charms on his watch-chain. She was carried away by what she was saying, and by being near the man she loved, and probably because her tears had cleared and refreshed her soul, there was a note of wonderful candour and sincerity in her voice. And Orlov played with her chestnut hair and kissed her hands, noiselessly pressing them to his lips.

Then they had tea in the study, and Zinaida Fyodorovna read aloud some letters. Soon after midnight they went to bed. I had a fearful pain in my side that night, and I not get warm or go to sleep till morning. I could hear Orlov go from the bedroom into his study. After sitting there about an hour, he rang the bell. In my pain and exhaustion I forgot all the rules and conventions, and went to his study in my night attire, barefooted. Orlov, in his dressing-gown and cap, was standing in the doorway, waiting for me.

"When you are sent for you should come dressed," he said sternly.

"Bring some fresh candles."

I was about to apologise, but suddenly broke into a violent cough, and clutched at the side of the door to save myself from falling.

"Are you ill?" said Orlov.

I believe it was the first time of our acquaintance that he addressed me not in the singular—goodness knows why. Most likely, in my night clothes and with my face distorted by coughing, I played my part poorly, and was very little like a flunkey.

"If you are ill, why do you take a place?" he said.

"That I may not die of starvation," I answered.

"How disgusting it all is, really!" he said softly, going up to his table.

While hurriedly getting into my coat, I put up and lighted fresh candles. He was sitting at the table, with feet stretched out on a low chair, cutting a book.

I left him deeply engrossed, and the book did not drop out of his hands as it had done in the evening.

VII

Now that I am writing these lines I am restrained by that dread of appearing sentimental and ridiculous, in which I have been trained from childhood; when I want to be affectionate or to say anything tender, I don't know how to be natural. And it is that dread, together with lack of practice, that prevents me from being able to express with perfect clearness what was passing in my soul at that time.

I was not in love with Zinaida Fyodorovna, but in the ordinary human feeling I had for her, there was far more youth, freshness, and joyousness than in Orlov's love.

As I worked in the morning, cleaning boots or sweeping the rooms, I waited with a thrill at my heart for the moment when I should hear her voice and her footsteps. To stand watching her as she drank her coffee in the morning or ate her lunch, to hold her fur coat for her in the hall, and to put the goloshes on her little feet while she rested her hand on my shoulder; then to wait till the hall porter rang up for me, to meet her at the door, cold, and rosy, powdered with the snow, to listen to her brief exclamations about the frost or the cabman—if only you knew how much all that meant to me! I longed to be in love, to have a wife and child of my own. I wanted my future wife to have just such a face, such a voice. I dreamed of it at dinner, and in the street when I was sent on some errand, and when I lay awake at night. Orlov rejected with disgust children, cooking, copper saucepans, and feminine knicknacks and I gathered them all up, tenderly cherished them in my dreams, loved them, and begged them of destiny. I had visions of a wife, a nursery, a little house with garden paths. . . .

I knew that if I did love her I could never dare hope for the miracle of her returning my love, but that reflection did not worry me. In my quiet, modest feeling akin to ordinary affection, there was no jealousy of Orlov or even envy of him, since I realised that for a wreck like me happiness was only to be found in dreams.

When Zinaida Fyodorovna sat up night after night for her *George*, looking immovably at a book of which she never turned a page, or when she shuddered and turned pale at Polya's crossing the room, I suffered with her, and the idea occurred to me to lance this festering wound as quickly as possible by letting her know what was said here at supper on Thursdays; but—how was it to be done? More and more often I saw her tears. For the first weeks she laughed and sang to herself, even when Orlov was not at home, but by the second month there was a mournful stillness in our flat broken only on Thursday evenings.

She flattered Orlov, and to wring from him a counterfeit smile or kiss, was ready to go on her knees to him, to fawn on him like a dog. Even when her heart was heaviest, she could not resist glancing into a looking-glass if she passed one and straightening her hair. It seemed strange to me that she could still take an interest in clothes and go into ecstasies over her purchases. It did not seem in keeping with her genuine grief. She paid attention to the fashions and ordered expensive dresses. What for? On whose account? I particularly remember one dress which cost four hundred roubles. To give four hundred roubles for an unnecessary, useless dress while women for their hard day's work get only twenty kopecks a day without food, and the makers of Venice and Brussels lace are only paid half a franc a day on the supposition that they can earn the rest by immorality! And it seemed strange to me that Zinaida Fyodorovna was not conscious of it; it vexed me. But she had only to go out of the house for me to find excuses and explanations for everything, and to be waiting eagerly for the hall porter to ring for me.

She treated me as a flunkey, a being of a lower order. One may pat a dog, and yet not notice it; I was given orders and asked questions, but my presence was not observed. My master and mistress thought it unseemly to say more to me than is usually said to servants; if when waiting at dinner I had laughed or put in my word in the conversation, they would certainly have thought I was mad and have dismissed me. Zinaida Fyodorovna was favourably disposed to me, all the same. When she was sending me on some errand or explaining to me the working of a new lamp or anything of that sort, her face was extraordinarily kind, frank, and cordial, and her eyes looked me straight in the face. At such moments I always fancied she remembered with gratitude how I used to bring her letters to Znamensky Street. When she rang the bell, Polya, who considered me her favourite and hated me for it, used to say with a jeering smile:

"Go along, *your* mistress wants you."

Zinaida Fyodorovna considered me as a being of a lower order, and did not suspect that if any one in the house were in a humiliating position it was she. She did not know that I, a footman, was unhappy on her account, and used to ask myself twenty times a day what was in store for her and how it would all end. Things were growing visibly worse day by day. After the evening on which they had talked of his official work, Orlov, who could not endure tears, unmistakably began to avoid conversation with her; whenever Zinaida Fyodorovna began to argue, or to beseech him, or seemed on the point of crying, he seized some plausible excuse for retreating to his study or going out. He more and more rarely slept at home, and still more rarely dined there: on Thursdays he was the one to suggest some expedition to his friends. Zinaida Fyodorovna was still dreaming of having the cooking done at home, of moving to a new flat, of travelling abroad, but her dreams remained dreams. Dinner was sent in from the restaurant. Orlov asked her not to broach the question of moving until after they had come back from abroad, and apropos of their foreign tour, declared that they could not go till his hair had grown long, as one could not go trailing from hotel to hotel and serving the idea without long hair.

To crown it all, in Orlov's absence, Kukushkin began calling at the flat in the evening. There was nothing exceptional in his behaviour, but I could never forget the conversation in which he had offered to cut Orlov out. He was regaled with tea and red wine, and he used to titter and, anxious to say something pleasant, would declare that a free union was superior in every respect to legal marriage, and that all decent people ought really to come to Zinaida Fyodorovna and fall at her feet.

VIII

Christmas was spent drearily in vague anticipations of calamity. On New Year's Eve Orlov unexpectedly announced at breakfast that he was being sent to assist a senator who was on a revising commission in a certain province.

"I don't want to go, but I can't find an excuse to get off," he said with vexation. "I must go; there's nothing for it."

Such news instantly made Zinaida Fyodorovna's eyes look red. "Is it for long?" she asked.

"Five days or so."

"I am glad, really, you are going," she said after a moment's thought. "It will be a change for you. You will fall in love with some one on the way, and tell me about it afterwards."

At every opportunity she tried to make Orlov feel that she did not restrict his liberty in any way, and that he could do exactly as he liked, and this artless, transparent strategy deceived no one, and only unnecessarily reminded Orlov that he was not free.

"I am going this evening," he said, and began reading the paper.

Zinaida Fyodorovna wanted to see him off at the station, but he dissuaded her, saying that he was not going to America, and not going to be away five years, but only five days—possibly less.

The parting took place between seven and eight. He put one arm round her, and kissed her on the lips and on the forehead.

"Be a good girl, and don't be depressed while I am away," he said in a warm, affectionate tone which touched even me. "God keep you!"

She looked greedily into his face, to stamp his dear features on her memory, then she put her arms gracefully round his neck and laid her head on his breast.

"Forgive me our misunderstandings," she said in French. "Husband and wife cannot help quarrelling if they love each other, and I love you madly. Don't forget me. . . . Wire to me often and fully."

Orlov kissed her once more, and, without saying a word, went out in confusion. When he heard the click of the lock as the door closed, he stood still in the middle of the staircase in hesitation and glanced upwards. It seemed to me that if a sound had reached him at that moment from above, he would have turned back. But all was quiet. He straightened his coat and went downstairs irresolutely.

The sledges had been waiting a long while at the door. Orlov got into one, I got into the other with two portmanteaus. It was a hard frost and there were fires smoking at the cross-roads. The cold wind nipped my face and hands, and took my breath away as we drove rapidly along; and, closing my eyes, I thought what a splendid woman she was. How she loved him! Even useless rubbish is collected in the courtyards nowadays and used for some purpose, even broken glass is considered a useful commodity, but something so precious, so rare, as the love of a refined, young, intelligent, and good woman is utterly thrown away and wasted. One of the early sociologists regarded every evil passion as a force which might by judicious management be turned to good, while among us even a fine, noble passion springs up and dies away in impotence, turned to no account, misunderstood or vulgarised. Why is it?

The sledges stopped unexpectedly. I opened my eyes and I saw that we had come to a standstill in Sergievsky Street, near a big house where Pekarsky lived. Orlov got out of the sledge and vanished into the entry. Five minutes later Pekarsky's footman came out, bareheaded, and, angry with the frost, shouted to me:

"Are you deaf? Pay the cabmen and go upstairs. You are wanted!"

At a complete loss, I went to the first storey. I had been to Pekarsky's flat before—that is, I had stood in the hall and looked into the drawing-room, and, after the damp, gloomy street, it always struck me by the brilliance of its picture-frames, its bronzes and expensive furniture. To-day in the midst of this splendour I saw Gruzin, Kukushkin, and, after a minute, Orlov.

"Look here, Stepan," he said, coming up to me. "I shall be staying here till Friday or Saturday. If any letters or telegrams come, you must bring them here every day. At home, of course you will say that I have gone, and send my greetings. Now you can go."

When I reached home Zinaida Fyodorovna was lying on the sofa in the drawing-room, eating a pear. There was only one candle burning in the candelabra.

"Did you catch the train?" asked Zinaida Fyodorovna.

"Yes, madam. His honour sends his greetings."

I went into my room and I, too, lay down. I had nothing to do, and I did not want to read. I was not surprised and I was not indignant. I only racked my brains to think why this deception was necessary. It is only boys in their teens who deceive their mistresses like that. How was it that a man who had thought and read so much could not imagine anything more sensible? I must confess I had by no means a poor opinion of his intelligence. I believe if he had had to deceive his minister or any other influential person he would have put a great deal of skill and energy into doing so; but to deceive a woman, the first idea that occurred to him was evidently good enough. If it succeeded—well and good; if it did not, there would be no harm done—he could tell some other lie just as quickly and simply, with no mental effort.

At midnight when the people on the floor overhead were moving their chairs and shouting hurrah to welcome the New Year, Zinaida Fyodorovna rang for me from the room next to the study. Languid from lying down so long, she was sitting at the table, writing something on a scrap of paper.

"I must send a telegram," she said, with a smile. "Go to the station as quick as you can and ask them to send it after him."

Going out into the street, I read on the scrap of paper:

"May the New Year bring new happiness. Make haste and telegraph; I miss you dreadfully. It seems an eternity. I am only sorry I can't send a thousand kisses and my very heart by telegraph. Enjoy yourself, my darling.—ZINA."

I sent the telegram, and next morning I gave her the receipt.

IX

The worst of it was that Orlov had thoughtlessly let Polya, too, into the secret of his deception, telling her to bring his shirts to Sergievsky Street. After that, she looked at Zinaida Fyodorovna with a malignant joy and hatred I could not understand, and was never tired of snorting with delight to herself in her own room and in the hall.

"She's outstayed her welcome; it's time she took herself off!" she would say with zest. "She ought to realise that herself. . . ."

She already divined by instinct that Zinaida Fyodorovna would not be with us much longer, and, not to let the chance slip, carried off everything she set her eyes on—smelling-bottles, tortoise-shell hairpins, handkerchiefs, shoes! On the day after New Year's Day, Zinaida Fyodorovna summoned me to her room and told me in a low voice that she missed her black dress. And then she walked through all the rooms, with a pale, frightened, and indignant face, talking to herself:

"It's too much! It's beyond everything. Why, it's unheard-of insolence!"

At dinner she tried to help herself to soup, but could not—her hands were trembling. Her lips were trembling, too. She looked helplessly at the soup and at the little pies, waiting for the trembling to pass off, and suddenly she could not resist looking at Polya.

"You can go, Polya," she said. "Stepan is enough by himself."

"I'll stay; I don't mind," answered Polya.

"There's no need for you to stay. You go away altogether," Zinaida Fyodorovna went on, getting up in great agitation. "You may look out for another place. You can go at once."

"I can't go away without the master's orders. He engaged me. It must be as he orders."

"You can take orders from me, too! I am mistress here!" said Zinaida Fyodorovna, and she flushed crimson.

"You may be the mistress, but only the master can dismiss me. It was he engaged me."

"You dare not stay here another minute!" cried Zinaida Fyodorovna, and she struck the plate with her knife. "You are a thief! Do you hear?"

Zinaida Fyodorovna flung her dinner-napkin on the table, and with a pitiful, suffering face, went quickly out of the room. Loudly sobbing and wailing something indistinct, Polya, too, went away. The soup and the grouse got cold. And for some reason all the restaurant dainties on the table struck me as poor, thievish, like Polya. Two pies on a plate had a particularly miserable and guilty air. "We shall be taken back to the restaurant to-day," they seemed to be saying, "and to-morrow we shall be put on the table again for some official or celebrated singer."

"She is a fine lady, indeed," I heard uttered in Polya's room. "I could have been a lady like that long ago, but I have some self-respect! We'll see which of us will be the first to go!"

Zinaida Fyodorovna rang the bell. She was sitting in her room, in the corner, looking as though she had been put in the corner as a punishment.

"No telegram has come?" she asked.

"No, madam."

"Ask the porter; perhaps there is a telegram. And don't leave the house," she called after me. "I am afraid to be left alone."

After that I had to run down almost every hour to ask the porter whether a telegram had come. I must own it was a dreadful time! To avoid seeing Polya, Zinaida Fyodorovna dined and had tea in her own room; it was here that she slept, too, on a short sofa like a half-moon, and she made her own bed. For the first days I took the telegrams; but, getting no answer, she lost her faith in me and began telegraphing herself. Looking at her, I, too, began impatiently hoping for a telegram. I hoped he would contrive some deception, would make arrangements, for instance, that a telegram should be sent to her from some station. If he were too much engrossed with cards or had been attracted by some other woman, I thought that both Gruzin and Kukushkin would remind him of us. But our expectations were vain. Five times a day I would go in to Zinaida Fyodorovna, intending to tell her the truth, But her eyes looked piteous as a fawn's, her shoulders seemed to droop, her lips were moving, and I went away again without saying a word. Pity and sympathy seemed to rob me of all manliness. Polya, as cheerful and well satisfied with herself as though nothing had happened, was tidying the master's study and the bedroom, rummaging in the cupboards, and making the crockery jingle, and when she passed Zinaida Fyodorovna's door, she hummed something and coughed. She was pleased that her mistress was hiding from her. In the evening she would go out somewhere, and rang at two or three o'clock in the morning, and I had to open the door to her and listen to remarks about my cough. Immediately afterwards I would hear another ring; I would run to the room next to the study, and Zinaida Fyodorovna, putting her head out of the door, would ask, "Who was it rung?" while she looked at my hands to see whether I had a telegram.

When at last on Saturday the bell rang below and she heard the familiar voice on the stairs, she was so delighted that she broke into sobs. She rushed to meet him, embraced him, kissed him on the breast and sleeves, said something one could not understand. The hall porter brought up the portmanteaus; Polya's cheerful voice was heard. It was as though some one had come home for the holidays.

"Why didn't you wire?" asked Zinaida Fyodorovna, breathless with joy. "Why was it? I have been in misery; I don't know how I've lived through it. . . . Oh, my God!"

"It was very simple! I returned with the senator to Moscow the very first day, and didn't get your telegrams," said Orlov. "After dinner, my love, I'll give you a full account of my doings, but now I must sleep and sleep. . . . I am worn out with the journey."

It was evident that he had not slept all night; he had probably been playing cards and drinking freely. Zinaida Fyodorovna put him to bed, and we all walked about on tiptoe all that day. The dinner went off quite satisfactorily, but when they went into the study and had coffee the explanation began. Zinaida Fyodorovna began talking of something rapidly in a low voice; she spoke in French, and her words flowed like a stream. Then I heard a loud sigh from Orlov, and his voice.

"My God!" he said in French. "Have you really nothing fresher to tell me than this everlasting tale of your servant's misdeeds?"

"But, my dear, she robbed me and said insulting things to me."

"But why is it she doesn't rob me or say insulting things to me?

Why is it I never notice the maids nor the porters nor the footmen? My dear, you are simply capricious and refuse to know your own mind . . . . I really begin to suspect that you must be in a certain condition. When I offered to let her go, you insisted on her remaining, and now you want me to turn her away. I can be obstinate, too, in such cases. You want her to go, but I want her to remain. That's the only way to cure you of your nerves."

"Oh, very well, very well," said Zinaida Fyodorovna in alarm. "Let us say no more about that. . . . Let us put it off till to-morrow . . . . Now tell me about Moscow. . . . What is going on in Moscow?"

X

After lunch next day—it was the seventh of January, St. John the Baptist's Day—Orlov put on his black dress coat and his decoration to go to visit his father and congratulate him on his name day. He had to go at two o'clock, and it was only half-past one when he had finished dressing. What was he to do for that half-hour? He walked about the drawing-room, declaiming some congratulatory verses which he had recited as a child to his father and mother.

Zinaida Fyodorovna, who was just going out to a dressmaker's or to the shops, was sitting, listening to him with a smile. I don't know how their conversation began, but when I took Orlov his gloves, he was standing before her with a capricious, beseeching face, saying:

"For God's sake, in the name of everything that's holy, don't talk of things that everybody knows! What an unfortunate gift our intellectual thoughtful ladies have for talking with enthusiasm and an air of profundity of things that every schoolboy is sick to death of! Ah, if only you would exclude from our conjugal programme all these serious questions! How grateful I should be to you!"

"We women may not dare, it seems, to have views of our own."

"I give you full liberty to be as liberal as you like, and quote from any authors you choose, but make me one concession: don't hold forth in my presence on either of two subjects: the corruption of the upper classes and the evils of the marriage system. Do understand me, at last. The upper class is always abused in contrast with the world of tradesmen, priests, workmen and peasants, Sidors and Nikitas of all sorts. I detest both classes, but if I had honestly to choose between the two, I should without hesitation, prefer the upper class, and there would be no falsity or affectation about it, since all my tastes are in that direction. Our world is trivial and empty, but at any rate we speak French decently, read something, and don't punch each other in the ribs even in our most violent quarrels, while the Sidors and the Nikitas and their worships in trade talk about 'being quite agreeable,' 'in a jiffy,' 'blast your eyes,' and display the utmost license of pothouse manners and the most degrading superstition."

"The peasant and the tradesman feed you."

"Yes, but what of it? That's not only to my discredit, but to theirs too. They feed me and take off their caps to me, so it seems they have not the intelligence and honesty to do otherwise. I don't blame or praise any one: I only mean that the upper class and the lower are as bad as one another. My feelings and my intelligence are opposed to both, but my tastes lie more in the direction of the former. Well, now for the evils of marriage," Orlov went on, glancing at his watch. "It's high time for you to understand that there are no evils in the system itself; what is the matter is that you don't know yourselves what you want from marriage. What is it you want? In legal and illegal cohabitation, in every sort of union and cohabitation, good or bad, the underlying reality is the same. You ladies live for that underlying reality alone: for you it's everything; your existence would have no meaning for you without it. You want nothing but that, and you get it; but since you've taken to reading novels you are ashamed of it: you rush from pillar to post, you recklessly change your men, and to justify this turmoil you have begun talking of the evils of marriage. So long as you can't and won't renounce what underlies it all, your chief foe, your devil so long as you serve that slavishly, what use is there in discussing the matter seriously? Everything you may say to me will be falsity and affectation. I shall not believe you."

I went to find out from the hall porter whether the sledge was at the door, and when I came back I found it had become a quarrel. As sailors say, a squall had blown up.

"I see you want to shock me by your cynicism today," said Zinaida Fyodorovna, walking about the drawing-room in great emotion. "It revolts me to listen to you. I am pure before God and man, and have nothing to repent of. I left my husband and came to you, and am proud of it. I swear, on my honour, I am proud of it!"

"Well, that's all right, then!"

"If you are a decent, honest man, you, too, ought to be proud of what I did. It raises you and me above thousands of people who would like to do as we have done, but do not venture through cowardice or petty prudence. But you are not a decent man. You are afraid of freedom, and you mock the promptings of genuine feeling, from fear that some ignoramus may suspect you of being sincere. You are afraid to show me to your friends; there's no greater infliction for you than to go about with me in the street. . . . Isn't that true? Why haven't you introduced me to your father or your cousin all this time? Why is it? No, I am sick of it at last," cried Zinaida Fyodorovna, stamping. "I demand what is mine by right. You must present me to your father."

"If you want to know him, go and present yourself. He receives visitors every morning from ten till half-past."

"How base you are!" said Zinaida Fyodorovna, wringing her hands in despair. "Even if you are not sincere, and are not saying what you think, I might hate you for your cruelty. Oh, how base you are!"

"We keep going round and round and never reach the real point. The real point is that you made a mistake, and you won't acknowledge it aloud. You imagined that I was a hero, and that I had some extraordinary ideas and ideals, and it has turned out that I am a most ordinary official, a cardplayer, and have no partiality for ideas of any sort. I am a worthy representative of the rotten world from which you have run away because you were revolted with its triviality and emptiness. Recognise it and be just: don't be indignant with me, but with yourself, as it is your mistake, and not mine."

"Yes, I admit I was mistaken."

"Well, that's all right, then. We've reached that point at last, thank God. Now hear something more, if you please: I can't rise to your level—I am too depraved; you can't descend to my level, either, for you are too exalted. So there is only one thing left to do. . . ."

"What?" Zinaida Fyodorovna asked quickly, holding her breath and turning suddenly as white as a sheet of paper.

"To call logic to our aid. . . ."

"Georgy, why are you torturing me?" Zinaida Fyodorovna said suddenly in Russian in a breaking voice. "What is it for? Think of my misery . . . ."

Orlov, afraid of tears, went quickly into his study, and I don't know why—whether it was that he wished to cause her extra pain, or whether he remembered it was usually done in such cases—he locked the door after him. She cried out and ran after him with a rustle of her skirt.

"What does this mean?" she cried, knocking at his door. "What . . . what does this mean?" she repeated in a shrill voice breaking with indignation. "Ah, so this is what you do! Then let me tell you I hate you, I despise you! Everything is over between us now."

I heard hysterical weeping mingled with laughter. Something small in the drawing-room fell off the table and was broken. Orlov went out into the hall by another door, and, looking round him nervously, he hurriedly put on his great-coat and went out.

Half an hour passed, an hour, and she was still weeping. I remembered that she had no father or mother, no relations, and here she was living between a man who hated her and Polya, who robbed her—and how desolate her life seemed to me! I do not know why, but I went into the drawing-room to her. Weak and helpless, looking with her lovely hair like an embodiment of tenderness and grace, she was in anguish, as though she were ill; she was lying on a couch, hiding her face, and quivering all over.

"Madam, shouldn't I fetch a doctor?" I asked gently.

"No, there's no need . . . it's nothing," she said, and she looked at me with her tear-stained eyes. "I have a little headache. . . . Thank you."

I went out, and in the evening she was writing letter after letter, and sent me out first to Pekarsky, then to Gruzin, then to Kukushkin, and finally anywhere I chose, if only I could find Orlov and give him the letter. Every time I came back with the letter she scolded me, entreated me, thrust money into my hand—as though she were in a fever. And all the night she did not sleep, but sat in the drawing-room, talking to herself.

Orlov returned to dinner next day, and they were reconciled.

The first Thursday afterwards Orlov complained to his friends of the intolerable life he led; he smoked a great deal, and said with irritation:

"It is no life at all; it's the rack. Tears, wailing, intellectual conversations, begging for forgiveness, again tears and wailing; and the long and the short of it is that I have no flat of my own now. I am wretched, and I make her wretched. Surely I haven't to live another month or two like this? How can I? But yet I may have to."

"Why don't you speak, then?" said Pekarsky.

"I've tried, but I can't. One can boldly tell the truth, whatever it may be, to an independent, rational man; but in this case one has to do with a creature who has no will, no strength of character, and no logic. I cannot endure tears; they disarm me. When she cries, I am ready to swear eternal love and cry myself."

Pekarsky did not understand; he scratched his broad forehead in perplexity and said:

"You really had better take another flat for her. It's so simple!"

"She wants me, not the flat. But what's the good of talking?" sighed Orlov. "I only hear endless conversations, but no way out of my position. It certainly is a case of 'being guilty without guilt.' I don't claim to be a mushroom, but it seems I've got to go into the basket. The last thing I've ever set out to be is a hero. I never could endure Turgenev's novels; and now, all of a sudden, as though to spite me, I've heroism forced upon me. I assure her on my honour that I'm not a hero at all, I adduce irrefutable proofs of the same, but she doesn't believe me. Why doesn't she believe me? I suppose I really must have something of the appearance of a hero."

"You go off on a tour of inspection in the provinces," said Kukushkin, laughing.

"Yes, that's the only thing left for me."

A week after this conversation Orlov announced that he was again ordered to attend the senator, and the same evening he went off with his portmanteaus to Pekarsky.

XI

An old man of sixty, in a long fur coat reaching to the ground, and a beaver cap, was standing at the door.

"Is Georgy Ivanitch at home?" he asked.

At first I thought it was one of the moneylenders, Gruzin's creditors, who sometimes used to come to Orlov for small payments on account; but when he came into the hall and flung open his coat, I saw the thick brows and the characteristically compressed lips which I knew so well from the photographs, and two rows of stars on the uniform. I recognised him: it was Orlov's father, the distinguished statesman.

I answered that Georgy Ivanitch was not at home. The old man pursed up his lips tightly and looked into space, reflecting, showing me his dried-up, toothless profile.

"I'll leave a note," he said; "show me in."

He left his goloshes in the hall, and, without taking off his long, heavy fur coat, went into the study. There he sat down before the table, and, before taking up the pen, for three minutes he pondered, shading his eyes with his hand as though from the sun— exactly as his son did when he was out of humour. His face was sad, thoughtful, with that look of resignation which I have only seen on the faces of the old and religious. I stood behind him, gazed at his bald head and at the hollow at the nape of his neck, and it was clear as daylight to me that this weak old man was now in my power. There was not a soul in the flat except my enemy and me. I had only to use a little physical violence, then snatch his watch to disguise the object of the crime, and to get off by the back way, and I should have gained infinitely more than I could have imagined possible when I took up the part of a footman. I thought that I could hardly get a better opportunity. But instead of acting, I looked quite unconcernedly, first at his bald patch and then at his fur, and calmly meditated on this man's relation to his only son, and on the fact that people spoiled by power and wealth probably don't want to die. . . .

"Have you been long in my son's service?" he asked, writing a large hand on the paper.

"Three months, your High Excellency."

He finished the letter and stood up. I still had time. I urged myself on and clenched my fists, trying to wring out of my soul some trace of my former hatred; I recalled what a passionate, implacable, obstinate hate I had felt for him only a little while before. . . . But it is difficult to strike a match against a crumbling stone. The sad old face and the cold glitter of his stars roused in me nothing but petty, cheap, unnecessary thoughts of the transitoriness of everything earthly, of the nearness of death. . . .

"Good-day, brother," said the old man. He put on his cap and went out.

There could be no doubt about it: I had undergone a change; I had become different. To convince myself, I began to recall the past, but at once I felt uneasy, as though I had accidentally peeped into a dark, damp corner. I remembered my comrades and friends, and my first thought was how I should blush in confusion if ever I met any of them. What was I now? What had I to think of and to do? Where was I to go? What was I living for?

I could make nothing of it. I only knew one thing—that I must make haste to pack my things and be off. Before the old man's visit my position as a flunkey had a meaning; now it was absurd. Tears dropped into my open portmanteau; I felt insufferably sad; but how I longed to live! I was ready to embrace and include in my short life every possibility open to man. I wanted to speak, to read, and to hammer in some big factory, and to stand on watch, and to plough. I yearned for the Nevsky Prospect, for the sea and the fields— for every place to which my imagination travelled. When Zinaida Fyodorovna came in, I rushed to open the door for her, and with peculiar tenderness took off her fur coat. The last time!

We had two other visitors that day besides the old man. In the evening when it was quite dark, Gruzin came to fetch some papers for Orlov. He opened the table-drawer, took the necessary papers, and, rolling them up, told me to put them in the hall beside his cap while he went in to see Zinaida Fyodorovna. She was lying on the sofa in the drawing-room, with her arms behind her head. Five or six days had already passed since Orlov went on his tour of inspection, and no one knew when he would be back, but this time she did not send telegrams and did not expect them. She did not seem to notice the presence of Polya, who was still living with us. "So be it, then," was what I read on her passionless and very pale face. Like Orlov, she wanted to be unhappy out of obstinacy. To spite herself and everything in the world, she lay for days together on the sofa, desiring and expecting nothing but evil for herself. Probably she was picturing to herself Orlov's return and the inevitable quarrels with him; then his growing indifference to her, his infidelities; then how they would separate; and perhaps these agonising thoughts gave her satisfaction. But what would she have said if she found out the actual truth?

"I love you, Godmother," said Gruzin, greeting her and kissing her hand. "You are so kind! And so dear *George* has gone away," he lied. "He has gone away, the rascal!"

He sat down with a sigh and tenderly stroked her hand.

"Let me spend an hour with you, my dear," he said. "I don't want to go home, and it's too early to go to the Birshovs'. The Birshovs are keeping their Katya's birthday today. She is a nice child!"

I brought him a glass of tea and a decanter of brandy. He slowly and with obvious reluctance drank the tea, and returning the glass to me, asked timidly:

"Can you give me . . . something to eat, my friend? I have had no dinner."

We had nothing in the flat. I went to the restaurant and brought him the ordinary rouble dinner.

"To your health, my dear," he said to Zinaida Fyodorovna, and he tossed off a glass of vodka. "My little girl, your godchild, sends you her love. Poor child! she's rickety. Ah, children, children!" he sighed. "Whatever you may say, Godmother, it is nice to be a father. Dear *George* can't understand that feeling."

He drank some more. Pale and lean, with his dinner-napkin over his chest like a little pinafore, he ate greedily, and raising his eyebrows, kept looking guiltily, like a little boy, first at Zinaida Fyodorovna and then at me. It seemed as though he would have begun crying if I had not given him the grouse or the jelly. When he had satisfied his hunger he grew more lively, and began laughingly telling some story about the Birshov household, but perceiving that it was tiresome and that Zinaida Fyodorovna was not laughing, he ceased. And there was a sudden feeling of dreariness. After he had finished his dinner they sat in the drawing-room by the light of a single lamp, and did not speak; it was painful to him to lie to her, and she wanted to ask him something, but could not make up her mind to. So passed half an hour. Gruzin glanced at his watch.

"I suppose it's time for me to go."

"No, stay a little. . . . We must have a talk."

Again they were silent. He sat down to the piano, struck one chord, then began playing, and sang softly, "What does the coming day bring me?" but as usual he got up suddenly and tossed his head.

"Play something," Zinaida Fyodorovna asked him.

"What shall I play?" he asked, shrugging his shoulders. "I have forgotten everything. I've given it up long ago."

Looking at the ceiling as though trying to remember, he played two pieces of Tchaikovsky with exquisite expression, with such warmth, such insight! His face was just as usual—neither stupid nor intelligent—and it seemed to me a perfect marvel that a man whom I was accustomed to see in the midst of the most degrading, impure surroundings, was capable of such purity, of rising to a feeling so lofty, so far beyond my reach. Zinaida Fyodorovna's face glowed, and she walked about the drawing-room in emotion.

"Wait a bit, Godmother; if I can remember it, I will play you something," he said; "I heard it played on the violoncello."

Beginning timidly and picking out the notes, and then gathering confidence, he played Saint-Saens's "Swan Song." He played it through, and then played it a second time.

"It's nice, isn't it?" he said.

Moved by the music, Zinaida Fyodorovna stood beside him and asked:

"Tell me honestly, as a friend, what do you think about me?"

"What am I to say?" he said, raising his eyebrows. "I love you and think nothing but good of you. But if you wish that I should speak generally about the question that interests you," he went on, rubbing his sleeve near the elbow and frowning, "then, my dear, you know . . . . To follow freely the promptings of the heart does not always give good people happiness. To feel free and at the same time to be happy, it seems to me, one must not conceal from oneself that life is coarse, cruel, and merciless in its conservatism, and one must retaliate with what it deserves—that is, be as coarse and as merciless in one's striving for freedom. That's what I think."

"That's beyond me," said Zinaida Fyodorovna, with a mournful smile. "I am exhausted already. I am so exhausted that I wouldn't stir a finger for my own salvation."

"Go into a nunnery."

He said this in jest, but after he had said it, tears glistened in Zinaida Fyodorovna's eyes and then in his.

"Well," he said, "we've been sitting and sitting, and now we must go. Good-bye, dear Godmother. God give you health."

He kissed both her hands, and stroking them tenderly, said that he should certainly come to see her again in a day or two. In the hall, as he was putting on his overcoat, that was so like a child's pelisse, he fumbled long in his pockets to find a tip for me, but found nothing there.

"Good-bye, my dear fellow," he said sadly, and went away.

I shall never forget the feeling that this man left behind him.

Zinaida Fyodorovna still walked about the room in her excitement. That she was walking about and not still lying down was so much to the good. I wanted to take advantage of this mood to speak to her openly and then to go away, but I had hardly seen Gruzin out when I heard a ring. It was Kukushkin.

"Is Georgy Ivanitch at home?" he said. "Has he come back? You say no? What a pity! In that case, I'll go in and kiss your mistress's hand, and so away. Zinaida Fyodorovna, may I come in?" he cried. "I want to kiss your hand. Excuse my being so late."

He was not long in the drawing-room, not more than ten minutes, but I felt as though he were staying a long while and would never go away. I bit my lips from indignation and annoyance, and already hated Zinaida Fyodorovna. "Why does she not turn him out?" I thought indignantly, though it was evident that she was bored by his company.

When I held his fur coat for him he asked me, as a mark of special good-will, how I managed to get on without a wife.

"But I don't suppose you waste your time," he said, laughingly. "I've no doubt Polya and you are as thick as thieves. . . . You rascal!"

In spite of my experience of life, I knew very little of mankind at that time, and it is very likely that I often exaggerated what was of little consequence and failed to observe what was important. It seemed to me it was not without motive that Kukushkin tittered and flattered me. Could it be that he was hoping that I, like a flunkey, would gossip in other kitchens and servants' quarters of his coming to see us in the evenings when Orlov was away, and staying with Zinaida Fyodorovna till late at night? And when my tittle-tattle came to the ears of his acquaintance, he would drop his eyes in confusion and shake his little finger. And would not he, I thought, looking at his little honeyed face, this very evening at cards pretend and perhaps declare that he had already won Zinaida Fyodorovna from Orlov?

That hatred which failed me at midday when the old father had come, took possession of me now. Kukushkin went away at last, and as I listened to the shuffle of his leather goloshes, I felt greatly tempted to fling after him, as a parting shot, some coarse word of abuse, but I restrained myself. And when the steps had died away on the stairs, I went back to the hall, and, hardly conscious of what I was doing, took up the roll of papers that Gruzin had left behind, and ran headlong downstairs. Without cap or overcoat, I ran down into the street. It was not cold, but big flakes of snow were falling and it was windy.

"Your Excellency!" I cried, catching up Kukushkin. "Your Excellency!"

He stopped under a lamp-post and looked round with surprise. "Your Excellency!" I said breathless, "your Excellency!"

And not able to think of anything to say, I hit him two or three times on the face with the roll of paper. Completely at a loss, and hardly wondering—I had so completely taken him by surprise—he leaned his back against the lamp-post and put up his hands to protect his face. At that moment an army doctor passed, and saw how I was beating the man, but he merely looked at us in astonishment and went on. I felt ashamed and I ran back to the house.

XII

With my head wet from the snow, and gasping for breath, I ran to my room, and immediately flung off my swallow-tails, put on a reefer jacket and an overcoat, and carried my portmanteau out into the passage; I must get away! But before going I hurriedly sat down and began writing to Orlov:

"I leave you my false passport," I began. "I beg you to keep it as a memento, you false man, you Petersburg official!

"To steal into another man's house under a false name, to watch under the mask of a flunkey this person's intimate life, to hear everything, to see everything in order later on, unasked, to accuse a man of lying—all this, you will say, is on a level with theft. Yes, but I care nothing for fine feelings now. I have endured dozens of your dinners and suppers when you said and did what you liked, and I had to hear, to look on, and be silent. I don't want to make you a present of my silence. Besides, if there is not a living soul at hand who dares to tell you the truth without flattery, let your flunkey Stepan wash your magnificent countenance for you."

I did not like this beginning, but I did not care to alter it.

Besides, what did it matter?

The big windows with their dark curtains, the bed, the crumpled dress coat on the floor, and my wet footprints, looked gloomy and forbidding. And there was a peculiar stillness.

Possibly because I had run out into the street without my cap and goloshes I was in a high fever. My face burned, my legs ached. . . . My heavy head drooped over the table, and there was that kind of division in my thought when every idea in the brain seemed dogged by its shadow.

"I am ill, weak, morally cast down," I went on; "I cannot write to you as I should like to. From the first moment I desired to insult and humiliate you, but now I do not feel that I have the right to do so. You and I have both fallen, and neither of us will ever rise up again; and even if my letter were eloquent, terrible, and passionate, it would still seem like beating on the lid of a coffin: however one knocks upon it, one will not wake up the dead! No efforts could warm your accursed cold blood, and you know that better than I do. Why write? But my mind and heart are burning, and I go on writing; for some reason I am moved as though this letter still might save you and me. I am so feverish that my thoughts are disconnected, and my pen scratches the paper without meaning; but the question I want to put to you stands before me as clear as though in letters of flame.

"Why I am prematurely weak and fallen is not hard to explain. Like Samson of old, I have taken the gates of Gaza on my shoulders to carry them to the top of the mountain, and only when I was exhausted, when youth and health were quenched in me forever, I noticed that that burden was not for my shoulders, and that I had deceived myself. I have been, moreover, in cruel and continual pain. I have endured cold, hunger, illness, and loss of liberty. Of personal happiness I know and have known nothing. I have no home; my memories are bitter, and my conscience is often in dread of them. But why have you fallen—you? What fatal, diabolical causes hindered your life from blossoming into full flower? Why, almost before beginning life, were you in such haste to cast off the image and likeness of God, and to become a cowardly beast who backs and scares others because he is afraid himself? You are afraid of life—as afraid of it as an Oriental who sits all day on a cushion smoking his hookah. Yes, you read a great deal, and a European coat fits you well, but yet with what tender, purely Oriental, pasha-like care you protect yourself from hunger, cold, physical effort, from pain and uneasiness! How early your soul has taken to its dressing-gown! What a cowardly part you have played towards real life and nature, with which every healthy and normal man struggles! How soft, how snug, how warm, how comfortable—and how bored you are! Yes, it is deathly boredom, unrelieved by one ray of light, as in solitary confinement; but you try to hide from that enemy, too, you play cards eight hours out of twenty-four.

"And your irony? Oh, but how well I understand it! Free, bold, living thought is searching and dominating; for an indolent, sluggish mind it is intolerable. That it may not disturb your peace, like thousands of your contemporaries, you made haste in youth to put it under bar and bolt. Your ironical attitude to life, or whatever you like to call it, is your armour; and your thought, fettered and frightened, dare not leap over the fence you have put round it; and when you jeer at ideas which you pretend to know all about, you are like the deserter fleeing from the field of battle, and, to stifle his shame, sneering at war and at valour. Cynicism stifles pain. In some novel of Dostoevsky's an old man tramples underfoot the portrait of his dearly loved daughter because he had been unjust to her, and you vent your foul and vulgar jeers upon the ideas of goodness and truth because you have not the strength to follow them. You are frightened of every honest and truthful hint at your degradation, and you purposely surround yourself with people who do nothing but flatter your weaknesses. And you may well, you may well dread the sight of tears!

"By the way, your attitude to women. Shamelessness has been handed down to us in our flesh and blood, and we are trained to shamelessness; but that is what we are men for—to subdue the beast in us. When you reached manhood and *all* ideas became known to you, you could not have failed to see the truth; you knew it, but you did not follow it; you were afraid of it, and to deceive your conscience you began loudly assuring yourself that it was not you but woman that was to blame, that she was as degraded as your attitude to her. Your cold, scabrous anecdotes, your coarse laughter, all your innumerable theories concerning the underlying reality of marriage and the definite demands made upon it, concerning the ten *sous* the French workman pays his woman; your everlasting attacks on female logic, lying, weakness and so on—doesn't it all look like a desire at all costs to force woman down into the mud that she may be on the same level as your attitude to her? You are a weak, unhappy, unpleasant person!"

Zinaida Fyodorovna began playing the piano in the drawing-room, trying to recall the song of Saint Saens that Gruzin had played. I went and lay on my bed, but remembering that it was time for me to go, I got up with an effort and with a heavy, burning head went to the table again.

"But this is the question," I went on. "Why are we worn out? Why are we, at first so passionate so bold, and so full of faith, complete bankrupts at thirty or thirty-five? Why does one waste in consumption, another put a bullet through his brains, a third seeks forgetfulness in vodka and cards, while the fourth tries to stifle his fear and misery by cynically trampling underfoot the pure image of his fair youth? Why is it that, having once fallen, we do not try to rise up again, and, losing one thing, do not seek something else? Why is it?

"The thief hanging on the Cross could bring back the joy of life and the courage of confident hope, though perhaps he had not more than an hour to live. You have long years before you, and I shall probably not die so soon as one might suppose. What if by a miracle the present turned out to be a dream, a horrible nightmare, and we should wake up renewed, pure, strong, proud of our righteousness? Sweet visions fire me, and I am almost breathless with emotion. I have a terrible longing to live. I long for our life to be holy, lofty, and majestic as the heavens above. Let us live! The sun doesn't rise twice a day, and life is not given us again—clutch at what is left of your life and save it. . . ."

I did not write another word. I had a multitude of thoughts in my mind, but I could not connect them and get them on to paper. Without finishing the letter, I signed it with my name and rank, and went into the study. It was dark. I felt for the table and put the letter on it. I must have stumbled against the furniture in the dark and made a noise.

"Who is there?" I heard an alarmed voice in the drawing-room.

And the clock on the table softly struck one at the moment.

XIII

For at least half a minute I fumbled at the door in the dark, feeling for the handle; then I slowly opened it and walked into the drawing-room. Zinaida Fyodorovna was lying on the couch, and raising herself on her elbow, she looked towards me. Unable to bring myself to speak, I walked slowly by, and she followed me with her eyes. I stood for a little time in the dining-room and then walked by her again, and she looked at me intently and with perplexity, even with alarm. At last I stood still and said with an effort:

"He is not coming back."

She quickly got on to her feet, and looked at me without understanding.

"He is not coming back," I repeated, and my heart beat violently. "He will not come back, for he has not left Petersburg. He is staying at Pekarsky's."

She understood and believed me—I saw that from her sudden pallor, and from the way she laid her arms upon her bosom in terror and entreaty. In one instant all that had happened of late flashed through her mind; she reflected, and with pitiless clarity she saw the whole truth. But at the same time she remembered that I was a flunkey, a being of a lower order. . . . A casual stranger, with hair ruffled, with face flushed with fever, perhaps drunk, in a common overcoat, was coarsely intruding into her intimate life, and that offended her. She said to me sternly:

"It's not your business: go away."

"Oh, believe me!" I cried impetuously, holding out my hands to her.

"I am not a footman; I am as free as you."

I mentioned my name, and, speaking very rapidly that she might not interrupt me or go away, explained to her who I was and why I was living there. This new discovery struck her more than the first. Till then she had hoped that her footman had lied or made a mistake or been silly, but now after my confession she had no doubts left. From the expression of her unhappy eyes and face, which suddenly lost its softness and beauty and looked old, I saw that she was insufferably miserable, and that the conversation would lead to no good; but I went on impetuously:

"The senator and the tour of inspection were invented to deceive you. In January, just as now, he did not go away, but stayed at Pekarsky's, and I saw him every day and took part in the deception. He was weary of you, he hated your presence here, he mocked at you . . . . If you could have heard how he and his friends here jeered at you and your love, you would not have remained here one minute! Go away from here! Go away."

"Well," she said in a shaking voice, and moved her hand over her hair. "Well, so be it."

Her eyes were full of tears, her lips were quivering, and her whole face was strikingly pale and distorted with anger. Orlov's coarse, petty lying revolted her and seemed to her contemptible, ridiculous: she smiled and I did not like that smile.

"Well," she repeated, passing her hand over her hair again, "so be it. He imagines that I shall die of humiliation, and instead of that I am . . . amused by it. There's no need for him to hide." She walked away from the piano and said, shrugging her shoulders:

"There's no need. . . . It would have been simpler to have it out with me instead of keeping in hiding in other people's flats. I have eyes; I saw it myself long ago. . . . I was only waiting for him to come back to have things out once for all."

Then she sat down on a low chair by the table, and, leaning her head on the arm of the sofa, wept bitterly. In the drawing-room there was only one candle burning in the candelabra, and the chair where she was sitting was in darkness; but I saw how her head and shoulders were quivering, and how her hair, escaping from her combs, covered her neck, her face, her arms. . . . Her quiet, steady weeping, which was not hysterical but a woman's ordinary weeping, expressed a sense of insult, of wounded pride, of injury, and of something helpless, hopeless, which one could not set right and to which one could not get used. Her tears stirred an echo in my troubled and suffering heart; I forgot my illness and everything else in the world; I walked about the drawing-room and muttered distractedly:

"Is this life? . . . Oh, one can't go on living like this, one can't. . . . Oh, it's madness, wickedness, not life."

"What humiliation!" she said through her tears. "To live together, to smile at me at the very time when I was burdensome to him, ridiculous in his eyes! Oh, how humiliating!"

She lifted up her head, and looking at me with tear-stained eyes through her hair, wet with her tears, and pushing it back as it prevented her seeing me, she asked:

"They laughed at me?"

"To these men you were laughable—you and your love and Turgenev; they said your head was full of him. And if we both die at once in despair, that will amuse them, too; they will make a funny anecdote of it and tell it at your requiem service. But why talk of them?" I said impatiently. "We must get away from here—I cannot stay here one minute longer."

She began crying again, while I walked to the piano and sat down.

"What are we waiting for?" I asked dejectedly. "It's two o'clock."

"I am not waiting for anything," she said. "I am utterly lost."

"Why do you talk like that? We had better consider together what we are to do. Neither you nor I can stay here. Where do you intend to go?"

Suddenly there was a ring at the bell. My heart stood still. Could it be Orlov, to whom perhaps Kukushkin had complained of me? How should we meet? I went to open the door. It was Polya. She came in shaking the snow off her pelisse, and went into her room without saying a word to me. When I went back to the drawing-room, Zinaida Fyodorovna, pale as death, was standing in the middle of the room, looking towards me with big eyes.

"Who was it?" she asked softly.

"Polya," I answered.

She passed her hand over her hair and closed her eyes wearily.

"I will go away at once," she said. "Will you be kind and take me to the Petersburg Side? What time is it now?"

"A quarter to three."

XIV

When, a little afterwards, we went out of the house, it was dark and deserted in the street. Wet snow was falling and a damp wind lashed in one's face. I remember it was the beginning of March; a thaw had set in, and for some days past the cabmen had been driving on wheels. Under the impression of the back stairs, of the cold, of the midnight darkness, and the porter in his sheepskin who had questioned us before letting us out of the gate, Zinaida Fyodorovna was utterly cast down and dispirited. When we got into the cab and the hood was put up, trembling all over, she began hurriedly saying how grateful she was to me.

"I do not doubt your good-will, but I am ashamed that you should be troubled," she muttered. "Oh, I understand, I understand. . . . When Gruzin was here to-day, I felt that he was lying and concealing something. Well, so be it. But I am ashamed, anyway, that you should be troubled."

She still had her doubts. To dispel them finally, I asked the cabman to drive through Sergievsky Street; stopping him at Pekarsky's door, I got out of the cab and rang. When the porter came to the door, I asked aloud, that Zinaida Fyodorovna might hear, whether Georgy Ivanitch was at home.

"Yes," was the answer, "he came in half an hour ago. He must be in bed by now. What do you want?"

Zinaida Fyodorovna could not refrain from putting her head out.

"Has Georgy Ivanitch been staying here long?" she asked.

"Going on for three weeks."

"And he's not been away?"

"No," answered the porter, looking at me with surprise.

"Tell him, early to-morrow," I said, "that his sister has arrived from Warsaw. Good-bye."

Then we drove on. The cab had no apron, the snow fell on us in big flakes, and the wind, especially on the Neva, pierced us through and through. I began to feel as though we had been driving for a long time, that for ages we had been suffering, and that for ages I had been listening to Zinaida Fyodorovna's shuddering breath. In semi-delirium, as though half asleep, I looked back upon my strange, incoherent life, and for some reason recalled a melodrama, "The Parisian Beggars," which I had seen once or twice in my childhood. And when to shake off that semi-delirium I peeped out from the hood and saw the dawn, all the images of the past, all my misty thoughts, for some reason, blended in me into one distinct, overpowering thought: everything was irrevocably over for Zinaida Fyodorovna and for me. This was as certain a conviction as though the cold blue sky contained a prophecy, but a minute later I was already thinking of something else and believed differently.

"What am I now?" said Zinaida Fyodorovna, in a voice husky with the cold and the damp. "Where am I to go? What am I to do? Gruzin told me to go into a nunnery. Oh, I would! I would change my dress, my face, my name, my thoughts . . . everything—everything, and would hide myself for ever. But they will not take me into a nunnery. I am with child."

"We will go abroad together to-morrow," I said.

"That's impossible. My husband won't give me a passport."

"I will take you without a passport."

The cabman stopped at a wooden house of two storeys, painted a dark colour. I rang. Taking from me her small light basket—the only luggage we had brought with us—Zinaida Fyodorovna gave a wry smile and said:

"These are my *bijoux*."

But she was so weak that she could not carry these *bijoux*.

It was a long while before the door was opened. After the third or fourth ring a light gleamed in the windows, and there was a sound of steps, coughing and whispering; at last the key grated in the lock, and a stout peasant woman with a frightened red face appeared at the door. Some distance behind her stood a thin little old woman with short grey hair, carrying a candle in her hand. Zinaida Fyodorovna ran into the passage and flung her arms round the old woman's neck.

"Nina, I've been deceived," she sobbed loudly. "I've been coarsely, foully deceived! Nina, Nina!"

I handed the basket to the peasant woman. The door was closed, but still I heard her sobs and the cry "Nina!"

I got into the cab and told the man to drive slowly to the Nevsky Prospect. I had to think of a night's lodging for myself.

Next day towards evening I went to see Zinaida Fyodorovna. She was terribly changed. There were no traces of tears on her pale, terribly sunken face, and her expression was different. I don't know whether it was that I saw her now in different surroundings, far from luxurious, and that our relations were by now different, or perhaps that intense grief had already set its mark upon her; she did not strike me as so elegant and well dressed as before. Her figure seemed smaller; there was an abruptness and excessive nervousness about her as though she were in a hurry, and there was not the same softness even in her smile. I was dressed in an expensive suit which I had bought during the day. She looked first of all at that suit and at the hat in my hand, then turned an impatient, searching glance upon my face as though studying it.

"Your transformation still seems to me a sort of miracle," she said. "Forgive me for looking at you with such curiosity. You are an extraordinary man, you know."

I told her again who I was, and why I was living at Orlov's, and I told her at greater length and in more detail than the day before. She listened with great attention, and said without letting me finish:

"Everything there is over for me. You know, I could not refrain from writing a letter. Here is the answer."

On the sheet which she gave there was written in Orlov's hand:

"I am not going to justify myself. But you must own that it was your mistake, not mine. I wish you happiness, and beg you to make haste and forget.

"Yours sincerely,

"G. O.

"P. S.—I am sending on your things."

The trunks and baskets despatched by Orlov were standing in the passage, and my poor little portmanteau was there beside them.

"So . . ." Zinaida Fyodorovna began, but she did not finish.

We were silent. She took the note and held it for a couple of minutes before her eyes, and during that time her face wore the same haughty, contemptuous, proud, and harsh expression as the day before at the beginning of our explanation; tears came into her eyes—not timid, bitter tears, but proud, angry tears.

"Listen," she said, getting up abruptly and moving away to the window that I might not see her face. "I have made up my mind to go abroad with you tomorrow."

"I am very glad. I am ready to go to-day."

"Accept me as a recruit. Have you read Balzac?" she asked suddenly, turning round. "Have you? At the end of his novel 'Pere Goriot' the hero looks down upon Paris from the top of a hill and threatens the town: 'Now we shall settle our account,' and after this he begins a new life. So when I look out of the train window at Petersburg for the last time, I shall say, 'Now we shall settle our account!'"

Saying this, she smiled at her jest, and for some reason shuddered all over.

XV

At Venice I had an attack of pleurisy. Probably I had caught cold in the evening when we were rowing from the station to the Hotel Bauer. I had to take to my bed and stay there for a fortnight. Every morning while I was ill Zinaida Fyodorovna came from her room to drink coffee with me, and afterwards read aloud to me French and Russian books, of which we had bought a number at Vienna. These books were either long, long familiar to me or else had no interest for me, but I had the sound of a sweet, kind voice beside me, so that the meaning of all of them was summed up for me in the one thing—I was not alone. She would go out for a walk, come back in her light grey dress, her light straw hat, gay, warmed by the spring sun; and sitting by my bed, bending low down over me, would tell me something about Venice or read me those books—and I was happy.

At night I was cold, ill, and dreary, but by day I revelled in life I can find no better expression for it. The brilliant warm sunshine beating in at the open windows and at the door upon the balcony, the shouts below, the splash of oars, the tinkle of bells, the prolonged boom of the cannon at midday, and the feeling of perfect, perfect freedom, did wonders with me; I felt as though I were growing strong, broad wings which were bearing me God knows whither. And what charm, what joy at times at the thought that another life was so close to mine! that I was the servant, the guardian, the friend, the indispensable fellow-traveller of a creature, young, beautiful, wealthy, but weak, lonely, and insulted! It is pleasant even to be ill when you know that there are people who are looking forward to your convalescence as to a holiday. One day I heard her whispering behind the door with my doctor, and then she came in to me with tear-stained eyes. It was a bad sign, but I was touched, and there was a wonderful lightness in my heart.

But at last they allowed me to go out on the balcony. The sunshine and the breeze from the sea caressed and fondled my sick body. I looked down at the familiar gondolas, which glide with feminine grace smoothly and majestically as though they were alive, and felt all the luxury of this original, fascinating civilisation. There was a smell of the sea. Some one was playing a stringed instrument and two voices were singing. How delightful it was! How unlike it was to that Petersburg night when the wet snow was falling and beating so rudely on our faces. If one looks straight across the canal, one sees the sea, and on the wide expanse towards the horizon the sun glittered on the water so dazzlingly that it hurt one's eyes to look at it. My soul yearned towards that lovely sea, which was so akin to me and to which I had given up my youth. I longed to live—to live—and nothing more.

A fortnight later I began walking freely. I loved to sit in the sun, and to listen to the gondoliers without understanding them, and for hours together to gaze at the little house where, they said, Desdemona lived—a naive, mournful little house with a demure expression, as light as lace, so light that it looked as though one could lift it from its place with one hand. I stood for a long time by the tomb of Canova, and could not take my eyes off the melancholy lion. And in the Palace of the Doges I was always drawn to the corner where the portrait of the unhappy Marino Faliero was painted over with black. "It is fine to be an artist, a poet, a dramatist," I thought, "but since that is not vouchsafed to me, if only I could go in for mysticism! If only I had a grain of some faith to add to the unruffled peace and serenity that fills the soul!"

In the evening we ate oysters, drank wine, and went out in a gondola. I remember our black gondola swayed softly in the same place while the water faintly gurgled under it. Here and there the reflection of the stars and the lights on the bank quivered and trembled. Not far from us in a gondola, hung with coloured lanterns which were reflected in the water, there were people singing. The sounds of guitars, of violins, of mandolins, of men's and women's voices, were audible in the dark. Zinaida Fyodorovna, pale, with a grave, almost stern face, was sitting beside me, compressing her lips and clenching her hands. She was thinking about something; she did not stir an eyelash, nor hear me. Her face, her attitude, and her fixed, expressionless gaze, and her incredibly miserable, dreadful, and icy-cold memories, and around her the gondolas, the lights, the music, the song with its vigorous passionate cry of " Jam-mo! Jam-mo!"—what contrasts in life! When she sat like that, with tightly clasped hands, stony, mournful, I used to feel as though we were both characters in some novel in the old-fashioned style called "The Ill-fated," "The Abandoned," or something of the sort. Both of us: she—the ill-fated, the abandoned; and I—the faithful, devoted friend, the dreamer, and, if you like it, a superfluous man, a failure capable of nothing but coughing and dreaming, and perhaps sacrificing myself.

But who and what needed my sacrifices now? And what had I to sacrifice, indeed?

When we came in in the evening we always drank tea in her room and talked. We did not shrink from touching on old, unhealed wounds— on the contrary, for some reason I felt a positive pleasure in telling her about my life at Orlov's, or referring openly to relations which I knew and which could not have been concealed from me.

"At moments I hated you," I said to her. "When he was capricious, condescending, told you lies, I marvelled how it was you did not see, did not understand, when it was all so clear! You kissed his hands, you knelt to him, you flattered him. . ."

"When I . . . kissed his hands and knelt to him, I loved him . . ." she said, blushing crimson.

"Can it have been so difficult to see through him? A fine sphinx! A sphinx indeed—a kammer-junker! I reproach you for nothing, God forbid," I went on, feeling I was coarse, that I had not the tact, the delicacy which are so essential when you have to do with a fellow-creature's soul; in early days before I knew her I had not noticed this defect in myself. "But how could you fail to see what he was," I went on, speaking more softly and more diffidently, however.

"You mean to say you despise my past, and you are right," she said, deeply stirred. "You belong to a special class of men who cannot be judged by ordinary standards; your moral requirements are exceptionally rigorous, and I understand you can't forgive things. I understand you, and if sometimes I say the opposite, it doesn't mean that I look at things differently from you; I speak the same old nonsense simply because I haven't had time yet to wear out my old clothes and prejudices. I, too, hate and despise my past, and Orlov and my love. . . . What was that love? It's positively absurd now," she said, going to the window and looking down at the canal. "All this love only clouds the conscience and confuses the mind.

The meaning of life is to be found only in one thing—fighting. To get one's heel on the vile head of the serpent and to crush it! That's the meaning of life. In that alone or in nothing."

I told her long stories of my past, and described my really astounding adventures. But of the change that had taken place in me I did not say one word. She always listened to me with great attention, and at interesting places she rubbed her hands as though vexed that it had not yet been her lot to experience such adventures, such joys and terrors. Then she would suddenly fall to musing and retreat into herself, and I could see from her face that she was not attending to me.

I closed the windows that looked out on the canal and asked whether we should not have the fire lighted.

"No, never mind. I am not cold," she said, smiling listlessly. "I only feel weak. Do you know, I fancy I have grown much wiser lately. I have extraordinary, original ideas now. When I think of my past, of my life then . . . people in general, in fact, it is all summed up for me in the image of my stepmother. Coarse, insolent, soulless, false, depraved, and a morphia maniac too. My father, who was feeble and weak-willed, married my mother for her money and drove her into consumption; but his second wife, my stepmother, he loved passionately, insanely. . . . What I had to put up with! But what is the use of talking! And so, as I say, it is all summed up in her image. . . . And it vexes me that my stepmother is dead. I should like to meet her now!"

"Why?"

"I don't know," she answered with a laugh and a graceful movement of her head. "Good-night. You must get well. As soon as you are well, we'll take up our work. . . It's time to begin."

After I had said good-night and had my hand on the door-handle, she said:

"What do you think? Is Polya still living there?"

"Probably."

And I went off to my room. So we spent a whole month. One grey morning when we both stood at my window, looking at the clouds which were moving up from the sea, and at the darkening canal, expecting every minute that it would pour with rain, and when a thick, narrow streak of rain covered the sea as though with a muslin veil, we both felt suddenly dreary. The same day we both set off for Florence.

XVI

It was autumn, at Nice. One morning when I went into her room she was sitting on a low chair, bent together and huddled up, with her legs crossed and her face hidden in her hands. She was weeping bitterly, with sobs, and her long, unbrushed hair fell on her knees. The impression of the exquisite marvellous sea which I had only just seen and of which I wanted to tell her, left me all at once, and my heart ached.

"What is it?" I asked; she took one hand from her face and motioned me to go away. "What is it?" I repeated, and for the first time during our acquaintance I kissed her hand.

"No, it's nothing, nothing," she said quickly. "Oh, it's nothing, nothing. . . . Go away. . . . You see, I am not dressed."

I went out overwhelmed. The calm and serene mood in which I had been for so long was poisoned by compassion. I had a passionate longing to fall at her feet, to entreat her not to weep in solitude, but to share her grief with me, and the monotonous murmur of the sea already sounded a gloomy prophecy in my ears, and I foresaw fresh tears, fresh troubles, and fresh losses in the future. "What is she crying about? What is it?" I wondered, recalling her face and her agonised look. I remembered she was with child. She tried to conceal her condition from other people, and also from herself. At home she went about in a loose wrapper or in a blouse with extremely full folds over the bosom, and when she went out anywhere she laced herself in so tightly that on two occasions she fainted when we were out. She never spoke to me of her condition, and when I hinted that it might be as well to see a doctor, she flushed crimson and said not a word.

When I went to see her next time she was already dressed and had her hair done.

"There, there," I said, seeing that she was ready to cry again. "We had better go to the sea and have a talk."

"I can't talk. Forgive me, I am in the mood now when one wants to be alone. And, if you please, Vladimir Ivanitch, another time you want to come into my room, be so good as to give a knock at the door."

That "be so good" had a peculiar, unfeminine sound. I went away. My accursed Petersburg mood came back, and all my dreams were crushed and crumpled up like leaves by the heat. I felt I was alone again and there was no nearness between us. I was no more to her than that cobweb to that palm-tree, which hangs on it by chance and which will be torn off and carried away by the wind. I walked about the square where the band was playing, went into the Casino; there I looked at overdressed and heavily perfumed women, and every one of them glanced at me as though she would say: "You are alone; that's all right." Then I went out on the terrace and looked for a long time at the sea. There was not one sail on the horizon. On the left bank, in the lilac-coloured mist, there were mountains, gardens, towers, and houses, the sun was sparkling over it all, but it was all alien, indifferent, an incomprehensible tangle.

XVII

She used as before to come into my room in the morning to coffee, but we no longer dined together, as she said she was not hungry; and she lived only on coffee, tea, and various trifles such as oranges and caramels.

And we no longer had conversations in the evening. I don't know why it was like this. Ever since the day when I had found her in tears she had treated me somehow lightly, at times casually, even ironically, and for some reason called me "My good sir." What had before seemed to her terrible, heroic, marvellous, and had stirred her envy and enthusiasm, did not touch her now at all, and usually after listening to me, she stretched and said:

"Yes, 'great things were done in days of yore,' my good sir."

It sometimes happened even that I did not see her for days together.
I would knock timidly and guiltily at her door and get no answer;
I would knock again—still silence. . . . I would stand near the door and listen; then the chambermaid would pass and say coldly, " Madame est partie." Then I would walk about the passages of the hotel, walk and walk. . . . English people, full-bosomed ladies, waiters in swallow-tails. . . . And as I keep gazing at the long striped rug that stretches the whole length of the corridor, the idea occurs to me that I am playing in the life of this woman a strange, probably false part, and that it is beyond my power to alter that part. I run to my room and fall on my bed, and think and think, and can come to no conclusion; and all that is clear to me is that I want to live, and that the plainer and the colder and the harder her face grows, the nearer she is to me, and the more intensely and painfully I feel our kinship. Never mind "My good sir," never mind her light careless tone, never mind anything you like, only don't leave me, my treasure. I am afraid to be alone.
Then I go out into the corridor again, listen in a tremor. . . . I have no dinner; I don't notice the approach of evening. At last about eleven I hear the familiar footstep, and at the turn near the stairs Zinaida Fyodorovna comes into sight.

"Are you taking a walk?" she would ask as she passes me. "You had better go out into the air. . . . Good-night!"

"But shall we not meet again to-day?"

"I think it's late. But as you like."

"Tell me, where have you been?" I would ask, following her into the room.

"Where? To Monte Carlo." She took ten gold coins out of her pocket and said: "Look, my good sir; I have won. That's at roulette."

"Nonsense! As though you would gamble."

"Why not? I am going again to-morrow."

I imagined her with a sick and morbid face, in her condition, tightly laced, standing near the gaming-table in a crowd of cocottes, of old women in their dotage who swarm round the gold like flies round the honey. I remembered she had gone off to Monte Carlo for some reason in secret from me.

"I don't believe you," I said one day. "You wouldn't go there."

"Don't agitate yourself. I can't lose much."

"It's not the question of what you lose," I said with annoyance. "Has it never occurred to you while you were playing there that the glitter of gold, all these women, young and old, the croupiers, all the surroundings—that it is all a vile, loathsome mockery at the toiler's labour, at his bloody sweat?

"If one doesn't play, what is one to do here?" she asked. "The toiler's labour and his bloody sweat—all that eloquence you can put off till another time; but now, since you have begun, let me go on. Let me ask you bluntly, what is there for me to do here, and what am I to do?"

"What are you to do?" I said, shrugging my shoulders. "That's a question that can't be answered straight off."

"I beg you to answer me honestly, Vladimir Ivanitch," she said, and her face looked angry. "Once I have brought myself to ask you this question, I am not going to listen to stock phrases. I am asking you," she went on, beating her hand on the table, as though marking time, "what ought I to do here? And not only here at Nice, but in general?"

I did not speak, but looked out of window to the sea. My heart was beating terribly.

"Vladimir Ivanitch," she said softly and breathlessly; it was hard for her to speak— "Vladimir Ivanitch, if you do not believe in the cause yourself, if you no longer think of going back to it, why . . . why did you drag me out of Petersburg? Why did you make me promises, why did you rouse mad hopes? Your convictions have changed; you have become a different man, and nobody blames you for it— our convictions are not always in our power. But . . . but, Vladimir Ivanitch, for God's sake, why are you not sincere?" she went on softly, coming up to me. "All these months when I have been dreaming aloud, raving, going into raptures over my plans, remodelling my life on a new pattern, why didn't you tell me the truth? Why were you silent or encouraged me by your stories, and behaved as though you were in complete sympathy with me? Why was it? Why was it necessary?"

"It's difficult to acknowledge one's bankruptcy," I said, turning round, but not looking at her. "Yes, I have no faith; I am worn out. I have lost heart. . . . It is difficult to be truthful— very difficult, and I held my tongue. God forbid that any one should have to go through what I have been through."

I felt that I was on the point of tears, and ceased speaking.

"Vladimir Ivanitch," she said, and took me by both hands, "you have been through so much and seen so much of life, you know more than I do; think seriously, and tell me, what am I to do? Teach me! If you haven't the strength to go forward yourself and take others with you, at least show me where to go. After all, I am a living, feeling, thinking being. To sink into a false position . . . to play an absurd part . . . is painful to me. I don't reproach you, I don't blame you; I only ask you."

Tea was brought in.

"Well?" said Zinaida Fyodorovna, giving me a glass. "What do you say to me?"

"There is more light in the world than you see through your window," I answered. "And there are other people besides me, Zinaida Fyodorovna."

"Then tell me who they are," she said eagerly. "That's all I ask of you."

"And I want to say, too," I went on, "one can serve an idea in more than one calling. If one has made a mistake and lost faith in one, one may find another. The world of ideas is large and cannot be exhausted."

"The world of ideas!" she said, and she looked into my face sarcastically. "Then we had better leave off talking. What's the use? . . ."

She flushed.

"The world of ideas!" she repeated. She threw her dinner-napkin aside, and an expression of indignation and contempt came into her face. "All your fine ideas, I see, lead up to one inevitable, essential step: I ought to become your mistress. That's what's wanted. To be taken up with ideas without being the mistress of an honourable, progressive man, is as good as not understanding the ideas. One has to begin with that . . . that is, with being your mistress, and the rest will come of itself."

"You are irritated, Zinaida Fyodorovna," I said.

"No, I am sincere!" she cried, breathing hard. "I am sincere!"

"You are sincere, perhaps, but you are in error, and it hurts me to hear you."

"I am in error?" she laughed. "Any one else might say that, but not you, my dear sir! I may seem to you indelicate, cruel, but I don't care: you love me? You love me, don't you?"

I shrugged my shoulders.

"Yes, shrug your shoulders!" she went on sarcastically. "When you were ill I heard you in your delirium, and ever since these adoring eyes, these sighs, and edifying conversations about friendship, about spiritual kinship. . . . But the point is, why haven't you been sincere? Why have you concealed what is and talked about what isn't? Had you said from the beginning what ideas exactly led you to drag me from Petersburg, I should have known. I should have poisoned myself then as I meant to, and there would have been none of this tedious farce. . . . But what's the use of talking!"

With a wave of the hand she sat down.

"You speak to me as though you suspected me of dishonourable intentions," I said, offended.

"Oh, very well. What's the use of talking! I don't suspect you of intentions, but of having no intentions. If you had any, I should have known them by now. You had nothing but ideas and love. For the present—ideas and love, and in prospect—me as your mistress. That's in the order of things both in life and in novels. . . . Here you abused him," she said, and she slapped the table with her hand, "but one can't help agreeing with him. He has good reasons for despising these ideas."

"He does not despise ideas; he is afraid of them," I cried. "He is a coward and a liar."

"Oh, very well. He is a coward and a liar, and deceived me. And you? Excuse my frankness; what are you? He deceived me and left me to take my chance in Petersburg, and you have deceived me and abandoned me here. But he did not mix up ideas with his deceit, and you . . ."

"For goodness' sake, why are you saying this?" I cried in horror, wringing my hands and going up to her quickly. "No, Zinaida Fyodorovna, this is cynicism. You must not be so despairing; listen to me," I went on, catching at a thought which flashed dimly upon me, and which seemed to me might still save us both. "Listen. I have passed through so many experiences in my time that my head goes round at the thought of them, and I have realised with my mind, with my racked soul, that man finds his true destiny in nothing if not in self-sacrificing love for his neighbour. It is towards that we must strive, and that is our destination! That is my faith!"

I wanted to go on to speak of mercy, of forgiveness, but there was an insincere note in my voice, and I was embarrassed

"I want to live!" I said genuinely. "To live, to live! I want peace, tranquillity; I want warmth—this sea here—to have you near. Oh, how I wish I could rouse in you the same thirst for life! You spoke just now of love, but it would be enough for me to have you near, to hear your voice, to watch the look in your face . . . !"

She flushed crimson, and to hinder my speaking, said quickly:

"You love life, and I hate it. So our ways lie apart."

She poured herself out some tea, but did not touch it, went into the bedroom, and lay down.

"I imagine it is better to cut short this conversation," she said to me from within. "Everything is over for me, and I want nothing . . . . What more is there to say?"

"No, it's not all over!"

"Oh, very well! . . . I know! I am sick of it. . . . That's enough."

I got up, took a turn from one end of the room to the other, and went out into the corridor. When late at night I went to her door and listened, I distinctly heard her crying.

Next morning the waiter, handing me my clothes, informed me, with a smile, that the lady in number thirteen was confined. I dressed somehow, and almost fainting with terror ran to Zinaida Fyodorovna. In her room I found a doctor, a midwife, and an elderly Russian lady from Harkov, called Darya Milhailovna. There was a smell of ether. I had scarcely crossed the threshold when from the room where she was lying I heard a low, plaintive moan, and, as though it had been wafted me by the wind from Russia, I thought of Orlov, his irony, Polya, the Neva, the drifting snow, then the cab without an apron, the prediction I had read in the cold morning sky, and the despairing cry "Nina! Nina!"

"Go in to her," said the lady.

I went in to see Zinaida Fyodorovna, feeling as though I were the father of the child. She was lying with her eyes closed, looking thin and pale, wearing a white cap edged with lace. I remember there were two expressions on her face: one—cold, indifferent, apathetic; the other—a look of childish helplessness given her by the white cap. She did not hear me come in, or heard, perhaps, but did not pay attention. I stood, looked at her, and waited.

But her face was contorted with pain; she opened her eyes and gazed at the ceiling, as though wondering what was happening to her. . . . There was a look of loathing on her face.

"It's horrible . . ." she whispered.

"Zinaida Fyodorovna." I spoke her name softly. She looked at me indifferently, listlessly, and closed her eyes. I stood there a little while, then went away.

At night, Darya Mihailovna informed me that the child, a girl, was born, but that the mother was in a dangerous condition. Then I heard noise and bustle in the passage. Darya Mihailovna came to me again and with a face of despair, wringing her hands, said:

"Oh, this is awful! The doctor suspects that she has taken poison!

Oh, how badly Russians do behave here!"

And at twelve o'clock the next day Zinaida Fyodorovna died.

XVIII

Two years had passed. Circumstances had changed; I had come to Petersburg again and could live here openly. I was no longer afraid of being and seeming sentimental, and gave myself up entirely to the fatherly, or rather idolatrous feeling roused in me by Sonya, Zinaida Fyodorovna's child. I fed her with my own hands, gave her her bath, put her to bed, never took my eyes off her for nights together, and screamed when it seemed to me that the nurse was just going to drop her. My thirst for normal ordinary life became stronger and more acute as time went on, but wider visions stopped short at Sonya, as though I had found in her at last just what I needed. I loved the child madly. In her I saw the continuation of my life, and it was not exactly that I fancied, but I felt, I almost believed, that when I had cast off at last my long, bony, bearded frame, I should go on living in those little blue eyes, that silky flaxen hair, those dimpled pink hands which stroked my face so lovingly and were clasped round my neck.

Sonya's future made me anxious. Orlov was her father; in her birth certificate she was called Krasnovsky, and the only person who knew of her existence, and took interest in her—that is, I—was at death's door. I had to think about her seriously.

The day after I arrived in Petersburg I went to see Orlov. The door was opened to me by a stout old fellow with red whiskers and no moustache, who looked like a German. Polya, who was tidying the drawing-room, did not recognise me, but Orlov knew me at once.

"Ah, Mr. Revolutionist!" he said, looking at me with curiosity, and laughing. "What fate has brought you?"

He was not changed in the least: the same well-groomed, unpleasant face, the same irony. And a new book was lying on the table just as of old, with an ivory paper-knife thrust in it. He had evidently been reading before I came in. He made me sit down, offered me a cigar, and with a delicacy only found in well-bred people, concealing the unpleasant feeling aroused by my face and my wasted figure, observed casually that I was not in the least changed, and that he would have known me anywhere in spite of my having grown a beard. We talked of the weather, of Paris. To dispose as quickly as possible of the oppressive, inevitable question, which weighed upon him and me, he asked:

"Zinaida Fyodorovna is dead?"

"Yes," I answered.

"In childbirth?"

"Yes, in childbirth. The doctor suspected another cause of death, but . . . it is more comforting for you and for me to think that she died in childbirth."

He sighed decorously and was silent. The angel of silence passed over us, as they say.

"Yes. And here everything is as it used to be—no changes," he said briskly, seeing that I was looking about the room. "My father, as you know, has left the service and is living in retirement; I am still in the same department. Do you remember Pekarsky? He is just the same as ever. Gruzin died of diphtheria a year ago. . . . Kukushkin is alive, and often speaks of you. By the way," said Orlov, dropping his eyes with an air of reserve, "when Kukushkin heard who you were, he began telling every one you had attacked him and tried to murder him . . . and that he only just escaped with his life."

I did not speak.

"Old servants do not forget their masters. . . . It's very nice of you," said Orlov jocosely. "Will you have some wine and some coffee, though? I will tell them to make some."

"No, thank you. I have come to see you about a very important matter, Georgy Ivanitch."

"I am not very fond of important matters, but I shall be glad to be of service to you. What do you want?"

"You see," I began, growing agitated, "I have here with me Zinaida Fyodorovna's daughter. . . . Hitherto I have brought her up, but, as you see, before many days I shall be an empty sound. I should like to die with the thought that she is provided for."

Orlov coloured a little, frowned a little, and took a cursory and sullen glance at me. He was unpleasantly affected, not so much by the "important matter" as by my words about death, about becoming an empty sound.

"Yes, it must be thought about," he said, screening his eyes as though from the sun. "Thank you. You say it's a girl?"

"Yes, a girl. A wonderful child!"

"Yes. Of course, it's not a lap-dog, but a human being. I understand we must consider it seriously. I am prepared to do my part, and am very grateful to you."

He got up, walked about, biting his nails, and stopped before a picture.

"We must think about it," he said in a hollow voice, standing with his back to me. "I shall go to Pekarsky's to-day and will ask him to go to Krasnovsky's. I don't think he will make much ado about consenting to take the child."

"But, excuse me, I don't see what Krasnovsky has got to do with it," I said, also getting up and walking to a picture at the other end of the room.

"But she bears his name, of course!" said Orlov.

"Yes, he may be legally obliged to accept the child—I don't know; but I came to you, Georgy Ivanitch, not to discuss the legal aspect."

"Yes, yes, you are right," he agreed briskly. "I believe I am talking nonsense. But don't excite yourself. We will decide the matter to our mutual satisfaction. If one thing won't do, we'll try another; and if that won't do, we'll try a third—one way or another this delicate question shall be settled. Pekarsky will arrange it all. Be so good as to leave me your address and I will let you know at once what we decide. Where are you living?"

Orlov wrote down my address, sighed, and said with a smile:

"Oh, Lord, what a job it is to be the father of a little daughter! But Pekarsky will arrange it all. He is a sensible man. Did you stay long in Paris?"

"Two months."

We were silent. Orlov was evidently afraid I should begin talking of the child again, and to turn my attention in another direction, said:

"You have probably forgotten your letter by now. But I have kept it. I understand your mood at the time, and, I must own, I respect that letter. 'Damnable cold blood,'

'Asiatic,' 'coarse laugh'— that was charming and characteristic," he went on with an ironical smile. "And the fundamental thought is perhaps near the truth, though one might dispute the question endlessly. That is," he hesitated, "not dispute the thought itself, but your attitude to the question—your temperament, so to say. Yes, my life is abnormal, corrupted, of no use to any one, and what prevents me from beginning a new life is cowardice—there you are quite right. But that you take it so much to heart, are troubled, and reduced to despair by it—that's irrational; there you are quite wrong."

"A living man cannot help being troubled and reduced to despair when he sees that he himself is going to ruin and others are going to ruin round him."

"Who doubts it! I am not advocating indifference; all I ask for is an objective attitude to life. The more objective, the less danger of falling into error. One must look into the root of things, and try to see in every phenomenon a cause of all the other causes. We have grown feeble, slack—degraded, in fact. Our generation is entirely composed of neurasthenics and whimperers; we do nothing but talk of fatigue and exhaustion. But the fault is neither yours nor mine; we are of too little consequence to affect the destiny of a whole generation. We must suppose for that larger, more general causes with a solid *raison d'etre* from the biological point of view. We are neurasthenics, flabby, renegades, but perhaps it's necessary and of service for generations that will come after us. Not one hair falls from the head without the will of the Heavenly Father—in other words, nothing happens by chance in Nature and in human environment. Everything has its cause and is inevitable. And if so, why should we worry and write despairing letters?"

"That's all very well," I said, thinking a little. "I believe it will be easier and clearer for the generations to come; our experience will be at their service. But one wants to live apart from future generations and not only for their sake. Life is only given us once, and one wants to live it boldly, with full consciousness and beauty. One wants to play a striking, independent, noble part; one wants to make history so that those generations may not have the right to say of each of us that we were nonentities or worse.... I believe what is going on about us is inevitable and not without a purpose, but what have I to do with that inevitability? Why should my ego be lost?"

"Well, there's no help for it," sighed Orlov, getting up and, as it were, giving me to understand that our conversation was over.

I took my hat.

"We've only been sitting here half an hour, and how many questions we have settled, when you come to think of it!" said Orlov, seeing me into the hall. "So I will see to that matter.... I will see Pekarsky to-day.... Don't be uneasy."

He stood waiting while I put on my coat, and was obviously relieved at the feeling that I was going away.

"Georgy Ivanitch, give me back my letter," I said.

"Certainly."

He went to his study, and a minute later returned with the letter.

I thanked him and went away.

The next day I got a letter from him. He congratulated me on the satisfactory settlement of the question. Pekarsky knew a lady, he wrote, who kept a school, something like a kindergarten, where she took quite little children. The lady could be entirely depended upon, but before concluding anything with her it would be as well to discuss the matter with Krasnovsky—it was a matter of form. He advised me to see Pekarsky at once and to take the birth certificate with me, if I had it. "Rest assured of the sincere respect and devotion of your humble servant. . . ."

I read this letter, and Sonya sat on the table and gazed at me attentively without blinking, as though she knew her fate was being decided.

THE HUSBAND

In the course of the maneuvres the N---- cavalry regiment halted for a night at the district town of K----. Such an event as the visit of officers always has the most exciting and inspiring effect on the inhabitants of provincial towns. The shopkeepers dream of getting rid of the rusty sausages and "best brand" sardines that have been lying for ten years on their shelves; the inns and restaurants keep open all night; the Military Commandant, his secretary, and the local garrison put on their best uniforms; the police flit to and fro like mad, while the effect on the ladies is beyond all description.

The ladies of K----, hearing the regiment approaching, forsook their pans of boiling jam and ran into the street. Forgetting their morning *deshabille* and general untidiness, they rushed breathless with excitement to meet the regiment, and listened greedily to the band playing the march. Looking at their pale, ecstatic faces, one might have thought those strains came from some heavenly choir rather than from a military brass band.

"The regiment!" they cried joyfully. "The regiment is coming!"

What could this unknown regiment that came by chance to-day and would depart at dawn to-morrow mean to them?

Afterwards, when the officers were standing in the middle of the square, and, with their hands behind them, discussing the question of billets, all the ladies were gathered together at the examining magistrate's and vying with one another in their criticisms of the regiment. They already knew, goodness knows how, that the colonel was married, but not living with his wife; that the senior officer's wife had a baby born dead every year; that the adjutant was hopelessly in love with some countess, and had even once attempted suicide. They knew everything. When a pock-marked soldier in a red shirt darted past the windows, they knew for certain that it was Lieutenant Rymzov's orderly running about the town, trying to get some English bitter ale on tick for his master. They had only caught a passing glimpse of the officers' backs, but had already decided that there was not one handsome or interesting man among them. . . . Having talked to their hearts' content, they sent for the Military Commandant and the committee of the club, and instructed them at all costs to make arrangements for a dance.

Their wishes were carried out. At nine o'clock in the evening the military band was playing in the street before the club, while in the club itself the officers were dancing with the ladies of K----. The ladies felt as though they were on wings. Intoxicated by the dancing, the music, and the clank of spurs, they threw themselves heart and soul into making the acquaintance of their new partners, and quite forgot their old civilian friends. Their fathers and husbands, forced temporarily into the background, crowded round the meagre refreshment table in the entrance hall. All these government cashiers, secretaries, clerks, and superintendents—stale, sickly-looking, clumsy figures—were perfectly well aware of their inferiority. They did not even enter the ball-room, but contented themselves with watching their wives and daughters in the distance dancing with the accomplished and graceful officers.

Among the husbands was Shalikov, the tax-collector—a narrow, spiteful soul, given to drink, with a big, closely cropped head, and thick, protruding lips. He had had a university education; there had been a time when he used to read progressive literature and sing students' songs, but now, as he said of himself, he was a tax-collector and nothing more.

He stood leaning against the doorpost, his eyes fixed on his wife, Anna Pavlovna, a little brunette of thirty, with a long nose and a pointed chin. Tightly laced, with her face carefully powdered, she danced without pausing for breath—danced till she was ready to drop exhausted. But though she was exhausted in body, her spirit was inexhaustible. . . . One could see as she danced that her thoughts were with the past, that faraway past when she used to dance at the "College for Young Ladies," dreaming of a life of luxury and gaiety, and never doubting that her husband was to be a prince or, at the worst, a baron.

The tax-collector watched, scowling with spite. . . .

It was not jealousy he was feeling. He was ill-humoured—first, because the room was taken up with dancing and there was nowhere he could play a game of cards; secondly, because he could not endure the sound of wind instruments; and, thirdly, because he fancied the officers treated the civilians somewhat too casually and disdainfully. But what above everything revolted him and moved him to indignation was the expression of happiness on his wife's face.

"It makes me sick to look at her!" he muttered. "Going on for forty, and nothing to boast of at any time, and she must powder her face and lace herself up! And frizzing her hair! Flirting and making faces, and fancying she's doing the thing in style! Ugh! you're a pretty figure, upon my soul!"

Anna Pavlovna was so lost in the dance that she did not once glance at her husband.

"Of course not! Where do we poor country bumpkins come in!" sneered the tax-collector.

"We are at a discount now. . . . We're clumsy seals, unpolished provincial bears, and she's the queen of the ball! She has kept enough of her looks to please even officers. . . They'd not object to making love to her, I dare say!"

During the mazurka the tax collector's face twitched with spite. A black-haired officer with prominent eyes and Tartar cheekbones danced the mazurka with Anna Pavlovna. Assuming a stern expression, he worked his legs with gravity and feeling, and so crooked his knees that he looked like a jack-a-dandy pulled by strings, while Anna Pavlovna, pale and thrilled, bending her figure languidly and turning her eyes up, tried to look as though she scarcely touched the floor, and evidently felt herself that she was not on earth, not at the local club, but somewhere far, far away—in the clouds. Not only her face but her whole figure was expressive of beatitude . . . . The tax-collector could endure it no longer; he felt a desire to jeer at that beatitude, to make Anna Pavlovna feel that she had forgotten herself, that life was by no means so delightful as she fancied now in her excitement. . . .

"You wait; I'll teach you to smile so blissfully," he muttered. "You are not a boarding-school miss, you are not a girl. An old fright ought to realise she is a fright!"

Petty feelings of envy, vexation, wounded vanity, of that small, provincial misanthropy engendered in petty officials by vodka and a sedentary life, swarmed in his heart like mice. Waiting for the end of the mazurka, he went into the hall and walked up to his wife. Anna Pavlovna was sitting with her partner, and, flirting her fan and coquettishly dropping her eyelids, was describing how she used to dance in Petersburg (her lips were pursed up like a rosebud, and she pronounced "at home in Puetuersburg").

"Anyuta, let us go home," croaked the tax-collector.

Seeing her husband standing before her, Anna Pavlovna started as though recalling the fact that she had a husband; then she flushed all over: she felt ashamed that she had such a sickly-looking, ill-humoured, ordinary husband.

"Let us go home," repeated the tax-collector.

"Why? It's quite early!"

"I beg you to come home!" said the tax-collector deliberately, with a spiteful expression.

"Why? Has anything happened?" Anna Pavlovna asked in a flutter.

"Nothing has happened, but I wish you to go home at once. . . . I wish it; that's enough, and without further talk, please."

Anna Pavlovna was not afraid of her husband, but she felt ashamed on account of her partner, who was looking at her husband with surprise and amusement. She got up and moved a little apart with her husband.

"What notion is this?" she began. "Why go home? Why, it's not eleven o'clock."

"I wish it, and that's enough. Come along, and that's all about it."

"Don't be silly! Go home alone if you want to."

"All right; then I shall make a scene."

The tax-collector saw the look of beatitude gradually vanish from his wife's face, saw how ashamed and miserable she was—and he felt a little happier.

"Why do you want me at once?" asked his wife.

"I don't want you, but I wish you to be at home. I wish it, that's all."

At first Anna Pavlovna refused to hear of it, then she began entreating her husband to let her stay just another half-hour; then, without knowing why, she began to apologise, to protest—and all in a whisper, with a smile, that the spectators might not suspect that she was having a tiff with her husband. She began assuring him she would not stay long, only another ten minutes, only five minutes; but the tax-collector stuck obstinately to his point.

"Stay if you like," he said, "but I'll make a scene if you do."

And as she talked to her husband Anna Pavlovna looked thinner, older, plainer. Pale, biting her lips, and almost crying, she went out to the entry and began putting on her things.

"You are not going?" asked the ladies in surprise. "Anna Pavlovna, you are not going, dear?"

"Her head aches," said the tax-collector for his wife.

Coming out of the club, the husband and wife walked all the way home in silence. The tax-collector walked behind his wife, and watching her downcast, sorrowful, humiliated little figure, he recalled the look of beatitude which had so irritated him at the club, and the consciousness that the beatitude was gone filled his soul with triumph. He was pleased and satisfied, and at the same time he felt the lack of something; he would have liked to go back to the club and make every one feel dreary and miserable, so that all might know how stale and worthless life is when you walk along the streets in the dark and hear the slush of the mud under your feet, and when you know that you will wake up next morning with nothing to look forward to but vodka and cards. Oh, how awful it is!

And Anna Pavlovna could scarcely walk. . . . She was still under the influence of the dancing, the music, the talk, the lights, and the noise; she asked herself as she walked along why God had thus afflicted her. She felt miserable, insulted, and choking with hate as she listened to her husband's heavy footsteps. She was silent, trying to think of the most offensive, biting, and venomous word she could hurl at her husband, and at the same time she was fully aware that no word could penetrate her tax-collector's hide. What did he care for words? Her bitterest enemy could not have contrived for her a more helpless position.

And meanwhile the band was playing and the darkness was full of the most rousing, intoxicating dance-tunes.

Anton Chekhov – A Biography

Anton Pavlovich Chekhov was born the third of six surviving children on 29th January 1860 in Taganrog, a port town on the Sea of Azov on the south coast of Russia. During his intense career he would make a name for himself as a playwright and author, though the whole time he practised as a physician. Indeed, he once wrote "medicine is my lawful wife, and literature is my mistress". This affair was an extended and colourful one, begun as a means of bolstering his income but developed as a form of artistic expression, through which he would make several key formal innovations which prevail in the writing of various authors who succeed him such as the method of stream-of-consciousness writing, heavily employed by the Irish novelist and poet James Joyce.

Chekhov's father Pavel Yegorovich, from whose Christian name Chekhov received his patronymic middle name, was the son of a former serf and ran a grocery store in Taganrog. As a devout orthodox Christian and director of the parish church choir in which Chekhov and his brothers sang, the stark contrast between this and his physically abusive attitude at home served as an example for many of Chekhov's portraits of hypocrisy, while also providing Chekhov with a model of how not to conduct himself in public and in private. This proved a valuable life lesson for him, for at every juncture Chekhov would treat those around him with dignity and respect. His mother, Yevgeniya, was a talented and passionate story-teller, and entertained the children with extensive stories about her travels across the entirety of Russia with her cloth merchant father. As his father provided character inspiration, his mother instilled in him a love of stories and a skill for telling them. He would later affirm that "our talents we got from our father, but our soul from our mother". The extent of the influence that this childhood had on him can be seen in his later chastisement of his elder brother Alexander, whose tyrannical treatment of his own wife and children reminded Chekhov all too painfully of their own fraught upbringing; he wrote, tentatively,

> Let me ask you to recall that it was despotism and lying that ruined your mother's youth. Despotism and lying so mutilated our childhood that it's sickening and frightening to think about it. Remember the horror and disgust we felt in those times when Father threw a tantrum at dinner over too much salt in the soup and called Mother a fool.

Between the ages of six and eight, he attended a Greek school in Taganrog, run by the Greek Church of Taganrog and funded by wealthy Greek merchants. Among the subjects taught were Greek language, God's law, mathematics, history, calligraphy and singing. Then, from 1868 he attended Taganrog gymnasium, the local grammar school, where he proved a distinctly average pupil. Despite being academically reserved and largely undemonstrative he nonetheless forged himself a reputation as a prankster, for making up humourous nicknames for his teachers and for being a reliable source of witty, satirical remarks. It soon became apparent that his interests lay away from academia for he became involved in amateur dramatics, frequently attending performances at the Taganrog Theatre. The first of these performances was Offenbach's operetta *Elena the Beautiful* which he saw when he was thirteen, and from then on he became an avid theatre attendee and spent much of his savings on visits, despite the theatre being out of bounds for Gymnasium students without special dispensation to visit; permission was rarely given, and mostly on weekends. So regular was he that he had a favourite seat, whose most attractive characteristic was its location; situated in the back gallery it was cheap, and being so far out of sight it proved an effective place to hide from the Gymnasium staff who would routinely check for unauthorised students. To further conceal themselves from these spot-checks, Anton and his schoolmates would disguise themselves with make-up, wigs and props such as spectacles and fake beards. Much of the savings which he spent at the theatre came from the annual 300 ruble grant he received from the Taganrog City Council after a failed assassination attempt on the then Tsar, Alexander II of Russia. Inspired by the drama he witnessed at the theatre, he tried his hand at writing short, amusing 'anecdotes' and stories. Alongside this he is known to have written a long, tragicomic play, entitled *Fatherless*, though he later destroyed it and no manuscript remains, and which his brother Alexander denounced as "an inexcusable though innocent fabrication".

His preoccupation with the theatre had a marked result on his school career, and the greatest blow came when he was fifteen and kept down a year for failing a Greek examination. During this time he sang under his Father's direction in the Greek orthodox ministry choir, a time which he would later recall as one of "suffering". A letter written in 1892 describes how "when my brothers and I used to stand in the middle of the church and sing the trio 'May my prayer be exalted', or 'The Archangel's Voice', everyone looked at us with emotion and envied our parents, but we at that moment felt like little convicts". The family gave an appearance of idyllic happiness and talent, though this contrast between this outward façade and the tyranny and despotism they experienced at home under Pavel's strict rule serves as another example of exactly the source of the picture of hypocrisy Chekhov paints in his work. When Chekhov was sixteen, Pavel mismanaged his own finances quite spectacularly during the process of building a new house which resulted in a declaration of bankruptcy and a subsequent fleeing to Moscow to avoid debtor's prison.

By now Chekhov's elder brothers Alexander and Nikolay were already studying at Moscow University so the majority of the family reunited there, living in poverty, a change of circumstance which left Yevgeniya in a state of emotional and physical infirmity. Chekhov, however, remained in Taganrog living with a man called Selivanov who, like Lopakhin in *The Cherry Orchard*, had bailed out the family for the price of their house, to complete his education. Although his board was free with Selivanov, he was left to pay for his schooling, covering the costs and surviving on a disparate income cobbled together from the selling off of family possessions and bolstered by private tutoring, catching and selling goldfinches, and by writing and selling short sketches to the newspapers. Every ruble he could spare from his education and his now less frequent theatre visits he sent to his family in Moscow, enclosed with humourous letters designed to cheer them up in their poverty and misery. He now began to take a more earnest interest in his education, reading extensively and analytically, including the works of Cervantes, Turgenev, Goncharov and Schopenhauer. Meanwhile he enjoyed a series of closeted love affairs, including one with the wife of one of his teachers. His schooling completed and a scholarship to Moscow University obtained, he moved there in 1879 and rejoined his family.

He now assumed responsibility for the family, supporting them by writing regular satirical sketches and vignettes of contemporary Russian lifestyle under pseudonyms such as 'Antosha Chekhonte' and 'Man Without a Spleen', and his prodigious output earned him first a reputation as a reputable chronicler and then, in 1882, a regular position writing for Oskolki, a journal owned by Nicolai Leykin, the most successful Russian publisher at the time. Although the wit and brevity of his work here prevails through much of his later writing, it was considerably harsher in tone, perhaps a reflection of the stressful position of poverty, study and patriarch in which he found himself. In 1884, he qualified as a physician and, although he earned little from the profession and often treated the poor free of charge, he considered this his principle profession. At this time and for the next two years he would regularly cough up blood, a symptom of tuberculosis with which he was all too familiar as a physician. However, not wishing to "submit himself to be sounded by his colleagues", he kept the condition to himself. The continued success of his periodical writing enabled him to move the family into progressively more comfortable accommodation, and then in 1886 he received an invitation to write for *Novoye Vremya* (*New Times*), owned and edited by the millionaire media magnate Alexey Suvorin. Paying double per line what Anton received from Leykin and being given three times the column inches he took the offer immediately and became close friends with Suvorin, a friendship which would last his lifetime.

His work at these periodicals was not the sole extent of his literary output, for in 1885 he published a short story, *The Huntsman*, which quickly attracted scholarly attention and recognition. The sixty-four year old celebrated writer Grigorovich wrote to him shortly after it first appeared on the shelves, saying "you have *real* talent—a talent which places you in the front rank among writers in the new generation." The letter continues in this effusive manner before resolving to offer Chekhov the practical advice to slow down, write less, and concentrate on literary quality. In reply, Chekhov admitted that he had been struck "like a thunderbolt" on reading the letter, confessing to hitherto writing his stories "the way reporters write up their notes about fires - mechanically, half-consciously, caring nothing about either the reader or myself." In making such an honest admission, Chekhov arguably undersold himself as a serious author, for despite the appearance of a nonchalant and casual approach, later analysis and comparison of early manuscripts reveals a huge extent of careful revision indicating a far more involved, authorial approach than he allows himself in correspondence with Grigorovich. Nonetheless, receiving such warm congratulation and encouragement along with such earnest advice from so respected an author caused Chekhov to sit up straight and approach his writing with far more serious, artistic ambition. Now twenty-six, and with the patronage of such a revered and loved author, his collection of short stories entitled *V Sumerkakh* (*At Dusk*) won him the much coveted Pushkin Prize, awarded "for the best literary production distinguished by high artistic worth".

Following this act of formal recognition and somewhat burnt out by the years of continued literary output his enduring success afforded him the time and the money to take a sabbatical, so he engaged in a journey to the Ukraine in 1887 whereupon he was reminded of the beauty of the Steppe. This excursion inspired the novella *The Steppe* which he started on his return, and which he described in a letter to Grigorovich as "something rather odd and much too original", and which was eventually published in *Severny Vestnik* (*The Northern Herald*). Later that year he was commissioned by a theatre manager to write a play, and a fortnight later Chekhov produced *Ivanov* which, though he considered the process "sickening" and described in a letter to his brother Alexander in the manner of a comic portrait, it was a huge success and was widely regarded as a work of excellent and noteworthy originality. Furthermore this period is considered the source of a literary device noted by Ilia Gurliand, who overheard it in conversation, as Chekhov's Gun; "if in act 1 you have a pistol hanging on the wall, then it must fire in the last act". Then, in 1889, his brother Nikolay died as a result of tuberculosis. Their brother Mikhail, who recorded Anton's depression during the period of mourning after the death, had been researching prisons as part of his studies in law, and Anton too became interested and eventually somewhat obsessed with the idea of prison reform.

This newfound interest in the humanitarian questions surrounding the prison system, combined with a conceivable yet subconscious desire to escape the close environment of mourning surrounding his brother's death, led Chekhov to journey to the penal colony Sakhalin, an island off the far East coast of Russia, where he spent three months interviewing convicts and settlers with the aim of compiling a census of the island. He made several now notorious remarks to his sister about what he witnessed (among others, a relatively lighthearted and blunt description of Tomsk, "a very dull town. To judge from the drunkards whose acquaintance I have made, and from the intellectual people who have come to the hotel to pay their respects to me, the inhabitants are very dull, too." [-the inhabitants of Tomsk later retaliated by erecting a mocking statue of Chekhov]). More seriously, though, many of the things he saw during this trip horrified him, writing that "there were times I felt that I saw before me the extreme limits of man's degradation." Among these was the plight of the children of the island, describing one such incident in his journals:

> On the Amur steamer going to Sakhalin, there was a convict who
> had murdered his wife and wore fetters on his legs. His daughter, a
> little girl of six, was with him. I noticed wherever the convict moved
> the little girl scrambled after him, holding on to his fetters. At night
> the child slept with the convicts and soldiers all in a heap together.

Concluding that the solution to this inhumanity lay not with charity and philanthropy, but with Government intervention and reform, he wrote *Ostrov Sakhalin* (*The Island of Sakhalin*), a work of social science which was praised, not for its literary brilliance, but for its steady and worthy informativeness, which was serialised and published in 1893-4. Though this initial work which stemmed from the trip was not literary in nature, the extended contact and expansive experience he received found itself expressed in *The Murder*, a story which, though longer than his others, is still considered short in nature.

In 1892 Chekhov had bought Melikhovo, a small country estate forty miles north of Moscow, which was his and his family's home until 1899. He joked about his residence there, quipping to his friend Ivan Leontyev that "it's nice to be a Lord" though this lighthearted remark belies the seriousness with which he undertook his responsibilities as a landlord. Within a few years of his taking residence there he had established his usefulness and sense of duty to the peasants, affording them relief from the 1892 outbreaks of cholera and bouts of famine, and building three schools, a fire station and a clinic, and offering his services as a physician to the peasantry of the surrounding countryside. Often he would find queues of patients lining up outside his door in the morning who had travelled by foot or by cart to receive treatment, and frequently he was called out to visit those too sick to travel. His brother Mikhail who resided with the family at Melikhovo recorded this honourable commitment to his role as estate physician, writing

> from the first day that Chekhov moved to Melikhovo, the sick began
> flocking to him from twenty miles around. They came on foot or
> were brought in carts, and often he was fetched to patients at a
> distance. Sometimes from early in the morning peasant women and
> children were standing before his door waiting.

Though these demanding hours left him with significantly less time for writing, they enriched his literary output for he was able to write informatively and genuinely about the peasantry and their living conditions, most notably in his short story *Peasants*. He did, however, visit those belonging to the upper-classes as well, though he was not enamoured by them, writing in his journal "Aristocrats? The same ugly bodies and physical uncleanliness, the same toothless old age and disgusting death, as with market-women".

He began to write arguably his most famous work, *The Seagull*, in 1894, in a lodge he had built himself in the orchard on the estate. Its first night on 17th October 1896 at the Alexandrinsky Theatre in Petersburg was something of a fiasco; it was booed by the audience, many of whom left, and this poor reception saw Chekhov fall out of love with the theatre. However, despite its poor reception by the play-going audience, it impressed the theatre director Vladimir Nemirovich-Danchenko so much that he proceeded to convince his colleague Constantin Stanislavski to take the play on and direct it in the innovative, progressive Moscow Art Theatre. This revival, in 1898, for the less-closeted Moscow audience was enormously well-received. Whereas the Petersburg performance had rendered the play literally and played down its more psychoanalytical aspects, Stanislavski payed far closer attention to the play's psychological realism and brought the deeply buried subtleties, lost on the Petersburg boards and on the audience's narrow-mindedness, to the surface. The play was such a success here that the Art Theatre commissioned further work from Chekhov, staging *Uncle Vanya* which he had completed in 1896. Furthermore, the positive critical reception had a restorative effect on Chekhov's interest in stage writing.

However, by now Chekhov's health condition was worsening, having suffered a major haemorrhage of the lungs in 1897 while visiting Moscow. His early reluctance to be seen by doctors prevailed and he protested to the notion of entering a clinic, though he eventually assented whereupon a formal diagnosis of the tuberculosis on the upper part of his lungs was reached, and the doctors ordered various changes in his lifestyle. His father then died in 1898, after which Chekhov bought a plot of land on the outskirts of Yalta and proceeded to build a villa, moving his mother and sister in with him the following year. Even though he pursued the enjoyment of gardening he had developed while at Melikhovo by planting trees and flowers, he kept dogs and tame cranes and regularly received highly regarded company such as Leo Tolstoy and Maxim Gorky, he spoke of a sense of relief upon each occasion of his leaving this "hot Siberia" for Moscow or to travel further afield. While here, he wrote two more plays for the Art Theatre, though these were composed with much greater difficulty; he remarked that unlike his youth when "[he] wrote serenely, the way [he eats] pancakes now". These two plays, *Three Sisters* and *The Cherry Orchard* took over a year each.

A quiet marriage to Olga Knipper on 25th May 1901 was performed in keeping with the position of suspicion he had always had towards weddings, with a small ceremony and little outside attention. Knipper was an actress whom he had met at the rehearsals for *The Seagull*, their marriage conformed to his stipulations;

> By all means I will be married if you wish it. But on these conditions: everything must be as it has been hitherto - that is, she must live in Moscow while I live in the country, and I will come and see her ... give me a wife who, like the moon, won't appear in my sky every day.

This proved convenient as Knipper remained in Moscow performing his work and that of contemporary playwrights, and their long-distance correspondence features various treasured pieces of writing, be they shared complaints about Stanislavski's method of direction or advice from Chekhov to Knipper as to her performances in his plays. Prior to the marriage, Chekhov had been considered "Russia's most elusive literary bachelor", preferring brief liaisons and dalliances with unknown women, or brothels, to commitment. Chekhov then wrote one of his most famous stories, *The Lady with the Dog*, depicting a casual encounter between two strangers who, despite their best efforts and risking the security, stability and respectability of their family lives, find themselves irrevocably drawn to one another.

Chekhov's tuberculosis was finally getting the better of him, and by May 1904 it was quite clear that his death was imminent. Despite this, Mikhail recorded that "everyone who saw him secretly thought the end was not far off, but the nearer [he] was to the end, the less he seemed to realise it". He set off for the German town Badenweiler on 3rd June, writing cheerful, witty letters to his sister describing variously the food and the surroundings, while assuring both her and his mother that his health was improving; his last letter contained a sardonic complaint about the German women's fashion. The circumstances of his death have become one of "the greatest set pieces of literary history", and are most accurately recorded in this, Knipper's own account from her diaries, written in 1908:

> Anton sat up unusually straight and said loudly and clearly (although he knew almost no German): *Ich sterbe* ("I'm dying"). The doctor calmed him, took a syringe, gave him an injection of camphor and ordered champagne. Anton took a full glass, examined it, smiled at me and said: 'It's a long time since I drank champagne.' He drained it, lay quietly on his left side, and I just had time to run to him and lean across the bed and call to him, but he had stopped breathing and was sleeping peacefully as a child.

His body, transferred to Moscow in a refrigerated railway car whose purpose was for fresh oysters, was then interred next to his father at Novodevichy Cemetery in Moscow. Although thousands of mourners mistakenly followed the pomp and circumstance of the military funeral procession for the also deceased General Keller, many hundreds of thousands of readers, writers and actors have followed correctly the path he pioneered for the short story and for twentieth century realism.

A Biography of Anton Chekov & List of His Most Famous Quotes

Anton Pavlovich Chekhov was born the third of six surviving children on 29th January 1860 in Taganrog, a port town on the Sea of Azov on the south coast of Russia. During his intense career he would make a name for himself as a playwright and author, though the whole time he practised as a physician. Indeed, he once wrote "medicine is my lawful wife, and literature is my mistress". This affair was an extended and colourful one, begun as a means of bolstering his income but developed as a form of artistic expression, through which he would make several key formal innovations which prevail in the writing of various authors who succeed him such as the method of stream-of-consciousness writing, heavily employed by the Irish novelist and poet James Joyce.

Chekhov's father Pavel Yegorovich, from whose Christian name Chekhov received his patronymic middle name, was the son of a former serf and ran a grocery store in Taganrog. As a devout orthodox Christian and director of the parish church choir in which Chekhov and his brothers sang, the stark contrast between this and his physically abusive attitude at home served as an example for many of Chekhov's portraits of hypocrisy, while also providing Chekhov with a model of how not to conduct himself in public and in private. This proved a valuable life lesson for him, for at every juncture Chekhov would treat those around him with dignity and respect. His mother, Yevgeniya, was a talented and passionate story-teller, and entertained the children with extensive stories about her travels across the entirety of Russia with her cloth merchant father. As his father provided character inspiration, his mother instilled in him a love of stories and a skill for telling them. He would later affirm that "our talents we got from our father, but our soul from our mother". The extent of the influence that this childhood had on him can be seen in his later chastisement of his elder brother Alexander, whose tyrannical treatment of his own wife and children reminded Chekhov all too painfully of their own fraught upbringing; he wrote, tentatively,

> Let me ask you to recall that it was despotism and lying that ruined your mother's youth. Despotism and lying so mutilated our childhood that it's sickening and frightening to think about it. Remember the horror and disgust we felt in those times when Father threw a tantrum at dinner over too much salt in the soup and called Mother a fool.

Between the ages of six and eight, he attended a Greek school in Taganrog, run by the Greek Church of Taganrog and funded by wealthy Greek merchants. Among the subjects taught were Greek language, God's law, mathematics, history, calligraphy and singing. Then, from 1868 he attended Taganrog gymnasium, the local grammar school, where he proved a distinctly average pupil. Despite being academically reserved and largely undemonstrative he nonetheless forged himself a reputation as a prankster, for making up humourous nicknames for his teachers and for being a reliable source of witty, satirical remarks. It soon became apparent that his interests lay away from academia for he became involved in amateur dramatics, frequently attending performances at the Taganrog Theatre. The first of these performances was Offenbach's operetta *Elena the Beautiful* which he saw when he was thirteen, and from then on he became an avid theatre attendee and spent much of his savings on visits, despite the theatre being out of bounds for Gymnasium students without special dispensation to visit; permission was rarely given, and mostly on weekends. So regular was he that he had a favourite seat, whose most attractive characteristic was its location; situated in the back gallery it was cheap, and being so far out of sight it proved an effective place to hide from the Gymnasium staff who would routinely check for unauthorised students. To further conceal themselves from these spot-checks, Anton and his schoolmates would disguise themselves with make-up, wigs and props such as spectacles and fake beards. Much of the savings which he spent at the theatre came from the annual 300 ruble grant he received from the Taganrog City Council after a failed assassination attempt on the then Tsar, Alexander II of Russia.

Inspired by the drama he witnessed at the theatre, he tried his hand at writing short, amusing 'anecdotes' and stories. Alongside this he is known to have written a long, tragicomic play, entitled *Fatherless*, though he later destroyed it and no manuscript remains, and which his brother Alexander denounced as "an inexcusable though innocent fabrication".

His preoccupation with the theatre had a marked result on his school career, and the greatest blow came when he was fifteen and kept down a year for failing a Greek examination. During this time he sang under his Father's direction in the Greek orthodox ministry choir, a time which he would later recall as one of "suffering". A letter written in 1892 describes how "when my brothers and I used to stand in the middle of the church and sing the trio 'May my prayer be exalted', or 'The Archangel's Voice', everyone looked at us with emotion and envied our parents, but we at that moment felt like little convicts". The family gave an appearance of idyllic happiness and talent, though this contrast between this outward façade and the tyranny and despotism they experienced at home under Pavel's strict rule serves as another example of exactly the source of the picture of hypocrisy Chekhov paints in his work. When Chekhov was sixteen, Pavel mismanaged his own finances quite spectacularly during the process of building a new house which resulted in a declaration of bankruptcy and a subsequent fleeing to Moscow to avoid debtor's prison.

By now Chekhov's elder brothers Alexander and Nikolay were already studying at Moscow University so the majority of the family reunited there, living in poverty, a change of circumstance which left Yevgeniya in a state of emotional and physical infirmity. Chekhov, however, remained in Taganrog living with a man called Selivanov who, like Lopakhin in *The Cherry Orchard*, had bailed out the family for the price of their house, to complete his education. Although his board was free with Selivanov, he was left to pay for his schooling, covering the costs and surviving on a disparate income cobbled together from the selling off of family possessions and bolstered by private tutoring, catching and selling goldfinches, and by writing and selling short sketches to the newspapers. Every ruble he could spare from his education and his now less frequent theatre visits he sent to his family in Moscow, enclosed with humourous letters designed to cheer them up in their poverty and misery. He now began to take a more earnest interest in his education, reading extensively and analytically, including the works of Cervantes, Turgenev, Goncharov and Schopenhauer. Meanwhile he enjoyed a series of closeted love affairs, including one with the wife of one of his teachers. His schooling completed and a scholarship to Moscow University obtained, he moved there in 1879 and rejoined his family.

He now assumed responsibility for the family, supporting them by writing regular satirical sketches and vignettes of contemporary Russian lifestyle under pseudonyms such as 'Antosha Chekhonte' and 'Man Without a Spleen', and his prodigious output earned him first a reputation as a reputable chronicler and then, in 1882, a regular position writing for Oskolki, a journal owned by Nicolai Leykin, the most successful Russian publisher at the time. Although the wit and brevity of his work here prevails through much of his later writing, it was considerably harsher in tone, perhaps a reflection of the stressful position of poverty, study and patriarch in which he found himself. In 1884, he qualified as a physician and, although he earned little from the profession and often treated the poor free of charge, he considered this his principle profession. At this time and for the next two years he would regularly cough up blood, a symptom of tuberculosis with which he was all too familiar as a physician. However, not wishing to "submit himself to be sounded by his colleagues", he kept the condition to himself. The continued success of his periodical writing enabled him to move the family into progressively more comfortable accommodation, and then in 1886 he received an invitation to write for *Novoye Vremya* (*New Times*), owned and edited by the millionaire media magnate Alexey Suvorin. Paying double per line what Anton received from Leykin and being given three times the column inches he took the offer immediately and became close friends with Suvorin, a friendship which would last his lifetime.

His work at these periodicals was not the sole extent of his literary output, for in 1885 he published a short story, *The Huntsman*, which quickly attracted scholarly attention and recognition. The sixty-four year old celebrated writer Grigorovich wrote to him shortly after it first appeared on the shelves, saying "you have *real* talent—a talent which places you in the front rank among writers in the new generation." The letter continues in this effusive manner before resolving to offer Chekhov the practical advice to slow down, write less, and concentrate on literary quality. In reply, Chekhov admitted that he had been struck "like a thunderbolt" on reading the letter, confessing to hitherto writing his stories "the way reporters write up their notes about fires - mechanically, half-consciously, caring nothing about either the reader or myself." In making such an honest admission, Chekhov arguably undersold himself as a serious author, for despite the appearance of a nonchalant and casual approach, later analysis and comparison of early manuscripts reveals a huge extent of careful revision indicating a far more involved, authorial approach than he allows himself in correspondence with Grigorovich. Nonetheless, receiving such warm congratulation and encouragement along with such earnest advice from so respected an author caused Chekhov to sit up straight and approach his writing with far more serious, artistic ambition. Now twenty-six, and with the patronage of such a revered and loved author, his collection of short stories entitled *V Sumerkakh* (*At Dusk*) won him the much coveted Pushkin Prize, awarded "for the best literary production distinguished by high artistic worth".

Following this act of formal recognition and somewhat burnt out by the years of continued literary output his enduring success afforded him the time and the money to take a sabbatical, so he engaged in a journey to the Ukraine in 1887 whereupon he was reminded of the beauty of the Steppe. This excursion inspired the novella *The Steppe* which he started on his return, and which he described in a letter to Grigorovich as "something rather odd and much too original", and which was eventually published in *Severny Vestnik* (*The Northern Herald*). Later that year he was commissioned by a theatre manager to write a play, and a fortnight later Chekhov produced *Ivanov* which, though he considered the process "sickening" and described in a letter to his brother Alexander in the manner of a comic portrait, it was a huge success and was widely regarded as a work of excellent and noteworthy originality. Furthermore this period is considered the source of a literary device noted by Ilia Gurliand, who overheard it in conversation, as Chekhov's Gun; "if in act 1 you have a pistol hanging on the wall, then it must fire in the last act". Then, in 1889, his brother Nikolay died as a result of tuberculosis. Their brother Mikhail, who recorded Anton's depression during the period of mourning after the death, had been researching prisons as part of his studies in law, and Anton too became interested and eventually somewhat obsessed with the idea of prison reform.

This newfound interest in the humanitarian questions surrounding the prison system, combined with a conceivable yet subconscious desire to escape the close environment of mourning surrounding his brother's death, led Chekhov to journey to the penal colony Sakhalin, an island off the far East coast of Russia, where he spent three months interviewing convicts and settlers with the aim of compiling a census of the island. He made several now notorious remarks to his sister about what he witnessed (among others, a relatively lighthearted and blunt description of Tomsk, "a very dull town. To judge from the drunkards whose acquaintance I have made, and from the intellectual people who have come to the hotel to pay their respects to me, the inhabitants are very dull, too." [-the inhabitants of Tomsk later retaliated by erecting a mocking statue of Chekhov]). More seriously, though, many of the things he saw during this trip horrified him, writing that "there were times I felt that I saw before me the extreme limits of man's degradation." Among these was the plight of the children of the island, describing one such incident in his journals:

> On the Amur steamer going to Sakhalin, there was a convict who had murdered his wife and wore fetters on his legs. His daughter, a little girl of six, was with him. I noticed wherever the convict moved the little girl scrambled after him, holding on to his fetters. At night the child slept with the convicts and soldiers all in a heap together.

Concluding that the solution to this inhumanity lay not with charity and philanthropy, but with Government intervention and reform, he wrote *Ostrov Sakhalin* (*The Island of Sakhalin*), a work of social science which was praised, not for its literary brilliance, but for its steady and worthy informativeness, which was serialised and published in 1893-4. Though this initial work which stemmed from the trip was not literary in nature, the extended contact and expansive experience he received found itself expressed in *The Murder*, a story which, though longer than his others, is still considered short in nature.

In 1892 Chekhov had bought Melikhovo, a small country estate forty miles north of Moscow, which was his and his family's home until 1899. He joked about his residence there, quipping to his friend Ivan Leontyev that "it's nice to be a Lord" though this lighthearted remark belies the seriousness with which he undertook his responsibilities as a landlord. Within a few years of his taking residence there he had established his usefulness and sense of duty to the peasants, affording them relief from the 1892 outbreaks of cholera and bouts of famine, and building three schools, a fire station and a clinic, and offering his services as a physician to the peasantry of the surrounding countryside. Often he would find queues of patients lining up outside his door in the morning who had travelled by foot or by cart to receive treatment, and frequently he was called out to visit those too sick to travel. His brother Mikhail who resided with the family at Melikhovo recorded this honourable commitment to his role as estate physician, writing

> from the first day that Chekhov moved to Melikhovo, the sick began flocking to him from twenty miles around. They came on foot or were brought in carts, and often he was fetched to patients at a

distance. Sometimes from early in the morning peasant women and children were standing before his door waiting.

Though these demanding hours left him with significantly less time for writing, they enriched his literary output for he was able to write informatively and genuinely about the peasantry and their living conditions, most notably in his short story *Peasants*. He did, however, visit those belonging to the upper-classes as well, though he was not enamoured by them, writing in his journal "Aristocrats? The same ugly bodies and physical uncleanliness, the same toothless old age and disgusting death, as with market-women".

He began to write arguably his most famous work, *The Seagull*, in 1894, in a lodge he had built himself in the orchard on the estate. Its first night on 17th October 1896 at the Alexandrinsky Theatre in Petersburg was something of a fiasco; it was booed by the audience, many of whom left, and this poor reception saw Chekhov fall out of love with the theatre. However, despite its poor reception by the play-going audience, it impressed the theatre director Vladimir Nemirovich-Danchenko so much that he proceeded to convince his colleague Constantin Stanislavski to take the play on and direct it in the innovative, progressive Moscow Art Theatre. This revival, in 1898, for the less-closeted Moscow audience was enormously well-received. Whereas the Petersburg performance had rendered the play literally and played down its more psychoanalytical aspects, Stanislavski payed far closer attention to the play's psychological realism and brought the deeply buried subtleties, lost on the Petersburg boards and on the audience's narrow-mindedness, to the surface. The play was such a success here that the Art Theatre commissioned further work from Chekhov, staging *Uncle Vanya* which he had completed in 1896. Furthermore, the positive critical reception had a restorative effect on Chekhov's interest in stage writing.

However, by now Chekhov's health condition was worsening, having suffered a major haemorrhage of the lungs in 1897 while visiting Moscow. His early reluctance to be seen by doctors prevailed and he protested to the notion of entering a clinic, though he eventually assented whereupon a formal diagnosis of the tuberculosis on the upper part of his lungs was reached, and the doctors ordered various changes in his lifestyle. His father then died in 1898, after which Chekhov bought a plot of land on the outskirts of Yalta and proceeded to build a villa, moving his mother and sister in with him the following year. Even though he pursued the enjoyment of gardening he had developed while at Melikhovo by planting trees and flowers, he kept dogs and tame cranes and regularly received highly regarded company such as Leo Tolstoy and Maxim Gorky, he spoke of a sense of relief upon each occasion of his leaving this "hot Siberia" for Moscow or to travel further afield. While here, he wrote two more plays for the Art Theatre, though these were composed with much greater difficulty; he remarked that unlike his youth when "[he] wrote serenely, the way [he eats] pancakes now". These two plays, *Three Sisters* and *The Cherry Orchard* took over a year each.

A quiet marriage to Olga Knipper on 25th May 1901 was performed in keeping with the position of suspicion he had always had towards weddings, with a small ceremony and little outside attention. Knipper was an actress whom he had met at the rehearsals for *The Seagull*, their marriage conformed to his stipulations;

By all means I will be married if you wish it. But on these conditions: everything must be as it has been hitherto - that is, she must live in Moscow while I live in the country, and I will come and see her ... give me a wife who, like the moon, won't appear in my sky every day.

This proved convenient as Knipper remained in Moscow performing his work and that of contemporary playwrights, and their long-distance correspondence features various treasured pieces of writing, be they shared complaints about Stanislavski's method of direction or advice from Chekhov to Knipper as to her performances in his plays. Prior to the marriage, Chekhov had been considered "Russia's most elusive literary bachelor", preferring brief liaisons and dalliances with unknown women, or brothels, to commitment. Chekhov then wrote one of his most famous stories, *The Lady with the Dog*, depicting a casual encounter between two strangers who, despite their best efforts and risking the security, stability and respectability of their family lives, find themselves irrevocably drawn to one another.

Chekhov's tuberculosis was finally getting the better of him, and by May 1904 it was quite clear that his death was imminent. Despite this, Mikhail recorded that "everyone who saw him secretly thought the end was not far off, but the nearer [he] was to the end, the less he seemed to realise it". He set off for the German town Badenweiler on 3rd June, writing cheerful, witty letters to his sister describing variously the food and the surroundings, while assuring both her and his mother that his health was improving; his last letter contained a sardonic complaint about the German women's fashion. The circumstances of his death have become one of "the greatest set pieces of literary history", and are most accurately recorded in this, Knipper's own account from her diaries, written in 1908:

Anton sat up unusually straight and said loudly and clearly (although he knew almost no German): *Ich sterbe* ("I'm dying"). The doctor calmed him, took a syringe, gave him an injection of camphor and ordered champagne. Anton took a full glass, examined it, smiled at me and said: 'It's a long time since I drank champagne.' He drained it, lay quietly on his left side, and I just had time to run to him and lean across the bed and call to him, but he had stopped breathing and was sleeping peacefully as a child.

His body, transferred to Moscow in a refrigerated railway car whose purpose was for fresh oysters, was then interred next to his father at Novodevichy Cemetery in Moscow. Although thousands of mourners mistakenly followed the pomp and circumstance of the military funeral procession for the also deceased General Keller, many hundreds of thousands of readers, writers and actors have followed correctly the path he pioneered for the short story and for twentieth century realism.

Quotes

Any idiot can face a crisis - it's day to day living that wears you out.

Medicine is my lawful wife and literature my mistress; when I get tired of one, I spend the night with the other.

People who lead a lonely existence always have something on their minds that they are eager to talk about.

Doctors are just the same as lawyers; the only difference is that lawyers merely rob you, whereas doctors rob you and kill you too.

If you are afraid of loneliness, do not marry.

Knowledge is of no value unless you put it into practice.

Don't tell me the moon is shining; show me the glint of light on broken glass.

I promise to be an excellent husband, but give me a wife who, like the moon, will not appear every day in my sky.

Let us learn to appreciate there will be times when the trees will be bare, and look forward to the time when we may pick the fruit.

Life does not agree with philosophy: There is no happiness that is not idleness, and only what is useless is pleasurable.

There is nothing new in art except talent.

A good upbringing means not that you won't spill sauce on the tablecloth, but that you won't notice it when someone else does.

Love, friendship and respect do not unite people as much as a common hatred for something.

The world perishes not from bandits and fires, but from hatred, hostility, and all these petty squabbles.

Advertising is the very essence of democracy.

Faith is an aptitude of the spirit. It is, in fact, a talent: you must be born with it.

People don't notice whether it's winter or summer when they're happy.

We shall find peace. We shall hear angels, we shall see the sky sparkling with diamonds.

You must trust and believe in people or life becomes impossible.

If you cry 'forward', you must without fail make plain in what direction to go.

No matter how corrupt and unjust a convict may be, he loves fairness more than anything else. If the people placed over him are unfair, from year to year he lapses into an embittered state characterized by an extreme lack of faith.

When you're thirsty and it seems that you could drink the entire ocean that's faith; when you start to drink and finish only a glass or two that's science.

All of life and human relations have become so incomprehensibly complex that, when you think about it, it becomes terrifying and your heart stands still.

How unbearable at times are people who are happy, people for whom everything works out.

Man is what he believes.

One must be a god to be able to tell successes from failures without making a mistake.

To advise is not to compel.

A fiancee is neither this nor that: he's left one shore, but not yet reached the other.

Money, like vodka, turns a person into an eccentric.

No psychologist should pretend to understand what he does not understand... Only fools and charlatans know everything and understand nothing.

Only entropy comes easy.

The more refined one is, the more unhappy.

The thirst for powerful sensations takes the upper hand both over fear and over compassion for the grief of others.

The University brings out all abilities, including incapability.

To judge between good or bad, between successful and unsuccessful would take the eye of a God.

We learn about life not from plusses alone, but from minuses as well.

When a woman isn't beautiful, people always say, 'You have lovely eyes, you have lovely hair.'

A writer is not a confectioner, a cosmetic dealer, or an entertainer.

Doctors are the same as lawyers; the only difference is that lawyers merely rob you, whereas doctors rob you and kill you too.

It's easier to write about Socrates than about a young woman or a cook.

Reason and justice tell me there's more love for humanity in electricity and steam than in chastity and vegetarianism.

The sea has neither meaning nor pity.

The wealthy are always surrounded by hangers-on; science and art are as well.

When a lot of remedies are suggested for a disease, that means it can't be cured.

When an actor has money he doesn't send letters, he sends telegrams.

About Us

We have many volumes of Chekhov available, together with other short story compilations, novels, essays and poetry from the most celebrated writers of all time. Use the search words 'miniature masterpieces' for other great short story compilations from incredible writers such as Arthur Conan Doyle, Joseph Conrad, Honore De Balzac, Robert Louis Stevenson and Rudyard Kipling among others. Use search words 'portable poetry' to find illuminating compositions by world renowned poets such as Rabindranth Tagore, Walt Whitman, Edgar Allan Poe, Thomas Hardy and Oscar Wilde among others. Use search words 'word to the wise' for some of the greatest novels, plays and essays ever written from history's very best including Jane Austen, Charles Dickens, Wilkie Collins, Elizabeth Gaskell, Anthony Trollope and Anthony Hope. Along with Anton Chekhov we offer many other foreign writers that have been translated to English such as Rumi, Henrik Ibsen, Miguel Cervantes, Dante Alighieri, Leo Tolstoy and Fyodor Dostoyevsky.